ALL THAT GLITTERS

HEATHER AMES

WELL OF IDEAS PRESS

CHAPTER ONE

Crystal Penney hugged a pair of splitting grocery sacks and staggered into the lobby of the Gold Rush Hotel. The screen door creaked ominously behind her, threatening to leave its hinges for the third time that week. She cast a quick look back at the lopsided door and the dilapidated scene beyond it. Owning half an Arizona ghost town was even more of a challenge than she had been prepared for, and at that moment, she definitely felt overwhelmed.

She sighed heavily, her spirits lower than they had been since she first arrived two weeks before. There had to be a better way of tackling the shopping than driving into Apache Junction every other day, especially in a battered, 1964-vintage green pickup truck without the benefit of air conditioning. The problem was, she couldn't come up with any better solutions for the growing needs of the town's guests.

The antiquated fan on the reception desk whirred noisily and blasted her with warm air. What she wouldn't give for the cool interior of her apartment in Paradise Valley and a tub with running water. She envisioned a long, luxurious bubble bath as she dropped the heavy bags onto the desk. The back of her shirt clung to her skin like a damp paper towel and sweat beaded her forehead. Crystal wished she had pulled her hair back into a ponytail before she left that morning.

"Hi, Crystal. Did you remember the dog food?"

She turned to face him. In the eight years they'd been apart, he hadn't matured one iota. While she'd been driving, shopping, toting and sweating, he'd been lazing yet again.

"Couldn't you do anything more constructive than lying around the lobby while I was gone?" Hands on hips, she confronted him. "Honestly, Cody Blye, you must think you're too good looking to work."

Sprawled nonchalantly across the faded green silk of the overstuffed Victorian sofa she had rescued from an upstairs bedroom, Cody's long, lean body resembled a stage prop left to enhance the old hotel's lobby. He wore a battered Stetson hat stained and aged to perfection, a fitted denim shirt, and jeans faded to a pale ice blue that matched his eyes. Worn, dusty boots rested on the recently-polished table.

When she glared pointedly at the boots, his eyes twinkled engagingly. With a lock of blond hair hanging casually over his forehead, Crystal thought Cody looked all of eighteen years old instead of thirty-three. He was a year older than she, for heaven's sake, and still acting like an adolescent.

He grinned disarmingly. "Tut-tut, Miss Crystal, honey. You're shootin' off your mouth without stoppin' to check first." He swung his legs off the furniture and planted his boots on the floor. "Come take a look in the kitchen before you get in an uproar."

With that, he stood up. No, Crystal thought. Standing up wasn't the right description. Flowed to his feet was more accurate. His body moved like molten lead beneath his clothes.

He handed her one of the grocery sacks and scooped up the other. Despite her resistance, he propelled her toward the back of the hotel. "There." He propped open the kitchen door and ushered her inside. "Now tell me I don't do anythin' around here."

He flipped a switch, flooding the kitchen with fluorescent light, and turned on the faucet over the sink. A stream of water spewed forth. "Not bad, huh?" His grin widened and took on a look of self-satisfaction. "I got the generator workin'."

Crystal sat down heavily on one of the old wooden chairs. "I-I don't believe it."

Just when she thought he'd be no help at all, Cody had rallied, and masterfully. Her bubble bath was more than a pipe dream. She could have purred.

"I'll expect no more complaints from you *or* the guests." Cody's eyes sparkled wickedly. "Doesn't that deserve a kiss at least, Miss Crystal?" He puckered his lips and lowered his face toward hers.

"Get away from me, Cody." Crystal leaped to her feet. Lowering her guard with him was always a mistake. He took advantage quicker than a rattler hidden under a rock. Her hands squarely on his shoulders, she pushed him away.

A snarl at knee-level told her she had committed an unforgivable sin. She stepped back carefully. "Call off your dog," she said.

"*Jackson.*" Cody sounded exasperated. "The only time Miss Crystal actually touches me, you have to ruin the moment." He looked down at the unkempt black and brown mutt standing by his feet.

The old dog had straggled in from his favorite place behind the reception desk, where he lurked in hopes of scaring off potential guests with a few well-chosen snarls and a spectacular baring of teeth. Jackson's hackles had risen, giving him the appearance of an untidy, slightly threadbare lion.

His yellow fangs made Crystal shudder. "I should have bought him a toothbrush instead of dog food," she said.

The dog resented her presence and displayed his opinion freely and often. Despite her best efforts, he had refused to bond with her even for table scraps, so she stepped around the table to give him as wide a berth as possible. "How about getting the rest of the groceries from the pickup for me, Cody? I'll make lunch if you do."

"That sounds like an offer I couldn't possibly refuse." He strode off.

"Take that miserable mutt with you," she called.

Cody gave a low whistle. Jackson aimed one last, baleful stare at Crystal before trotting unhurriedly out the door with his long, stringy tail bouncing like a ragged pennant.

Crystal smiled grudgingly. She had to admire Jackson's spirit, if nothing else. Since Cody had found him scavenging in the hotel trash a couple of days after their arrival in Cactus Station, the old dog had certainly carved himself a niche. Mostly with his teeth, she thought, shaking her head.

She stowed perishables in the humming refrigerator. Regardless of how annoying Cody and Jackson were, she had to give credit where it was due--Cody had done a fine job of coaxing life back into the generator.

She stopped to look out the window at the Superstition Mountains. Rising from the desert floor in tones of brown, rust and grey, they loomed glowering and formidable in the noontime heat. Their peaks sliced the vivid azure sky with the precision of razor- sharp knives. Heat quivered and pulsated under the relentless sun. The outdoor thermometer beside the kitchen window read one hundred and ten degrees, and the thermometer was in the shade.

She washed lettuce, took plates out of a cupboard and prepared to slice tomatoes. Where was Cody now? Crystal paused and glanced into the lobby. If he didn't get the rest of those groceries inside pretty quick, the meat she had purchased for the evening meal wouldn't need cooking--it would have slow-roasted in the truck.

She spotted him outside talking to a prospector, caked in dust and holding a pickaxe. Cody took a bottle of water from the case in the back of the truck and handed it to the man. Crystal shook her head. City folk got in so much trouble. They came ill-prepared for the punishing climate or the rocky, unforgiving terrain. Cactus Station needed a full- time medical clinic just to take care of the daily cases of dehydration, cuts and sprains. Maybe she needed to advertise for someone to fill that vacancy, along with a proprietor to open a general store and stop the time-consuming trips to get rations.

She dumped the lettuce into a bowl. Thinking about prospecting brought a familiar desire to head for the hills. Crystal gave herself a mental reprimand--she'd realized six months ago that her workaholic habits as a freelance geologist had brought her nothing but loneliness, and she had told herself she had to make changes in her life.

But had she made yet another mistake by taking possession of her inheritance from Uncle Dock? What made her believe she wouldn't exchange one frustration for another by trying to make a living out of one side of Cactus Station's Main Street when Cody had inherited the other from his Uncle Willy and apparently had no plans to redevelop it?

She knew the only reason the generator now operated was because they had to share the hotel and it was actually making money. Cody knew their profit margin could be increased by providing running water and electricity to the guests who thought they'd strike it rich in the Gold Rush Hills.

Two of them had already done so. They'd found sizeable nuggets while panning the creek that fed the town's water tank, and now the rush was on. Instead of ten people turning up to pan, Crystal and Cody had fifteen rooms rented at the hotel and another ten prospectors staying in the old boarding house down the street. Gold fever continued to draw people, and Cody was now working on the dilapidated brothel adjacent to the graveyard. Filled with vermin, bullet holes and dust, he had talked about demolishing it before need and greed threw common sense out the window.

While the rest of the newcomers waited for more permanent accommodations, they set up a tent city inside the parking lot at the other end of town. Crystal wondered whether self-preservation had stopped them squatting in the rest of what remained of Cactus Station, or if the ghost stories Cody told were more the cause. Even she had to admit that when night cloaked the town, the buildings took on a different appearance. Their decay masked, they appeared to be waiting for past inhabitants to come out of hiding and populate them again with laughter, music and altercations.

Crystal hadn't intended to get involved with yet another of Cody's seemingly endless schemes. But her plans to rehabilitate the hotel into a tourist attraction had been met far quicker than she had expected, and she knew Cody's scheming might be at the bottom of it. She strongly suspected he might have sacrificed a couple of his own nuggets to kick-start the gold rush fever.

As she opened the tuna can, she asked herself why she still felt so attracted to him. He was the same glib-talking, irresponsible man he had been when she came to stay with Uncle Dock and Uncle Willy the summer before grad school. She'd been too naïve then to see Cody would never amount to anything more, and she certainly mustn't repeat the same mistake now. At the end of that summer, she reminded herself, he'd wished her luck and disappeared into the mountains without a backward glance.

Crystal mixed mayonnaise with the tuna. She'd eagerly claimed her inheritance to begin a new life. And when she'd found out Cody owned the other half of the old town, she'd thought she might find an explanation for his behavior all those years ago. She beat the tuna with gusto, wishing she could whip Cody into shape with the same ease. Some hope. She couldn't even get him to stay serious long enough to have an intelligent conversation.

Her introspection ended when he dumped two boxes on the kitchen table.

"That's it for the food," he said. "I'll take the water out back and stow it in the coolers. The generator's got the pump goin', so we won't need all those bottles anymore." He took off his hat and wiped his forehead on his shirt sleeve. "Explain to me how you're gonna fit all this food into that old refrigerator."

"Can't you get the freezer working?" She tried smiling at him.

"Gettin' friendly because you want another job done?" Blond eyebrows rose mockingly over those insolent eyes. His lips quirked. "What would you do if I repaired your side of town?" He flipped his hat onto the top of the refrigerator.

"Marry you."

She regretted the words as soon as they'd left her mouth. Despite the intended flippancy of the remark, it hung between them with the consistency of lead.

"Is that so?" Cody folded his arms across his chest and leaned against the counter." Sure would be one hell of a way of solvin' the dispute over this hotel, wouldn't it?"

"There *is* no dispute."

Her face averted, she vented her anger by slashing her knife through celery stalks. That's all Cody wanted--to claim the only building worth anything and then sell his half of the town for whatever he could get for it. Her cheeks flamed, and her eyes burned.

"Under the terms of our uncles' wills, we share the hotel," she reminded him, her voice as on-edge as the rest of her. "That means I cook and clean for the guests, while you're in charge of maintenance."

Cody snorted his disgust with the whole arrangement. He'd made no bones about his opinion of the wills or about his future in Cactus Station, which was to be as short-lived as he could possibly make it.

Crystal bit back a caustic comment. She mustn't aggravate him when he was actually using the tool kit for something more than a place to prop his feet. "Speaking of maintenance..." With difficulty, she ignored the fact that he rolled his eyes. "If you don't fix that freezer, we're going to have the biggest dinner tonight that you've ever eaten. I made a mistake on the meat order and got double what I wanted."

"Why didn't you ask the store to take it back?" Cody shook his head. "You're an intelligent woman with a fancy degree, Crystal, but you don't have an ounce of plain horse-sense."

"I *would* have sent the extra back if I hadn't asked them to cut it especially for me," Crystal explained patiently. She chose not to comment on the gibe about her educational history. "I left the order and went to do the rest of the shopping. I didn't notice the mistake until the meat arrived at the check-out."

Cody sighed. "Don't know if I can handle doin' *two* jobs today." He took his tool kit from its perch on a stool. "Might destroy my image."

"One you're working overtime to maintain." Crystal sliced deftly through a dill pickle.

Cody watched, his eyes narrowed. "You bet, Miss Crystal."

The screen door slammed back into place, leaving her glaring at torn netting instead of his broad back.

"I hate it when he calls me that," she told Jackson.

He whined.

"Go away, mangy." She shook the knife at him since Cody was no longer within sight.

Jackson curled his lip and trotted away, taking the back stairs up to the second floor.

"Damn dog."

Crystal made sandwiches and added dill pickle slices to the plates. A resounding crash overhead startled her as she laid placemats on the scarred table.

There were no guests in the hotel at that time of day. Everyone was out making Swiss cheese of the Superstitions.

"Damn dog," she said louder. No doubt Jackson had put his dry, cracked nose where it didn't belong. She only hoped he hadn't broken some guest's prized possession.

Rhythmic banging on the back porch told her Cody was busy with the freezer. If she made him deal with Jackson, he'd probably take the opportunity to abandon his chores for the rest of the day. She shoved their lunch into the refrigerator and marched up the steep stairs.

"Jackson! What have you done now?" She stopped on the landing to listen. Silence greeted her. Dust motes floated in the hot, musty air. She sniffed and wrinkled her nose.

No matter how many times she swept the floor or polished the furniture, the place still smelled closed up. She took a few steps, the boards creaking in protest beneath her feet.

"Jackson?"

She heard a faint whine, but from the third floor, not the second. The attic door stood open.

Crystal stopped, puzzled. The attic door hadn't been open since they arrived. Then she thought again. Maybe Cody had been crawling around up there while he messed with the electrical system. She tried the light switch at the bottom of the stairs. Miraculously it worked--all ten watts of it. She peered up the stairs.

She had never been able to force herself up to the third floor. Not even during the time the uncles had owned the town. Enclosed spaces gave her more than chills--she suffered from claustrophobia. Warily, she placed her foot on the first stair. It held her weight with only a mild, protesting squeak.

Grasping the banister firmly, she took another step. A cobweb drifted across her face. Crystal brushed it away without thinking, and then looked at the grime already coating her palm. *Wonderful.* Now she was covering herself with dirt in an effort to find Cody's horrible excuse for a pet.

Reminding herself why she had chosen not to involve Cody, she hurried up the rest of the stairs. A thick, grey blanket coated the entire attic. Crystal sneezed loudly, four times in rapid succession. Jackson barked from the farthest corner.

"Come here," she pleaded in what she hoped was a tone suitable for attracting willful animals. "If you get hurt, Cody'll find some way to blame me."

Another bark answered her, but Jackson stayed hidden.

"I'll give you a big treat," she wheedled. "Tuna. An entire sandwich."

He made a noise she swore sounded like a long drawn out yawn of boredom.

Annoyed and already feeling short of breath, Crystal abandoned her attempts at coercion. "Stop fooling around and get over here!"

The dog whined plaintively.

Her exasperation changed to anxiety, and not because of the claustrophobia tightening her throat. Jackson *loved* tuna. He salivated even at the mention of it. He must be caught on something.

She tiptoed hesitantly past old furniture, piled up shutters, heaps of brocade drapes and rolled up, moth-eaten rugs. She brushed aside a hanging clump of muslin curtains and a shower of dust rained down on her head, bringing another bout of sneezing.

After that stopped, she wiped her eyes on a corner of her shirt. The roof sloped sharply toward the eaves and the curtains had dropped back into place, enhancing the enclosed, oppressive atmosphere. Crystal's heart pounded in an all-too-familiar fashion. *Not now.* She took deep, measured breaths, but dust tickled her nostrils and she sneezed again.

Jackson's shape loomed out of the shadows.

Crystal felt overwhelming relief. "Oh, thank goodness. What in the world are you doing up here, you bad dog?"

He barked again, his raucous voice echoing around the rafters as he sidled past her, his body brushing her leg.

"Let's get out of here," she said.

He butted her right behind the knees.

Crystal lost her balance, arms flailing as she clutched wildly for the support of anything within reach. Her outstretched hand caught a door handle and she swung, suspended in space. Saved! She congratulated herself and tried to get her feet back under her.

Jackson, obviously determined to help her break her neck, jumped, his paws landing on her shoulders.

Under the added weight, the door flew open. Something large and heavy fell out of the closet and landed on both of them. Crystal screamed desperately as they all fell to the floor.

CHAPTER TWO

Cody heard the scream. He scrambled up from his contorted position behind the freezer and tripped over his open tool kit. His head smacked the porch railing and he fell to his knees as tools went flying every which way, but he ignored the pain and regained his feet. He ripped the tattered screen door from its hinges and took the back stairs two and three at a time.

"Crystal!"

He paused on the landing while he tried to decide which of the many closed doors to kick open first. She must have put her foot through a rotten floor board and fallen, he thought, his heart racing. Or had the ceiling fallen in on her? "Crystal, for God's sake answer me!"

"Up here." Weak and shaky, her voice came from the attic.

Cody charged up the steps. What the devil was claustrophobic Crystal doing up there? Something must be really wrong.

"Are you okay?" He glanced around the dimly lit space. His flashlight lay beside the freezer, two floors below. He blinked in an effort to adjust his vision.

"I-I'm okay, I guess."

She sounded close to tears. Cody cursed under his breath. He couldn't handle Crystal if she was crying. He'd lose his detachment and make a complete fool of himself.

"Where are you?"

"Over here. In the corner."

He found her crouching beside a large object on the floor. Relief flooded him, along with anger. She should never have gone up there alone. She could have endangered herself and him, too.

"What are you doin'?" He grabbed her arm and hauled her to her feet. "You screamed so loud, I thought you were hurt."

For once, she didn't try to shake him off. In fact, she collapsed against him, her shoulders quivering under the thin cotton blouse.

"I-I opened the closet and something fell on top of me. I don't know what it was, but it...it felt...hideous."

Against his better judgment, Cody held her. He didn't care about unidentified objects falling out of closets. In fact, he was absurdly grateful to whatever had frightened Crystal. She'd kept her distance until now, suddenly and miraculously, she was in his arms.

He was treading on very dangerous ground, but he couldn't help himself. The clean, fresh scent of her dazzled his senses. The warmth of her body next to his stirred a familiar ache. He buried his face in her hair and allowed his memories to seep out of their hiding place deep inside him. He'd held her in just such a way all those years before. He remembered the sweetness and closed his eyes, resting his cheek against the top of her head.

"It'll be okay." His hands soothed her, stilling her tremors with their touch.

Crystal burrowed against his chest and sighed. "I was so scared," she whispered. "I heard a crash and came up here looking for Jackson."

"You should have called me."

"I know. I thought he'd gone into one of the guest's rooms and broken something. Then I heard him barking up here." She pulled away, sniffling. "Pretty stupid, huh?"

"We all make mistakes. I'm just glad you're okay."

He hated the way she'd broken contact. His arms felt empty. The old gnawing filled his gut. He thought he'd conquered that feeling, only to find it resurrected the moment he touched her again.

"Thanks for coming to save me." She patted his arm awkwardly.

Cody felt a glimmer of hope at her touch, but he forced himself not to push his advantage. *Step by small step,* he reminded himself. *Win back her trust first.*

"I think we'd better find out what fell on me," Crystal said.

"Then we need some more light. There's a flashlight in my tool kit."

"You'd better get it, then."

Did he imagine it, or was her voice husky? He thought again of her claustrophobia. "You want to come with me?"

"No thanks. I'm okay now."

Still he hesitated, unwilling to leave her alone in the darkness, the dust and the cobwebs.

"Really," she said. "I'll wait here."

Cody used the time he was gone to compose himself, and figured Crystal stayed in the attic to do the same thing. When he returned, they discovered the object was a rolled up maroon blanket.

"Is that all?" He breathed a sigh of relief.

"There's something in it." Crystal grabbed the flashlight from him. She sounded indignant. "It felt really heavy, and it knocked me over."

"A good gust of wind would knock you down," Cody said. "You're just as skinny now as you used to be."

"Don't be ridiculous. And don't be so rude, either, calling me skinny."

"It's easy to let your imagination run away with you when you're frightened," he reasoned.

"I'm not going to get thrown to the floor by a rolled up blanket," she snapped, their moment of shared intimacy suddenly no more than a memory. "Open it up." She kicked the blanket with her foot, but then stepped back. "Go ahead." She waved the flashlight at him. *"You* do it. You're the man around here, as you keep reminding me. Just be careful there aren't any scorpions or snakes in there."

Cody felt like shaking her until her teeth rattled. There she went again--ordering him around like he was the hired help instead of her partner. "Fine." He squatted down. "Leave all the dirty jobs for me." He shook his head at her. "You're startin' to believe all those ghost stories and tall tales, Miss Crystal. What do you think's in there...a body?"

"Very funny." But she continued to hang back.

"What happened to women's lib?" Cody asked.

"Forget it, Cody. I'm not falling for that trick." She folded her arms and shivered, despite the fact that the heat made it harder to breathe.

The atmosphere pressed in on him, too. He wasn't getting any satisfaction out of baiting her, and he was beginning to feel lightheaded. If they stayed up there much longer, they'd both pass out. He grabbed the end of the blanket and began unwrapping. Crystal directed the beam of light on the dirty and frayed wool as he cautiously peeled away the layers. And then she screamed and dropped the flashlight just as everything went dark in the attic.

Cody was in the middle of jumping to his feet when the light went out. He staggered back. Jackson let out a low howl that brought goose bumps onto Cody's arms and sent a chill up his back. Crystal ran into him, and he felt her fingernails bite into his flesh.

"Who's playin' with the light?" he shouted. "Turn it back on!"

The overhead light flickered back to life, not that it helped much.

"Sorry! I'm sorry." A man's voice came from the stairwell. "I didn't mean to frighten anyone, but what in hell are you doing up there, anyway?" he asked. "I can't see a thing."

Cody heard stumbling footsteps and a dull thud as someone fell.

"Isn't there any more light than this?" the man complained. "I came to ask if you're selling box lunches or something. I'm hungry."

CHAPTER THREE

"My nerves are about shot," Cody said when they were back in the kitchen. He opened the refrigerator. "You want a beer?"

"No, thanks. Lemonade. I'm really thirsty." Crystal finished washing her hands, wrapped a sandwich in a napkin and took it to the back door. "Here," she said to the prospector who had plunged the attic into darkness. "There's water in the coolers. Help yourself."

She looked at the screen door lying on the back porch and took a seat at the table. "What a day," she said, running her hands through her shoulder-length golden brown hair. "I was so scared when the light went out. If I hadn't run into you, I don't know what would've happened. I'd probably have fallen down those stairs trying to get out of the attic."

Cody watched her and remembered the pleasure of running his own hands through her hair after they made love. What a fool he had been, he thought. His pride had destroyed their relationship, and he'd paid for that mistake ever since.

He brought her the jug of lemonade and a glass. "Glad to be of service." He glanced at the indentations on his arms.

"I'm so sorry," she said. "You'd better wash. There's no telling what was under my fingernails after all that dirt up there."

He grinned at her. "No harm done. You didn't even break the skin.

An' you weren't the only one losin' your head. When Jackson howled, all the hair stood up on my arms." He straddled a chair and took a pull of the beer. "Those are bones up there, you know."

"I know. I saw." She wiped her dirt-smeared face with a napkin and drank an entire glass of lemonade without stopping. "We have to call Sheriff Dalton."

"An' tell him what? Someone left a pile of bones in the closet?"

"To tell him someone might have been murdered in the hotel, that's what." She shook her finger at Cody. "You don't think whoever's in that blanket did his own wrapping job and then managed to stand up in the closet and close the door, do you?"

"Of course not." Cody felt a flash of anger. She had a way of talking down to him sometimes, and he hated it.

"You call the sheriff while I go back up to see if we missed anything, like an ID." She got up.

"Crystal." He tried to keep his voice under control, despite his irritation. "It's hotter'n hell up there. I'm hungry, and you're dehydrated. You wait 'til it cools down; I'll go with you."

She made an exasperated noise, but she hesitated.

"Sheriff's gonna take at least an hour and a half to get here, even if we call him right now," Cody reasoned.

Crystal eyed the lemonade pitcher.

"There's no hurry, honey. That skeleton's not goin' anywhere."

As soon as he finished speaking, he knew he should have quit while he was ahead. Crystal's blue eyes told him just how self-centered she thought he was.

"How you can think about food at a time like this is beyond me." She snatched the flashlight off the table and left him.

"Women!" Cody watched Jackson cock one ear as he lay on the rag rug in front of the sink. "You caused all this, so don't you play innocent," he told the old dog.

Jackson half-heartedly thumped his tail. He yawned widely and closed his eyes.

"Now you're gonna take a nap while Crystal has me pokin' 'round that filthy attic," Cody complained.

Jackson ignored him.

Cody called Sheriff Dalton before he headed back upstairs.

"You've got what?" the sheriff demanded.

"A skeleton. I told you. It's in the hotel attic." Cody watched the first of the prospectors drag into the lobby after a day of fruitless digging. He lowered his voice. "Crystal's not gonna give me any rest 'til you get here, Reed. She thinks someone was murdered."

He waited while Reed Dalton digested that piece of information.

"Oh, all right. I'll get on my way. I'll bring the coroner. It'll take me a while to find him and get him moving. He hates driving out into the desert in the middle of the day."

"Fine. Somehow, I'm gonna make Crystal come out of the attic, and we'll be waitin' for you."

Cody put down the phone and headed back upstairs. Maybe Crystal hadn't made such a big mistake with the meat order after all. With Reed and the coroner arriving in Cactus Station late afternoon, they'd better plan to set a couple of extra places at the table.

CHAPTER FOUR

Crystal surveyed the interior of the closet, which appeared to be completely empty. She heard a rustle behind her, and her heart rate went from a fast trot into a full gallop.

"The sheriff wants you out of here," a voice said right by her ear.

She jumped like the Grim Reaper had put his hand on her shoulder.

"Sorry," Cody said. "It's just me."

"For God's sake!" She knew what people were talking about when they said their hearts were in their throats. "What's the matter with you?" she demanded. "Sneaking up on me like that!"

"Sheriff said he'll be here later," Cody said. "You need to stop pokin' around. You're tramplin' on any evidence that's left."

"I've been careful." She squatted down and shone the flashlight into the closet. "There's nothing else in here, anyway."

Cody squatted down beside her. His thigh inadvertently brushed hers, and before she could stop herself, she scooted away from him. He got back up.

"Come on, Crystal," he said. "Leave things be."

She knew he was being sensible, but just leaving human remains in the attic sounded callous to her. "We should cover it back up, at least," she said.

"I think Reed would prefer us not touchin' anythin' else." Cody held out his hand. "There's nothin' useful you can do up here, and you know it."

"Well...okay." She ignored his hand, stood up and dusted off her jeans. "Yuk, it's so filthy up here. Is there any way we can lock the door?"

"I don't think there's a key, an' the reason it's filthy is 'cause it's an attic. They're always dirty. I suppose you're gonna tell me you'll clean up here, too."

He sounded annoyed, and Crystal couldn't blame him. She'd acted as though he had some contagious disease when he'd accidentally come into contact with her.

"You've got some obsession about cleanin'," he told her.

"I can't stand dust. It makes me sneeze." Crystal rubbed her nose. "You're right, let's get out of here." She shuddered. "This place gives me the creeps, and my heart's pounding again."

"I'm surprised you volunteered to come back up here," Cody said as they headed down the steep staircase.

"Me, too," she admitted. "But you made me so mad, talking about eating instead of calling Sheriff Dalton."

"You take everythin' too seriously." When he looked at her, his expression wasn't mocking for once. "That's your trouble. Whoever's up there wouldn't object to us eatin' lunch before reportin' what we found. Those bones look old, so *if* there was a crime, whoever did it is long gone."

Crystal tried to detach herself from her knee-jerk reactions to Cody's suggestions. "I hate to admit it," she said. "But you're probably right."

The pounding sensation subsided once they were back on the landing. Damned claustrophobia, she thought. It had caused so many issues when she tried to go into the mines.

"I'm gonna eat." Cody closed the attic door. "Whether you come with me or not." He pulled a rag out of his back pocket and wiped his hands on it. "I've still got to work on the freezer, too," he reminded her.

"And I left the mail on the front desk." She refused to start arguing over his maintenance chores yet again. "I'd better check it while we're eating."

She ran ahead of him down the wide wooden staircase to the welcoming brightness of the lobby, where she paused to appreciate the breeze stirring her hair from the noisy blades of the old desk fan. She reacted so quickly to sensuous touches, whether those of nature or human hand. Probably because she rarely got enough of either, she decided regretfully.

As though interpreting her thoughts, Cody's fingers replaced the air flow, massaging her taut muscles with rhythmical strokes that made her eyes close in ecstasy. His touch worked all its old magic, drifting from her neck to her shoulders, easing the rigidity and dissolving the pent-up tension.

Crystal couldn't help herself. She leaned back against him, her mind soaring free. His lips found the special place behind her left ear that reduced her to pliant, supple quicksilver in his arms. His hands slid oh, so slowly down her arms to her wrists, then back up, milking the tension while the pressure of his lips destroyed the barrier she had so desperately erected between them. When she could barely stand, he stopped.

"Let's go into the kitchen," he said softly.

If he'd said "Let's go into the bedroom," she wouldn't have been surprised, and she was disturbed to find she would have followed him there, too.

"Okay," she managed.

She struggled to regain her poise as she followed his broad shoulders, built up by years of digging in the Superstitions. His back tapered into a lean waist and slender hips. His buttocks were rounded muscle, his thighs corded beneath his figure-hugging jeans. She knew how corded. Intimately.

"You want coffee?" He picked up the battered pot on the stove.

The last thing she needed was more heat.

"No. I'll get water from the cooler. You want one, too?" *Damn it, why did she have to sound so breathless? He'd be sure to notice.*

"Yeah, thanks; this tap water's gonna be warm." Without looking at her, he took the container over to the sink. "I'd still better make a pot if the sheriff's comin'. That man can drink ten cups by himself." Cody ran water.

"Who do you think it is?" Crystal asked when she returned with the bottles.

"Who?"

"The skeleton, of course. Don't play dumb with me." She watched him strike a match and light the vintage stove.

"I don't have to play dumb with you, Miss Crystal. We both know I *am* dumb." He kept his back turned while he dumped coffee into the pot. "I never had the benefit of a college education. I'm pure seventh grade, straight from Miss Hester Grandy's one room schoolhouse."

The bitterness in his voice felt like a slap. "That's never mattered to me, and you know it," she said. "You've got more knowledge about the mining business than I'll ever have." She watched coffee spill onto the stove as he ladled heaping spoonfuls into the pot.

"I guess it's some old prospector," Cody said. He put two cups on the table.

"Who?"

"The skeleton." He grinned at her. *"Now* look who's being dumb."

They were back to normal, Crystal thought with a twinge of regret. They'd sparred verbally since she arrived to find him already in residence at the hotel. "Fifty-fifty," he

had reminded her when she dumped her bags on the lobby floor. "I already claimed my room. Take whatever you like of what's left."

When she had seen her choices, she could have strangled him. He had taken the most habitable and luxurious bedroom, dubbed the presidential suite, with its four-poster bed, gilt furnishings and purple velvet drapes. The one she finally elected to make her own was the smallest room on the second floor. The third-floor staircase bit into available headroom, but it was the only other bedroom without holes in the ceiling or cracked glass at the window.

Crystal gave herself a mental shake. All that was old news. She gave him his drink and took their lunch out of the refrigerator. The cold interior felt good on her hot cheeks. She didn't want to face Cody across the table, but Hop Penney's daughter was no coward.

At least, she wasn't cowardly with anyone or anything but Cody, she told herself. She placed the food on the table and watched him drain the water bottle, get a soda out of the refrigerator and straddle a chair. He took one of the sandwiches and bit into it.

"Mm...'s good," he mumbled.

"Have some salad." She pushed the bowl across the table. "You never did eat enough greens."

"You don't get lettuce in the desert." He took a small helping and doused it with what looked like half a bottle of ranch dressing.

"That's disgusting." Crystal wrinkled her nose and spread a thin layer of dressing on her own salad.

"You eat the way you want to, an' I'll eat my way." He took a drink from the soda can, then popped the rest of the sandwich into his mouth.

Why did she feel he was purposely using sloppy table manners just to rile her? Crystal picked at her food and drank all the water. Her parched throat demanded more. She got up to fetch another bottle.

Cody finished his second sandwich and pushed aside the half-eaten salad. "Get me a beer while you're out there, would you?" he asked. "I put a six pack in the red cooler." His chair scraped on the worn wooden floor.

When Crystal returned, his legs were stretched out, his feet resting on one corner of the table.

"Cody." She kept the beer in her hand. "I'm still eating. Do I have to watch the dirt on your boots while I finish?"

"You're playin' with your food, Crystal, not eatin' it. Have a cup of coffee." He reached over and took the bubbling pot off the stove without getting to his feet.

She sat down and gave him her cup. "You're hopeless," she said.

"At what?" His eyebrows raised, pale question marks on his tanned face.

"Anything civilized." She took a sip of the dark, aromatic brew and almost gagged. She grabbed the first thing that came to hand--the beer bottle--and took a big swig. "Oh, my God, that coffee's awful--the worst thing I've ever tasted." She grimaced. "Like bitter oil or something."

"Sheriff Dalton likes it that way. I forgot your sensibilities again, Miss Crystal." Cody pushed his chair back until it balanced on two legs. He folded his arms and grinned at her discomfort. "Can I have my beer if you're finished with it?"

Crystal looked down at the bottle in her hand. "Here." She pushed it across the table. "A bad meal on top of a dreadful day."

She remembered thinking her spirits had been at their lowest when she got back with the shopping earlier. Not so, she decided, covering her face with her hands. They had sunk even lower after finding the skeleton and drinking that ghastly swill Cody had tried to pass off as coffee. What in the world was she doing with her life?

"Think I'll take a turn down the street while we wait for Reed and the coroner." Cody's voice intruded on her misery. "Want to come with me?"

"No, thanks." She pushed her depression aside and forced herself out of the chair. "I've got work to do." She took two roasts from the refrigerator. "Turn on the oven to three- fifty, would you?"

Cody opened the oven, struck a match and twisted the dial. "It's gonna be hotter than the attic in here," he warned. "Why don't you make a pot of beans an' some cornbread or somethin' instead? It'd be quicker, an' those greenhorn prospectors won't mind."

"Those prospectors are going to give us enough money to make the necessary repairs to this place." She took two large roasting pans from one of the cupboards and prepared them for the meat. She pushed past him to place the pans in the oven to preheat. "What we really need is a barbeque or a fire pit."

Cody grunted. "Which you expect me to build in my spare time." He silenced her with a look. "A couple of people findin' nuggets in a stream doesn't mean the hotel's gonna be filled with hundreds of people willin' to plunk down the bucks to stay. This sudden rush could be over tomorrow, an' you'll be stuck with fifty pounds of beef and a useless fire pit."

He propped one hip against the counter while she sprinkled the meat with aromatic herbs.

Crystal put down the spice containers. "Did you plant those nuggets?" she asked, intently watching his expression. Cody might be able to lie with impunity to anyone else, but not to her.

"Now why would I do that, even if I had the gold to throw away, which I don't?"

"I'm not sure," Crystal admitted. "But it sure seems odd that two people would find gold so close to town. The uncles never found anything, and they were up here for years."

Cody shrugged. "Some people look for gold all their lives an' never find it. Others are luckier. Doesn't mean prospectin' ain't excitin' or rewardin'. Uncle Dock and Uncle Willy were pretty much always happy."

"Which is more than you can say about their partner, Jake Carver." Crystal tapped Cody on the chest with her finger. "All those years of honeycombing the hills never got him anywhere. It didn't put any excitement into his life or give him a pleasant disposition." She opened the oven and felt the punishing blast of heat as she removed the pans. She quickly shut the door and loaded the meat into them.

"Oh, Jake was okay, Crystal." Cody grabbed one of the heavy pans. "Open the oven back up," he said. "I'll do this for you."

"He was the meanest man I ever met," Crystal insisted.

"You didn't think so when he brought you that piece of pyrite." Cody chuckled. "Remember?"

"The Fool's Gold? Yes, I remember." Crystal had to smile. "I thought I was rich. I ran all over camp and then down to the stream to find Uncle Dock. He laughed so hard when I showed him my treasure and told him all my plans for the future." Her smile crumpled. "I loved him, Cody. He was the stabilizing influence in my life. After my dad died, Uncle Dock stepped in and took care of me."

"I know what you mean." Cody spoke softly. "Uncle Willy was like a father to me, too. Hell, he *was* my father. I never knew my real dad."

Crystal laid a hand on his arm. She knew how much he'd loved his uncle.

Cody squeezed her hand and gave her a quick smile. "That's enough talkin' about the past. I'm takin' a walk." He grabbed the hat he'd thrown on top of the refrigerator earlier. "I'll finish workin' on the freezer when I get back. Sure you don't want to come with me?"

Crystal thought of the silence that would fall over the old hotel after he left her alone. She thought of the skeleton lying above her head in the attic. She wanted to forget the dinner preparations and go with him. But she shook her head. She'd already spent far too much time with him that day, and after the shock of the attic find, she still felt far too vulnerable.

"Suit yourself." He paused at the door, hat in hand. "You always did that, didn't you?" Without waiting for an answer, he left.

Crystal started peeling potatoes. She nicked her finger on the first one. The physical pain went very well with her emotional turmoil.

CHAPTER FIVE

Cody wondered if he could find anything that would help him relax. Dunking himself in the creek hadn't worked and walking didn't seem to be doing the trick, either. Shoving his hands deep in his pockets, he trudged along the sun-baked boards that served as Main Street's sidewalks.

In the harsh afternoon heat, the old buildings crouched like rows of battered war veterans squaring up against each other. Across the street from the hotel, the Nugget Saloon slumped, its doorway a gaping black hole and its battered, faded sign hanging by one nail. The remains of the dental office, long since in need of demolition, opened its roof to the sky while the assay office, with its boarded windows and peeling clapboards, struggled to maintain an air of dilapidated gentility.

Echoes of ghostly laughter seemed to float in the air above the saloon at certain times of the day. At night, a velvet silence blanketed the deserted stores and abandoned homes. Maybe the silence should remain, Cody mused. The town had died a natural death, and they were trying to bring it back. Maybe Cactus Station needed to decay and float away on the wind, instead of being resurrected.

A faint, rhythmical tapping reminded him of the prospectors filling the hills. All too soon they would be coming back to demand food and baths at the Gold Rush Hotel. The town was rising from the ashes whether he wanted it or not.

Crystal would never forgive him, he decided, kicking at a barrel outside Mason's Mercantile and Emporium. She'd never let him get close to her again. He'd blown his one chance for happiness when he'd walked out on her eight years before. The Crystal he knew now was distant and guarded, sharp as a cactus spine and hard as the rock of the Superstitions.

This Crystal thought he was a shallow, self-serving disappointment. After the way he'd treated her all those years ago, he couldn't blame her, he thought, staring blankly into the darkened interior of Diamond Della's House of Splendors. Well...maybe that wasn't true. He did blame her for one thing. Young as she had been, she should have realized they couldn't have a future together. Uncle Dock certainly made sure he understood that. Cody still remembered how humiliated he had been when Crystal's uncle took him aside and told him he wasn't going to ruin Crystal's life by marrying her.

He strolled morosely down to the end of the street and crossed from Crystal's side to his own. Uncle Willy must have thought leaving his nephew one side of the town would give him a second chance with Crystal. Some wishful thinking, Cody decided, his hands clenched at his sides. Uncle Willy must have forgotten how badly Crystal had been hurt.

Cody groaned under his breath. He'd never wanted to hurt Crystal. She'd been so young and so much in love with him. And he with her.

But he'd come to realize that Uncle Dock was right--she was so out of his league, it was laughable. He'd had nothing to offer Crystal except an unstable, nomadic existence gold prospecting, and an uncertain financial future. Instead, she'd become a geologist, while he'd stayed a penniless, seventh-grade drop-out who narrowly escaped jail-time in his last venture with the uncles.

Cody wiped sweat off his forehead. Uncle Willy's dream of finding the Lost Dutchman Mine hadn't produced anything but rocks and dirt. The backers Cody had convinced to fund the exploration had complained to the authorities. He'd been accused of fraud and narrowly escaped a prison sentence.

He ran out of street and struck out for the hills. That day, walking around town wasn't going to do it for him. He needed to tire himself out so he wouldn't feel so frustrated with his present position as a mainte- nance man, or want Crystal with the same biting need. Touching her had been the worst mistake he'd made since they both arrived in town.

When he'd placed his lips on her neck, his reaction had been so strong, it had practically knocked him off his feet.

He passed two men struggling along with pickaxes and buckets, ropes and pans. "Any luck?" he asked, knowing full well they couldn't have found anything.

"No."

The first man looked miserable, his dark hair plastered against his head, his face sunburned and peeling after only a couple of days spent prospecting. His partner, overweight and breathing in labored gasps, dropped the pickaxe he was carrying and licked dry lips.

"Wish it wasn't so hot," the second man said between gasps.

"You need hats," Cody said. "An' where's your water? You should be out early mornin' or late afternoon, when the sun's not blisterin.'"

The man with wet hair grimaced and shook his head wearily. "And while we're relaxing at the hotel, someone else might make a big find." He wiped his red, dirty face with the bottom of his t-shirt.

Cody shrugged. "Your funeral."

Then he thought about the sheriff's arrival, along with the coroner's wagon. Bad choice of words. Oh well, no doubt Crystal would stand at the door and explain the whole situation to the guests as they arrived. She was good at explaining; efficient.

"Why don't you walk back with us and have a beer?" the fat man asked, his voice wheezing into the air. "I'll buy."

"Thanks. I'll take a rain check." Cody tipped his hat at them and strode off.

Jackson joined him, trotting along with his long tongue lolling out of his mouth in an idiotic fashion. Cody grinned in spite of his sour mood. Animals didn't hold grudges for years, he thought, wishing humans didn't, either.

"Hey, Cody!"

He spotted Hoyle Bixby laboring down the trail. If some people were called long drinks of water, Hoyle would barely measure up to a few drops in the bottom of a glass. His wiry little body had practically disappeared under the mound of equipment he insisted on toting around on a daily basis. He refused to camp overnight in the hills. Hoyle had so many stories to tell of murder and mysterious disappearances in the Superstitions, it was amazing there were any guests left in town.

Hoyle waved and shouted, "What're you an' that ole dog doin' up here? Goin' out of the town ownership business an' back into prospectin'?"

"Naw. Takin' a walk, that's all." Cody stopped and waited for Hoyle to reach him. "Find anythin'?"

"You should know better'n that. I'd like to see where those guys found them nuggets. You an' your uncle an' his partners prospected 'round here for years without findin' nothin'. How come there're nuggets suddenly?" Hoyle unloaded his gear and pulled back his shoulders. A grimace deepened the lines around his mouth. His face, brown as an old leather saddle and cratered like the surface of the mountains behind his back, was streaked with sand and dirt.

"Maybe it's Cactus Station's last dyin' kick," Cody said.

A horn sounded, followed by the short burst of a siren. The noises echoed around the hills and down the canyons. Cody knew the origin even before he saw the sheriff's car parked in front of the hotel with the coroner's black wagon behind it.

Three figures stood in front of the hood, easily recognizable, even from that distance. One was unmistakably Crystal with her small, slender figure and shoulder-length brown hair blowing in the hot breeze. The other two figures were a tall, round-bellied man in a law-enforcement uniform and a short, bearded man with longish white hair touching the shoulders of his white shirt. He wore black pants and a black jacket hung over one arm. Cody had only seen the coroner once before, but he remembered the hair.

"What's goin' on? Social call or business?" Hoyle hitched up his pants and grabbed his gear.

"Bit of both." Cody helped Hoyle out by taking a heavy knapsack filled with tools. He watched as Crystal escorted the two men up the stairs and they disappeared inside the hotel.

Hoyle squinted. "Is that the coroner's wagon?" he asked. "I can't see without my glasses."

"Yeah," Cody said. He took two shovels and a pickaxe from his companion's grimy fingers. "Step it up or I'll leave you behind," he told Hoyle.

"I'm comin'." Hoyle broke into a rolling version of a trot. "Don't wanna miss out on anythin' good."

"That figures," Cody said under his breath.

"What?" Hoyle already sounded winded.

"I'll see you back at the hotel."

Cody increased his speed and easily left Hoyle behind. By the time he hit the front steps of the hotel, he was almost at a dead run. He stowed Hoyle's equipment behind the desk and followed the sound of voices through the kitchen and out to the back porch.

Sheriff Dalton held out one large, blunt-fingered hand. "'Afternoon, Cody. Interesting problem you've got here."

"Yeah, I guess you could say that." Cody shook hands. "You take a look?"

"Sure did." The sheriff nodded slowly, his deceptively mild hazel eyes fixed on Cody's face. "Coroner's still up there. I came down to get Crystal's statement."

Crystal handed Dalton a glass of lemonade. "Guests are beginning to come back. People are going to start asking questions," she said, her finely drawn brows pulling together. "What am I supposed to tell them? That there's an old, uninvited guest on the third floor?"

Her eyes, usually as blue as cornflowers on a summer day, were veiled and troubled. Her kissable mouth wore a dimple at one corner; a dimple that only appeared when Crystal was perturbed. Cody well remembered the depth of that dimple the day he told her summer was over and so was their affair. He shifted uncomfortably at the memory. Crystal evidently misinterpreted his body-language.

"I'm sorry this is so boring for you," she snapped. "I suppose you find skeletons in *your* closet every day of the week."

"All the time. Some are more trouble than others." The words were out before he could stop them.

Damn it! She'd needled him again, and he'd reacted with his usual

29

defensive sarcasm. Crystal needed sympathy and support at that moment, regardless of the way she reached for it. Her methods left much to be desired, that was for sure. By the time he had convinced her of his sincerity in wanting to mend his fences with her, he would be bruised, bleeding, and crawling on hands and knees. Even then he might not succeed, he realized with painful insight. Unless he was totally misinterpreting Crystal's signals, she wanted nothing to do with him at all.

To reinforce his train of thought, the look Crystal shot in his direction would have withered flowers if any had been growing in the arid desert soil. Cody could have kicked himself. He realized Reed was watching them both, his congenial face marred by a deep frown.

"I made coffee," Cody said. "I'll get you a cup." *Anything to beat a hasty retreat.*

But Crystal was already moving toward the back door. "I'll get it," she said. "Why don't you take the sheriff into the parlor? It's more private."

Cody nodded. "It's off the lobby," he told Reed.

Jackson lumbered to his feet and walked ahead of them through the brutally hot kitchen, now filled with a tantalizing aroma of roasting meat.

"Smells right good," Reed said.

"Yeah. Only Crystal would use an oven in mid-summer, though." Cody watched Jackson slump down in front of the reception desk. "Behave yourself," he admonished. "No threatening the guests today."

Jackson thumped his tail half-heartedly, head on paws. The breeze from the fan ruffled his matted coat.

Hoyle straggled in, his boots leaving a trail of sand. Cody wished Reed Dalton would move faster than a snail's pace. He'd prefer to miss the fireworks when Crystal spotted that dirt.

"Your gear's behind the desk," he told Hoyle. "You'd better get washed up for dinner, but do yourself and me a favor--ask Crystal for a broom an' take care of that mess before you do anythin' else. She'll be in a snit for the rest of the day, otherwise."

Hoyle looked behind him and his eyes turned into two big Goobers. He scurried off toward the kitchen.

"The parlor's over here." Cody slid open a pocket door and ushered Reed inside the darkened, musty room.

Reed sniffed. "You ever *been* in here before?" he asked. "It smells worse than the attic."

Cody opened the drapes and managed to push up a window, despite its squealing resistance. A slight breeze lifted the ragged net curtains and brought a breath of fresh air into the stagnant atmosphere.

Crystal placed her tray on the table in front of the high-backed, faded horsehair couch. Sounds of brisk sweeping came from the lobby.

"Thanks, Cody." She jerked her head in the direction of Hoyle's industrious little figure. And then she did something totally unexpected and more than welcome--she actually smiled.

Cody felt more relief than he had in two weeks. He pulled the pocket door closed while she poured coffee and handed it to Reed.

"Do you think the coroner would like some, too, when he comes back down from the attic?" she asked Dalton.

"Thanks." Reed checked the couch out before gently perching on the edge of it. "Walt's not one for coffee. He'll probably take a soda when he's finished up there."

Cody sank into the recesses of an old side chair. One of the springs poked his back, while another rammed him in the hip. "So, what do you think about our skeleton?" he asked the sheriff.

"Right now, I wouldn't even like to hazard a guess." Reed shook his head when Crystal offered him cream. "From the state of the thing, I'd say it's been dead for quite a while, but as to whether the body was stuffed in the closet right after death or brought there later, I wouldn't like to say, and we may never know." He shrugged. "I'm sure the coroner will want to send it for forensic testing. He already said it's an adult male--you can tell by the pelvic bones, and the length of the femurs." He looked at Cody. "Those are the long leg bones," he said.

"I know what they are," Cody said. "I've watched the crime shows on TV."

"Are you going to take it away today?" Crystal asked. She passed a mug of coffee to Cody.

Cody wondered if she was going to make another attempt at drinking the strong brew herself. Irreverently, he followed that thought with an image of her taking a big gulp from his beer earlier. The image brought a twitch to his lips.

Crystal raised her eyebrows at the smirk. Cody's mood deflated. He just couldn't stay on the right side of her for more than two minutes at a stretch. He took a gulp of his coffee. She must have thrown the old stuff out and brewed another pot while he was out walking. The liquid slipped down his throat in a pleasurable way instead of tearing its way down to his stomach like molten lava fresh from a volcano.

"Billy Ride's here to help the coroner transport the remains," Reed said. "He elected to stay up there with Walt. I don't see how they can do it. I had to come down for a break before I passed out." He shook his head. "I remember when nothing affected me--long, hot days out searching for lost tourists and prospectors, cold nights camping out with only a bedroll--"

"But the skeleton," Crystal interrupted.

"Yes, oh, sorry." He smiled and drank the last of his coffee. "I get side-tracked, sometimes."

He handed his mug to Crystal, who refilled it.

"Since we don't have the fancy facilities in Apache Junction, it'll have to go either to Phoenix or Tucson," he said. He took the sandwich Crystal offered him. "I left that part up to Walt." He bit into the sandwich. "Hmm. That's mighty good, Miss Crystal."

"Please, don't call me that." Crystal's lips tightened. "Cody calls me Miss Crystal to annoy me. It works very well."

Reed swallowed and almost choked.

Cody grinned. It was nice to see someone else in trouble, for a change. "You think there's a chance we could get the skeleton back after the investigation's finished?" he asked.

"*Cody!*" Crystal's coffee slopped all over the floor. She ignored the mess. "What are you thinking? We don't want that thing back here!"

Cody used the rag from his back pocket to mop up the spill. "Just a thought," he said. "If it's an old citizen of Cactus Station, it'd be right and proper to bring it back."

"For a decent burial, you mean?" She visibly relaxed. "I suppose that would be the thing to do, wouldn't it?" She looked helplessly at the sheriff.

"We can discuss that later. It's a mite premature now." He stood up. "I'm going to look around the attic again."

"Are you going to be dusting for fingerprints or something up there?" Crystal asked. "How long do you think the coroner's going to need before the remains can be brought down?"

Sheriff Dalton shrugged. "I'm not sure. Maybe a half hour or so? I've checked for fingerprints, but there's nothing up there that I can see. I don't think it's worth sending out a team from Phoenix, unless Walt thinks there really was foul play involved. Maybe whoever he was died of natural causes, but there wasn't time to bury him, so instead of leaving him where animals could get him, he got wrapped in a blanket and stored."

"Ugh. That's really horrible," Crystal said.

"Not in the middle of a gold rush. People didn't want to waste time and energy digging a grave when they could be out getting rich. Especially if it was someone they didn't particularly like. Out of sight, out of mind." Dalton headed for the stairs. "Why don't you come with me?" he asked Cody.

"Okay." Cody couldn't imagine why Reed needed him, but he went along.

"You're not talking about burying it, are you?" Reed Dalton asked when they reached the attic.

"This town needs a few attractions," Cody said.

"Did you plant those nuggets the prospectors found?"

Cody looked at the portly, middle-aged man with the narrowed eyes. He thought Reed was altogether too shrewd for an out-in-the-sticks law officer.

"Where would I find nuggets?" Cody asked in what he hoped was a casual tone.

"You've had plenty of opportunities to store up a few," Reed said. "It wouldn't take much to stir up gold fever around here."

Cody snorted. "You seriously think I'd be stayin' in this rat hole if I had gold to throw away?"

Frenzied barking interrupted further conversation.

"Cody?" Crystal called. "Could you come here for a moment?"

Relieved to escape Reed's questioning, Cody went to the head of the stairs. "Can't you stop Jackson barking without me?" he grumbled, but he went down to join her.

Crystal stood waiting on the landing. Unexpectedly, she smiled at him. "You've got dirt on your cheek." Her thumb rubbed it gently away. "You need a shave," she said, her voice softening. "And a cobweb remover." Her hand brushed them out of his hair.

"You're hired," he said. "The pay's no good, but there could be other perks." He reached out for her, and she didn't resist. "Crystal...I..."

"Well, I think I've got what I need," Sheriff Dalton said, his heavy footfalls assaulting the stairs. "Walt," he shouted. "I'll ask Crystal to give Billy sodas for both of you when he gets the body bag."

"Damn," Cody said under his breath. Always interruptions. And Jackson's ruckus was still going on in the background.

"Why is that dog barkin' his fool head off?" he asked Crystal.

She clapped one hand over her mouth. "What's the matter with me?" She grabbed Cody's hand. "The bus."

"Bus?" He allowed her to drag him over to the main staircase. "What bus?"

"That bus." Crystal pointed. "And all those people."

He saw Jackson standing on the threshold, teeth bared, hackles fully operational, all four legs planted in an aggressive stance as he held what appeared to be at least fifty people at bay.

Cody ran, taking the stairs two at a time and yelling at Jackson the whole way down to the lobby.

CHAPTER SIX

The thirty "bus people," as Crystal dubbed them, got housed in the old rooming house opposite the hotel. Barely fit for even Jackson to sleep in, the building was greeted with oohs and ahhs of delight by people looking for atmosphere at night and instant fortune in the hills during the day.

By the time the new guests had eaten, then settled in with their sleeping bags, backpacks and prospecting equipment, Crystal knew that intuition may have had more to do with that huge meat order mistake. Not only were the roasting pans empty, but so was the refrigerator--again.

Sheriff Dalton, the coroner and Billy Ride had all stayed to dinner, too. The skeleton was brought downstairs in a black body bag and stowed in the back of the coroner's wagon while the rest of the diners tucked into meat, mashed potatoes, gravy and salad either at picnic tables at the back of the hotel, seated on the rotting porches, or even perched on rocks. A festive atmosphere reigned at the back of the buildings, while the somber proceedings took place at the front.

Cody looked at the amassed garbage bags on the back porch and the pots and pans piled into the kitchen sink and spilling onto the counters, table and stove.

"Why don't you go to bed?" he told Crystal. "You look exhausted."

"I am." She stifled a yawn and pushed her hair back from her face. Bed sounded so good. Her back and shoulders ached, her feet hurt, and her head pounded. "I need Tylenol and a bath."

Cody's mouth quirked into a genuine smile instead of the usual smirk. The effect was devastating to Crystal's dangerously-compromised defenses.

"I can get you the Tylenol," he said. "But a bath? Sorry, the boiler's one thing I *can't* fix. We're gonna have to buy a replacement." He grabbed the biggest pot and started filling it with water. "Better get some hot water into the sink and start soakin' this stuff."

"What did you and the uncles do when you lived here before--bathe in cold water?" Crystal sat at the table and eased her throbbing feet out of her boots.

"Yeah. Mostly in the creek. Sometimes we brought a tin tub into the kitchen, heated buckets of water and scrubbed down. About once a year, because it was just too much trouble." He cleared a space on the stove and set the pot of water to heat. "The tub's still on the back porch. I can rinse it out and bring it inside for you."

Crystal rubbed her feet. No way. Not without curtains and locks on all the doors. "No, thanks. I'll pass."

"It doesn't take that long to heat water in buckets," Cody assured her. He rolled up his sleeves and began stacking the dirty pots and pans.

"Even though it sounds tempting, Cody, I'm not risking an audience." She pointed to the bare windows.

"I'll hang a sheet," he said.

"I'd still run the risk of someone walking into the kitchen." She could almost feel the water and see the bubbles.

"Not with me around. They wouldn't dare. I'd patrol and chase them off."

"And that's supposed to make me feel *so* much safer. You outside the window. Hmm. I think not." She could just imagine him taking the opportunity to see what he'd missed over the last few years.

"I promise I wouldn't look your way even once." He grinned, his eyes twinkling in that charming, irreverent way.

She felt the effects right down to her toes. It was rather like standing on a fault line in the middle of a major earthquake. At least an eight on the Richter scale. Well, closer to nine point five if she was totally honest with herself, she decided.

"I'll think about it." She managed a smile, even though the effort cost her more energy than she wanted to waste. "In the meantime, I have to do dishes."

"I'll take care of them," Cody said. "Go to bed, honey. It's been a long day."

Crystal looked at him carefully. He'd called her honey. That wasn't one of his usual expressions. His eyes were a soft and brilliant sapphire blue, arresting in his tanned face.

"Are you sure?" Her voice sounded as unsteady as the rest of her felt.

"Positive." His fingers pushed the tangle of hair from her brow. "We need help around here. Trouble is, we can't afford it."

"With all these guests?" She stood up and stretched, her hands in the small of her back. "That bus-load of people alone will bring in enough cash to hire someone to clean rooms and change sheets. I can't do all of this, and you've got your hands full trying to repair enough of Cactus Station to house everyone."

"I know it's too much, believe me. You don't need to keep hammerin' home your point."

He ran his hands through his hair. "Let's talk about it tomorrow, okay?"

He was right. They didn't need to talk business at the end of the day. Especially when he looked so appealingly tired and rumpled.

"Okay," she said.

She remembered the texture of his hair and his skin as though it were yesterday. When he suddenly enfolded her in his arms, the years fell away and she was a college student again, her head on his chest, her nose filled with his own particular scent, devoid of colognes or after-shave. The Cody she remembered felt the same as this one: strong and impenetrable outside, but soft and pliable inside.

"Do you remember how I used to hold you?" he whispered, as though he had interpreted her train of thought.

"Yes." Her voice was as soft as a sigh.

"Do you remember how I used to kiss you?"

She raised her face. The moonlight and the fatigue must be addling her brain, she decided as his lips touched hers, fiery magic, all warmth and power and longing. The kiss deepened in what felt like a natural progression. Her lips parted and she tasted his breath, lightly tinged with peppermint and promise.

"Oh, Cody," she wanted to say. *"I've missed you so much."* But she kept silent, her secrets intact. He had used her once; he wouldn't use her again. She pulled away.

Although he released her immediately, his eyes filled with sadness. "Good night," he said, his voice low.

"See you tomorrow." She turned away from him and from the emotions she couldn't deal with when she was under the influence of the desert's velvet night and her memories.

When she glanced back, he had already left the kitchen, disappearing into the darkness outside. She slowly climbed the stairs, her hand gliding along the banister. Then she remembered the pot of water still heating on the stove. What if he didn't come back for a while and the pot boiled dry? A fire would start and burn down the hotel.

She regretfully retraced her steps, filled the sink with the hot water and a generous squirt of liquid soap. She turned off the kitchen light, and the lower floor plunged into darkness. One of the guests must have turned out the light in the lobby.

Crystal decided to turn on the reception desk's lamp. She pushed open the door and heard muted voices. Cody and Sheriff Dalton were talking while the sheriff walked around to his car door. Crystal didn't plan to sneak around eavesdropping, but her bare feet made no noise as she walked across the lobby, and the doors of the hotel stood wide open.

"I don't care what you say, Cody." Reed let his cigarette drop and ground it out with his heel. "Planting nuggets isn't going to save this town. You've got far more at stake than guests at the hotel are going to pay for."

"Cactus Station is mine." Cody's voice was hard. "I plan to keep it that way. This town was part of my uncle's dream and I mean to keep it alive for him."

"What about Crystal?" Reed asked.

"I'll buy her out and send her back to civilization, where she belongs."

Cody's fist connected with the roof of the patrol car, making a hollow sound that echoed in Crystal's heart. "She should never have come back here. She knows that as well as I do."

"How do you plan to accomplish that?" Reed asked in a scoffing tone. "Plant a few nuggets in her back pack or simulate a gold rush, so she's got too many guests to handle?"

"Whatever it takes." Cody folded his arms across his chest. "She doesn't belong here, and I'm gonna make sure she leaves as fast as possible."

Crystal crept back to the kitchen, where she took the back stairs up to her room. She'd heard enough, and she'd been right to guard her emotions. She wouldn't make a fool of herself twice with the same man. Neither was he going to run her out of town, she vowed as she set the alarm for 5:00AM. She'd show him how well she could run the hotel, boarding house and any other building in Cactus Station.

CHAPTER SEVEN

Crystal awoke with a headache equal to the size of the grocery list she had to take to Apache Junction. She had totally over-stretched her resources, but she wasn't about to admit it.

If Cody had really planted those nuggets, she'd have his head, she thought as she opened the door of the pickup. As though he'd heard her, he came strolling around the side of the hotel with his tool kit slung over one shoulder and his hands shoved deep into the pockets of his jeans. He was whistling slightly off-key, which grated on Crystal's already frayed nerves.

"Goin' shoppin'?" He grinned and winked.

Crystal could have kicked herself for allowing moonlight to overcome her common sense the night before. She should never have allowed him to kiss her. He knew now that despite everything she said, he still had the power to ignite her body like a match to a powder keg.

"I don't have any choice with all these mouths to feed." She threw her purse onto the passenger's seat and climbed into the old truck. "I should have majored in hotel management or the culinary arts in college, instead of geology. I can tell you just how much dynamite it'll take to blast a hole in a pile of rock, but I have trouble figuring out what to make for dinner and how much food to buy."

"Why don't you take my Blazer today?" Cody dug around in his pockets as he stepped off the boardwalk. He pulled out his key ring. "Mine's got air conditionin' an' almost a full tank of gas. It won't tell you what to cook for dinner, but at least it'll make the drive a little easier."

Crystal hesitated. Despite her desire to remain self-sufficient, Uncle Dock's old pickup was an uncomfortable ride, and she'd waved her own car away at the back of a tow truck.

Just then, a tall, thin girl ambled across the street. Crystal watched her over Cody's shoulder. Dressed in skin-tight faded jeans, a black vest and a brown check shirt with the sleeves rolled up to the elbows, she managed to look cool and comfortable. Her long brown hair slid off her shoulders and streamed behind her as a hot wind gusted down the street.

Cody saw Crystal's preoccupation and turned. "Hi, Jolie," he greeted the girl. "Where's Harold?"

Jolie smiled a little thinly. "Out with the rest of 'em. He left before five this mornin'. Tryin' to get the jump on the others, I guess. I don't think he was too successful."

Her drawl, conjuring up visions of moss-covered trees and fog-shrouded bayous, sounded like East Texas or Louisiana to Crystal, who wondered if Jolie had arrived on the bus and when Cody had found time to meet her.

"Jolie, this is my partner, Crystal Penney," Cody said. He stepped aside so the two women got a clear view of each other. "Crystal, Jolie and her husband, Harold, rode all the way from Port Arthur, Texas on a motorcycle."

"I bet that was a hot trip," Crystal ventured.

Jolie's nose wrinkled in disgust. "Hot ain't the word for it. I told Harold if he thinks he's gettin' me back on that bike, he'd better think again. He's gotta hit pay dirt so's he can buy me a plane ticket home." She grinned at Crystal. "Men are so thick-headed sometimes."

"Sometimes!" Crystal shook her head. "I think they're always like that."

"Includin' Cody?" Jolie laughed and shot Cody a flirtatious look.

For some reason, Crystal didn't feel irritated. She couldn't say why, because to her chagrin, any other time another woman looked at Cody, she felt unreasonably jealous.

"He's at the front of the pack," Crystal said, unable to prevent herself smiling at Cody's wounded expression.

"You goin' somewhere?" Jolie asked.

"Apache Junction." Crystal took the keys out of Cody's hand. "But not in the pickup. Cody just offered me his Blazer with air conditioning."

"Want some company?" Jolie pulled a rubber band out of her vest pocket and drew her hair through it, making a loose pony tail.

"Sure." Crystal couldn't remember when she'd last spent time in the company of another woman. It seemed she'd been surrounded by men her entire life.

Cody watched them walk away, the tool kit swinging from one hand and a perplexed look on his face. Crystal wasn't sure whether it was because she'd just found a friend or because she'd taken him up on his offer without arguing about it first.

Jolie was articulate, sarcastic and open. Within thirty minutes she had let Crystal know that Harold was the man in her life, but if he ever let her down, she'd be after Cody in a heartbeat. Jolie also told Crystal she thought Cody wouldn't even spare her a second look.

"He's a one woman man, Crystal, and you're that woman," she said, energetically smacking gum.

"You don't know Cody." Crystal accelerated on the final stretch of single lane highway before Apache Junction. "Thinking he's capable of having a one woman, one man relationship is a bunch of nonsense."

"You think so, huh?" Jolie pushed wisps of hair away from her face. "I was thinkin' about gettin' my hair cut. Whadda ya think?"

"I don't think it would suit you, but that's only my opinion." Crystal glanced in the rearview mirror and wondered if she should change her own look. She'd been in some sort of rut over the last few years.

"You're fine just the way you are, hon," Jolie said, watching her. "You could do with a bit more meat on your bones, though. Have you been takin' care of all the cookin' an' chores by yourself?"

"Yes, and it's too much. I was complaining to Cody right before you arrived."

"Want to hire some help?" Jolie pulled out a cigarette, lit it and prepared to throw the match out the window.

"I don't so much mind your smoking," Crystal said. "But you can't throw anything out the window that would burn. We're always having brush fires around here in the dry season."

"Sorry." Jolie pulled open the ashtray. "Bad old habits. We get so much rain around where I'm from; I guess I'm not careful enough."

"I can't imagine living somewhere that has a lot of rain." Crystal smiled. "We think we're having a monsoon if we get one rainstorm a month."

"Where I come from, we get so much rain, we wonder if'n we should be buildin' an ark sometimes." Jolie blew smoke rings. "So, you need help with the cookin' an' such?" she pursued. "I'm pretty good in a kitchen. I grew up on a farm with eleven brothers an' sisters an' all the workers. My ma ran a soup kitchen three times a day, seemed like, an' I helped from the time I was big enough to stand on a chair an' wield a spoon."

"I'd *love* help. Did Harold get ESP when he made you climb on that motorcycle?"

"He had somethin', but I wouldn't call it ESP." Jolie laughed, her laugh as generous as her spirit. "If'n he don't find gold, he's gonna have somethin' a lot worse to worry 'bout, as my daddy used to say."

Crystal pulled the Blazer into the grocery store parking lot.

"Now." Jolie took a pen from the top pocket of her western-style shirt. "Let's look at your shoppin' list. Then we'll see if we can't buy enough groceries to last a couple of days instead of all this drivin' you've been doin'."

"How did you know I've been doing a lot of driving? I thought you only arrived yesterday." Crystal looked suspiciously at her companion. Who'd been talking about her business? Cody, she thought.

"Cody," Jolie affirmed. "He met Harold and me when we arrived late yesterday afternoon. He's concerned about you. He thinks you're gonna make yourself ill with the work."

"I already about did that," Crystal said before she could stop herself.

"Is that so?" Jolie stopped scribbling items on the grocery list. "What was the cause?"

"Business." Crystal grabbed her purse off the back seat.

A sickening twinge grabbed first her heart, then her stomach. Talking about her affairs was all too painful. Her nerve endings were still too raw. She couldn't even think about the events of the past six months when she was in her room, let alone discuss them with a stranger in a crowded parking lot.

"I'm fine," she said. "I don't want to talk about it with you. Let's pick up the groceries and head back, so I can clean the guests' rooms."

Jolie dropped the remains of her cigarette onto the blacktop and ground it out with her heel. "Let them clean their own rooms," she said. "You need to put up a sign that tells 'em to do everythin' themselves. All you should be providin' is the room an' an evenin' meal. Charge 'em for anythin' else."

Crystal frowned. What a radical idea, but what a pleasing one, too. She felt a heavy load shift on her shoulders.

"Hon, you're wearin' yourself out for no reason." Jolie grabbed an empty cart and started pushing it toward the store. "Most of these guys'd be thankful just to have a bed an' runnin' water at the end of a hard day out prospectin'."

"That's true," Crystal said slowly. "But I don't want the hotel turning into some flop house with dirty beds and filthy rooms."

"So charge more for the privilege of stayin' at the hotel. I'll help you keep it clean if you let me an' Harold stay for free. I need somethin' to occupy me while he's out diggin'."

"You don't have the urge to go out there, too?" Crystal knew if Cody announced he was going back into the mountains with a pickaxe, she'd have a lot of trouble stopping herself from joining him.

"No way. This heat's too much for me."

"But Texas is hot."

"Yeah, I know it is, and everyone says this is a *dry* heat." Jolie rolled her eyes. "I don't care what you Arizona folks say, Crystal. One hundred an' fifteen degrees is still one hundred an' fifteen degrees. Right now, bein' in this parking lot feels like the inside of an oven. Texas is humid, an' not as hot as Arizona, neither." Her expression grew wistful. "I wish I was back there, sippin' lemonade on my porch swing instead of waitin' around all day for Harold. How do you stand havin' your man gone for weeks on end in those mountains?"

"I think you're under some misapprehension," Crystal said. "Cody's not my man."

"Oh, yes he is, hon." Jolie pushed her cart up a short ramp and into the blissfully cool interior of the store. "I can see it all over your face when you look at him."

Oh God. Crystal stopped in front of a display of peaches and leaned against the cold metal. She could only hope Cody wasn't as perceptive as Jolie.

"Come on, girl. Step it up." Jolie headed for the meat counter. "We've got a lot to do."

CHAPTER EIGHT

Cody spent the morning putting all the old shutters back up on the ground floor of the hotel. Crystal would be able to close them and have privacy in the kitchen if she wanted to take a bath. He even installed a bolt on the swinging door between the kitchen and hallway.

He hoped she'd open up to Jolie. Crystal needed a friend, and he wasn't being too successful in that department. Despite all his efforts, she hadn't warmed up to him at all.

His thoughts returned to the night before. Laying down his hammer, he sat in the shade on the back porch steps and got water out of the cooler. He took off his hat and wiped his dust-caked forehead before draining the bottle. He'd seen another side of Crystal when he'd taken her in his arms and kissed her in the moonlight. No longer a young girl, she had responded to him as a woman. Her passion had taken him completely by surprise, and he'd felt himself react with the same urgency as a champagne bottle about to be uncorked. If she hadn't pulled away, he would have carried her up to his bed.

Without Crystal, his life had been empty, regardless of how many times he'd tried to fill it. He'd never found another woman who could thrill him like Crystal did with only a touch, a word, or a look. Cody closed his eyes and leaned back against the cooler, forgetting the heat and the dust. In his mind, he made love to Crystal slowly and completely, fulfilling every fantasy he'd ever held about her since she'd left Cactus Station all those years before.

What a fool he'd been, listening to his own fears and the uncles' dire predictions. He should have gone to Phoenix and gotten an education instead of following his uncle on that quest for the Lost Dutchman Mine. That damn mine had occupied most of Willy's waking hours and dominated his dreams. Cody felt resentment welling up.

Instead of settling down with Crystal and proving himself capable of supporting both of them, he'd used his slick tongue to talk people into investing money in Uncle Willy's hunt for the Dutchman. He'd been so successful, his name had become synonymous with large grub stakes. Cody sighed and opened his eyes. Uncle Willy was dead and he was no longer into glib talking. Maybe in a way he had to prove to himself as well as Crystal that he was capable of doing something other than panhandling for a living.

"What you doin' on them steps in the middle of the day?"

Cody squinted at Hoyle Bixby's weathered face. "And what are you doin' in town at this time, Hoyle? I thought you prospected from sun up to sundown."

"I came back for somethin' to eat. I was so excited last night, what with the skeleton an' all, I forgot to eat dinner. Then I overslept and missed breakfast. I'm starvin'." Hoyle hitched his baggy pants, held up only by a battered leather belt.

Cody couldn't help laughing. "You'd better come inside before a dust devil blows you away." He grabbed his tool belt and stood up, motioning Hoyle into the kitchen.

"Damn, Cody. I shouldn't be in here. If Miss Crystal sees me, she'll chase me out with a broom. I'm filthy and she don't like dirt in her kitchen."

"Relax. She's gone to Apache Junction with Jolie, Harold's wife. You know how women love to talk an' shop. They'll probably be gone half the day."

I hope, he added silently. He had a call in to Reed Dalton about getting the skeleton returned as soon as the investigation was completed. If he could put it on display in the lobby and concoct some yarn, he was sure more tourists would come to Cactus Station. The last thing he and Crystal needed was more folk like Hoyle, who could barely afford to pay his way.

Cody had to talk with Crystal about attracting more businesses. They needed convenience and hardware stores and a souvenir shop. Maybe even a small grocery store. They could rent the space out and take a percentage of the profits. He didn't know much about business, but it seemed to him that was the way it should be done. He made sandwiches while he thought. Hoyle kept prattling on in the background, Cody listening with only half an ear.

"So what does Miss Crystal say about your dog bein' in here?" Hoyle asked.

Cody snapped out of his introspection. Jackson lay beneath the table, his coat grey with dust. A fine layer of sand showed his path from the lobby.

"Damn!" Crystal was going to be furious. "Out, Jackson." He opened the screen door.

Jackson grunted and rolled onto his side, exposing his dirt-encrusted belly. As though that wasn't enough, he stretched and then rolled completely onto his back, kicking his legs.

"Dammit, Jackson." Cody crouched beside the table. "Will you please go outside an' shake yourself off so I can clean up before Crystal makes both of us regret livin'?"

Jackson yawned in response.

"If you don't do as I tell you, I swear I'll bathe you," Cody threatened.

Jackson whined and flipped right side up. He crawled out from under the table and ambled over to the screen door.

"I knew you'd see sense." Cody opened the door. Jackson energetically shook himself all over the threshold before heading for the porch railing, where he lifted his leg.

Cody swore under his breath. Now he had to clean the kitchen floor as well as the lobby, and then throw a bucket of detergent onto the wet wood outside.

He took the broom and dustpan into the kitchen. Hoyle was sinking his teeth into a ham sandwich. "Beer?" Cody asked.

"Nah, thanks. It'll make me sweat when I get back outside. But I'll take water."

"Sure." Cody took a jug out of the refrigerator and set it in front of Hoyle with a glass.

Hoyle poured water and raised his glass. "Here's to luck," he said.

"To luck," Cody agreed.

He decided his lunch could wait until he'd cleaned up Jackson's mess. He ran the broom under the table and something dragged against the bristles. Cody bent down and picked up a dirty coin.

He held it up between his fingers. "Is this yours?" he asked Hoyle.

"Nope," Hoyle mumbled around his sandwich. He wiped his mouth on the back of his hand. "What is it?"

"Probably some prospector's lucky piece," Cody said. "I bet Jackson found it lying around somewhere." He shoved it in his pocket.

Hoyle pointed to the other sandwich. "Are you gonna eat that?"

"I guess not," Cody said as Hoyle grabbed it.

CHAPTER NINE

Hoyle stayed long enough to consume both sandwiches, a wedge of pie, half a jug of water and three cups of black coffee. Cody barely managed to contain his temper. Now he had to add washing dishes to his 'to do' list, because the thought of a filthy Hoyle Bixby on kitchen detail repulsed him. When Hoyle finally bolted out the back door, it was because he heard Crystal and Jolie coming through the front.

Crystal came into the kitchen and placed two bags on the corner of the table. Her eyebrows lifted in disbelief at the mess of plates, crumbs and hacked out pie. The expression on her face would have sent Satan scurrying for cover. Cody wanted to join the Devil in hiding.

"I hope you had a good time while we were shopping." Her voice sounded like a blast of winter air at the North Pole. "It looks like you took Jackson out to roll in the dust and then used him to sweep the entire ground floor of the hotel. And now I see you must have also decided to have a picnic with the ham and apple pies I had planned to use for supper."

Cody's temper rose to the occasion. "Yeah, you would think that, wouldn't you?" he snapped just as Jolie walked in and dumped an armful of bags onto the counter.

"Don't you worry none about any of it, Crystal," she said as she started taking packages of hot dogs out of the bags and stacking them neatly in the refrigerator. "You go lie down and rest awhile. Cody and I'll clean this mess up and put the groceries away, won't we?" She winked at him from behind Crystal's back.

"Yeah, I suppose we will." He glared at Crystal before stomping out to unload the rest of the supplies from the Blazer. He shoved the screen door and it fell to the ground yet again. "Goddammit." Cody kicked the screen aside.

"Anger doesn't help much, but I guess you've gotta do somethin'," Jolie said from behind him.

"That Crystal. One of these days, I swear I'll...I'll..." He faltered and stopped, turning away to grab the rest of the groceries. He used his knee to close the Blazer's door.

"You? Lost for words?" Jolie grinned. "What were you gonna say? Kiss her and take her to bed?" She laughed outright at his expression. "What's the matter--afraid to say it yourself? Don't tell me you haven't thought about it."

"Not lately, I haven't." Cody hefted a box and three bags up the steps.

Jolie took two of the bags away from him. When he started to protest, she grinned.

"You've got a whole lot of work ahead of you this afternoon. Don't you worry your head 'bout me carryin' two little bags of groceries into the hotel."

She walked in front of him into the kitchen. "You've got that screen door to fix, Jackson to bathe an' the sweepin'," she listed, as though she was talking to some subordinate. "I'll put away the groceries an' make dinner. There are gonna be some changes 'round here startin' tomorrow mornin'. No more two an' three meals for every Tom, Dick an' Harry that comes into this town. Crystal agreed that was too much work for two women. We're gonna provide a room an' one meal a day."

"She hired you? Without consultin' me?" Cody threw the box onto a chair.

"I made her a good deal--room an' board for Harold an' me against helpin' her out with the hotel and the caterin'."

"She should have asked me first," Cody said. "We're partners."

"I reckon she knew you'd realize she needed help." Jolie continued unpacking bags as she talked. "Crystal don't look well."

"That's true enough," he admitted. "She doesn't." He'd felt worried about her himself, and although he still felt betrayed by the way Crystal had gone over his head about hiring Jolie, he could see by the way she was organizing the kitchen with lightning speed that things might get a whole lot less stressful if she was around. He watched Jolie start a pot of beans and his anger receded. She was doing what he'd told Crystal to do earlier--cut down on the time and effort involved in taking care of the guests. But he still had questions.

"So where do you think the prospectors are gonna get the rest of their food?" he asked.

Jolie tossed her hair back, the gesture annoyingly dismissive. "We made some contacts in Apache Junction. There's a couple that wants to open a convenience store out here. That'll solve the problem of gettin' supplies all the time."

"You've been busy." Cody thought Jolie sounded more and more like she was in charge of the whole operation.

"Crystal said you own one side of the street an' she owns the other." Jolie leaned against the counter. "That couple's comin' here to look for a suitable buildin' later this afternoon. If they decide on the saloon, that'd be on Crystal's side, and she might get kinda crabby 'bout you sharin' the rent."

"Are they planning on doing the remodeling themselves, or will they need me?" Cody glowered at her. "If Crystal gets difficult or those people bring in outsiders, the road into town might suddenly develop a few problems."

Jolie returned his glare with a cool, level gaze. A trace of a dimple sat beside her generous mouth. "She's right, you know. You *are* pigheaded sometimes."

"Me?" He couldn't believe Jolie was making fun of him. "You've been spendin' too much time out in the heat. Crystal's the one who's bein' pigheaded. She's not built for livin' like this. She needs to go back where she belongs."

"So's you won't keep gettin' tempted, huh?" Jolie turned away and began packing the cupboards with flour, beans, rice and cornmeal.

"Damn right," Cody said, annoyed past caring what came out of his mouth.

He stalked out. Pausing only long enough to grab some gold panning equipment he'd left in the saloon, he struck out for the hills, his legs moving like pistons and keeping time with the throb in his temples.

CHAPTER TEN

It was practically dark before he returned tired, aching and covered with dust. He'd found nothing. Not that he'd expected to. He'd been away from gold panning too long-- his body complained in every joint from spending hours in a cramped position.

The lights from the Gold Rush Hotel slanted across Main Street like oblongs of the elusive metal for which it had been named. Someone had put the screen door back on, and done it well. New holes had been drilled and the door mounted securely with reinforcements to stop it tearing off its hinges. Cody dumped his equipment behind the reception desk.

Voices came from both the parlor and the kitchen. He dragged himself up to his room, where he stripped off his clothes and fell onto the bed under the open window. A welcome breeze blew across his hot, naked body and soothed him into a light sleep.

The sound of his door opening jerked him wide awake. Clouds cast shadows over the moon, leaving the room in semi-darkness. The air felt unusually moist and heavy, hinting at rain.

Cody lay still, waiting to identify the person creeping across the worn wooden floor, which suddenly squeaked in protest. The figure stopped, waited a moment to see if he stirred, then continued over toward the bed.

"Cody," Crystal said softly. "Are you okay? We missed you at supper."

He closed his eyes and feigned sleep. Crystal gasped when she realized he was lying naked on top of the bedclothes. When she tried to pull the comforter from under him, he lost his composure.

"Dammit, Crystal. Haven't you seen me naked enough times before not to be acting like you're shocked?"

"You're awake? You...you..." Fists clenched, she turned to leave.

Cody grabbed her wrist and she lost her balance. She fell across him, her head landing beside his on the pillow, the rest of her body blanketing him with softness. Cody felt himself respond strongly to the contact. He rolled onto his side, taking her with him, until she was lying with her face only inches from his.

"Did you really miss me?" His voice sounded as breathless as he felt.

"You know I did. I was worried sick about you." She sounded out of breath herself. The clouds parted and he saw her moisten her lips, her tongue glistening in the moonlight.

"Is that so?"

He captured those moist lips with his own and fitted her body against his. One hand tangled in the fine hair at the nape of her neck, the other splayed across her back, feeling her warmth through the thin material of her blouse.

Crystal whimpered deep in her throat and opened her mouth to his. The kiss deepened. Cody pulled her shirt out of her pants and trailed his fingers up her back. Her skin felt velvet-soft beneath his callused palm. He caressed her buttocks, round and firm in the heavy denim.

Her arms slipped around his waist and ran the length of his bare back, chilled from the draft coming through the window. Her hands did things to him that he had only dreamed about for too long. He cupped her breast, the nipple hardening beneath its flimsy lace covering.

"Don't," she implored against his mouth, but he wouldn't, couldn't listen.

He found the buttons on her shirt, hurriedly unfastened them and unclasped her bra. Her breasts rose and fell quickly, her eyes shining with a diamond-like quality in the darkness. Powerless to stop, he pulled the lace out of his way.

"I must," he whispered against the delectable, cushioned surface before covering her breast with his mouth.

His tongue came into contact with the already-hardened nipple and raised it to the consistency of a pebble while she moaned and ground her hips against the heavy part of him that throbbed for release.

Barely able to catch his breath, he drew down her zipper and eased her pants over her hips. Crystal's mouth was on his neck, her breath fanning his passion, her lips accelerating his pulse to a dizzying speed as she kissed her way toward his chest. He pulled off her wispy panties and tossed them onto the floor with the rest of her clothes.

She was his at last, and he wouldn't ruin the moment for either of them by hurrying. He forced himself to hold back, even though he barely had enough control left. He gently parted her thighs and raised himself above her. But as she rose to meet his thrust, a shaft of lightning rent the sky, struck the mountain glowering over Cactus Station and splintered rock with a crack as loud as the coming of Judgment Day.

Cody pulled away as swiftly as though the lightning had struck him instead of the Superstitions. His befuddled brain registered the fact that a wizened tree above Diamond Della's House of Splendors had burst into orange flames that clawed at the night sky.

"It's an omen," Crystal whispered. She scrambled to gather her clothes.

"Nonsense," Cody protested, but a chill ran through him. He grabbed his jeans and pulled them on. He wanted to chide Crystal for being superstitious, but she'd call him a hypocrite. The uncles had filled both their heads with tales of myth, tradition and folklore. Stories of ghostly apparitions and Indian taboos ran rampant through the gold prospecting community. Omens were to be respected, their messages to be obeyed.

"I'll go check things out; make sure the town's in no danger of goin' up in flames." Cody put on a denim shirt and fumbled with the buttons as he headed for the door.

He cursed the storm and the tree. If lightning hadn't struck, he would have made love to Crystal just as sure as the sun was going to rise again.

In the lobby, guests milled around like cattle on the verge of a stampede. Harold was trying to assure everyone that they were in no danger, but no one looked convinced, including Harold himself.

Cody pushed his way through the throng without troubling to give them any reassurances of his own. Let Crystal do that. He strode off the porch and headed across the street toward the decaying Dry Dust Saloon, a smaller version of the Nugget and on the opposite side of the street. His side. It wasn't as pretentious as Crystal's; mimicking their characters and relationship, he thought with resentment. He quickened his pace. If he didn't get that fire put out, he might not even have a side left, however modest.

Harold ran up behind him. "Wait up, Cody. I'll help you."

"You don't even know what I'm plannin' to do," he told the biker, who still wore knee high black leather boots, a chain at his belt and a red bandana around his forehead to keep his long black hair off his face.

What in the name of heaven Harold and Jolie were doing in Cactus Station was beyond Cody's comprehension. Bikers weren't supposed to be up at the crack of dawn to go panning for gold in some creek in the Superstitions. Bikers were supposed to be riding around in a group, creating disturbances and drinking beer.

Cody came to an abrupt halt and turned to face the tall, thin man laboring up the barely- visible track behind the saloon. Harold, intent of finding his footing in the near darkness, almost ran into Cody.

"What are you stoppin' for?" Harold demanded, panting. "I just got my momentum goin'."

"Are you the scout for a pack of bikers that are gonna come here to cause trouble?" Cody asked.

Harold looked at Cody as though he'd lost his mind. "Why the hell are you askin' me that right now?"

"No time like the present." Cody blocked Harold's way. "You didn't answer my question."

"I *do* belong to a club, but they have no idea I'm up here with Jolie. I saw an article in the local paper about a gold rush in Cactus Station and we came." Harold jangled the chain looping from his belt and sighed. "I don't want to work for some fat ole slob in a bike shop for the rest of my life. I want my own shop an' a house for Jolie. She gives me hell about havin' no ambition. I want to prove to her that I can make somethin' of myself. Maybe then she'll consider startin' a family."

"Oh." Cody turned away and started climbing again. "You an' I have a few things in common. I've never amounted to anythin' either, accordin' to Crystal."

"Is that right?" Harold slid off the steep, narrow path.

Cody quickly grabbed his companion's arm. "You shouldn't have followed me," he said, pulling Harold upright. "I know these mountains; you don't. You'll fall down an' kill yourself, then I'll have to listen to Jolie as well as Crystal tellin' me off."

"I'll be more careful," Harold promised. He shook free from Cody's grip. "I'll try to step where you do."

"It's gonna get steeper from here on out," Cody warned. "That tree's on an overhang, which is what makes it so dangerous to the town. If it falls, it'll set light to this whole side of Main Street."

"Isn't that *your* side?" Harold sounded totally winded. He paused to catch his breath and started to look back.

"Keep lookin' ahead," Cody said sharply as Harold started to sway, his feet too close together.

Harold obeyed and regained his balance. He hurried to catch up with Cody, who had quickly lengthened the distance between them. Harold sounded like a pack of horses clattering up the loose rocks, which fell behind him with a cascading roll of stone on stone all the way back down the trail.

Cody kept climbing, unhesitatingly finding toe and hand holds. He had climbed that trail countless times before, and he knew Harold would have to give up very shortly. If his breath didn't give out first, his sense of self-preservation would take over and he'd realize how stupid it was to continue.

"Don't you like me or somethin'?"

Harold's voice floated up to Cody while he prepared to swing up to the next ledge under the tree, still flickering with intermittent leaps of flame that illuminated the rocks with tongues of orange, red and yellow.

Cody gritted his teeth. Why did he have to be cursed with a useless sidekick? "I don't even know you," he called. "You can't follow me up here. Accept that and wait for me to get you back down or try it yourself. I told you not to come."

"I think you must have had one hell of a time with Crystal since you both arrived here."

Harold's voice sounded further away. Cody stopped climbing and strained to listen.

"Somethin' happened tonight that's made you as angry as hell, but don't take it out on me." Harold's voice held a definite note of uncertainty. It quivered audibly around the edges. "I wanted to help you, and now you're leavin' me stuck on the side of some mountain until you decide you're feelin' charitable enough to come back'n pick me up."

Cody sat on the ledge and took a deep breath. Harold was right--he was taking his frustrations out on anyone and everyone except the person responsible.

"Harold, I think you and Jolie are either gonna be great friends or royal pains," he shouted, the corners of his mouth twitching and an almost unbearable urge to laugh overtaking him. "Okay, I'll come down an' get you, you hard-headed Texan."

"Good," Harold said. "'Cause I'm hangin' onto some itty bitty piece of rock an' my legs're swingin' in the middle of nowhere."

CHAPTER ELEVEN

"They shouldn't have gone up there in the dark." Crystal paced back past the table where Jolie sat, chin on hands, watching the bubbling coffee pot.

Jolie's green eyes shifted from the pot to Crystal. "Hon, would you please sit down. You're makin' me more an' more nervous. Didn't you tell me your Cody knows the Superstitions so well he could find his way 'round them with his eyes shut?"

"I did say that, but I wasn't talking about him finding his way with Harold hanging off his coat-tails."

Jolie sat up straight, her eyes flashing. "Harold's capable of takin' care of his self. He don't need Cody doin' it for him."

"I didn't mean to offend you," Crystal clarified, anxious not to upset her new friend. "But unless Harold's got some hidden talents, I don't think he's gone rock-climbing in a long while. I saw him slip and almost fall a couple of times today on the main trail back into town. Cody's on a path that leads up the mountain. Some of it has to be climbed. Can Harold do that in the dark?"

Jolie shook her head. "Probably not."

"And that's exactly why I'm worried about both of them."

Little creases formed at the corners of Jolie's eyes. She looked older that evening under the stark fluorescent kitchen light. "No, it's not." She shook her head again. "Somethin' went on between you an' Cody tonight. You're more worried 'bout what's gonna happen when he gets back than you are about what's happen' out there right now."

"That's not true!" Crystal took the coffee pot off the stove and nearly dropped it, her hands shaking. She grabbed another towel and held the pot from the bottom until it was safely on the table with the creamer and mugs.

"You're real good at denial," Jolie said.

"I think you were sent here to drive me insane," Crystal countered. "I thought I was going to have some peace and quiet."

"Life's not like that if you face up to it." Jolie poured coffee and pushed a mug toward Crystal.

"What makes *you* so capable of facing everything?" Crystal dumped creamer into her coffee and stirred.

All she needed right then was a caffeine buzz. She doubted she'd be able to sleep at all that night, between berating herself for almost letting Cody make love to her and then blaming herself for her cowardice in not offering to go with him instead of sending Harold, who would be more of a hindrance than a help.

Jolie traced the outline of a wood knot in the rough surface of the table before answering, her eyes meeting Crystal's with a hint of moisture in their depths. "I lost three of my younger brothers to Viral Meningitis when I was fifteen," she said.

Crystal tried to interrupt, but Jolie silenced her with an upheld hand.

"You asked," she said. She dabbed at her eyes with a napkin. "I married my first husband too young and found myself workin' two jobs to support us while he was out of work most of the time. Then he left me after I found out I was pregnant an' got fired from both my jobs because I was gettin' mornin' sickness all day long an' wasn't turnin' up. I lost the baby an' went back to live with my parents for a while before I met Harold."

"Oh, Jolie, I'm sorry. I shouldn't have pried." Crystal felt ashamed. Next to Jolie's life, hers had been a breeze, and her problems with Cody sounded so juvenile and stupid.

"Well, you did; so now you know," Jolie said. "Harold's a sweet guy.

He buys me stuff an' treats me good, but he can't seem to keep a job for more'n a few weeks, either, an' he spends a lot on his bike. He wants us to have children, but I'm not bringin' kids into the world until their daddy makes enough to support them."

Crystal sipped her coffee as she mentally compared notes with Jolie's description of Harold. "Cody's much the same way," she said finally. "He's so lazy and shiftless. He'll never amount to anything. His idea of ambition is to get people to grubstake mining ventures that net them nothing ninety percent of the time."

"He's a flimflam man, is what you're sayin', then." Jolie lit a cigarette.

"In some ways," Crystal admitted. "I don't think he's ever looked at it that way. He always tried to make his Uncle Willy's dreams come true by supplying him with the means to go out and search for the Lost Dutchman Mine. Cody always managed to talk people into giving him the money needed to finance the uncles' next expedition."

"Then his intentions were honorable, if misguided. You shouldn't blame him for that."

"I don't." Crystal's insides squirmed. She hated trading secrets with anyone, let alone someone she'd only just met, but the burden of keeping everything inside was becoming too much.

"That's not what worries you, is it?" Jolie prompted.

Crystal was about to spill more of her secrets, but Jackson interrupted, jumping up from under the table and breaking into ear-splitting barks. The back door opened.

"Stop that racket, Jackson," Cody said.

He walked into the room with his arm around Harold's waist. Hopping on one leg, every open area of flesh covered with scratches, Harold looked as pale as the moonlit landscape outside.

Jolie rose, her face draining.

"I'm okay," Harold said. "Cody rescued me after I fell."

"Fell?" Jolie rushed over to support Harold on the other side. "What do you mean? Fell where? How far?"

"Only a few feet," Cody said. He guided Harold over to a chair. "He got up to the tree okay. It was comin' down that did him in."

"Oh, Harold. Are you all right, hon?" Jolie dabbed his bleeding face with the cloth Crystal handed her.

Harold tried to smile but winced instead. "I'll be fine. It's my ankle that's killin' me. I twisted it when I landed."

"It was a good landing," Cody said, like that should be some sort of comfort. "He ended up right on the path, only about ten feet down."

"Harold!" Jolie stopped dabbing the cloth. "You could've been killed."

"Nice to know you care." Harold grinned. He slid the bandana off his head and used it to wipe his face. "I'm okay, sweetheart. Seriously. I just need to get this boot off before my ankle swells any more."

While Jolie struggled with the boot, Crystal took Cody outside.

"You should have stopped him following you," she hissed. "You know better."

A furrow of annoyance appeared on Cody's brow. "I'm not a babysitter for all these greenhorns. Harold should know his own limits, not expect me to."

"You're a native 'Zonie. You've been in these mountains since you were nine years old. You know how dangerous they are. Where's your conscience?"

He shrugged, his smirk returning. "On vacation. You drove it away earlier this evening."

She wanted to wipe that smirk right off his face. "This is no time to be flippant."

"Oh, give it a rest, Crystal. I'm tired and dirty. I just had to get rid of that damned tree and half-carry Harold back down the side of a hill. I'm gonna get some soap an' head over to the creek. Maybe you should come with me, so you can throw cold water on your temper."

"I could just slap you for that comment." She turned her face away and blinked back tears.

"I bet you'd love to, wouldn't you?" His face came within inches of hers. "Go ahead. I dare you."

She didn't want him to see the tears swimming in her eyes. She stepped further into the shadows. "I was brought up to avoid physical violence," she said stiffly.

"It's a pity you weren't brought up to show a little human kindness and love once in a while," Cody said. He left her, the screen door slamming behind him as he marched through the kitchen.

Crystal stayed on the porch and cried silently. She'd almost given herself to him that evening, and he was accusing her of being nothing more than cold and totally emotionless.

It would be a long, cold day in hell before she'd show him anything but contempt.

CHAPTER TWELVE

The following morning, Crystal looked at herself in the cracked mirror over her dresser before going downstairs to get breakfast started. A gaunt, troubled face stared back at her.

"You've got to stop this feuding with Cody," she told her reflection. "It's not doing you a bit of good. You look terrible, and you feel even worse."

She pinched her cheeks in a vain effort to put some color into them. Crystal had never been one to use makeup, but she wished she had some that morning. Why had she been so sure that coming to Cactus Station would solve all her problems? Hadn't she realized that seeing Cody again would give her even more?

Her stomach churned at the thought of confronting him. He'd been so angry, and justly so. She could have refused when he had tried to make love to her. Instead, she'd allowed things to progress toward their inevitable conclusion until the heat lightning had restored her senses.

She didn't love him, she swore as she tied a pink scarf around her neck to add a little color to her pale complexion. She needed to get outside, into the air and sunlight.

Maybe if she left the cooking and cleaning to Jolie she could help Cody. She was no stranger to a tool kit, and Harold certainly wasn't going to be able to do much until his ankle healed. Regretfully, she decided, thinking of the great job he'd done with that problematic screen door at the front of the building.

The hotel was ominously quiet, its corridors and lobby empty. When she pushed open the kitchen door, a mountain of clean dishes sat in the center of the table while Jolie tended a huge pot on the stove.

"What's going on?" Crystal glanced at her watch. It was only six o'clock.

"They all ate an' left. I wasn't gonna wake you up. Your light was still on at four o'clock this mornin', when I came down to get Harold somethin' for pain. I'm makin' a pot of soup for supper, an' cornbread. That'll do for today."

"You should have got me up," Crystal protested. "I don't sleep well, even when I don't have a reason to be restless."

"An' you look like it." Jolie tapped the spoon against the edge of the pot and put a lid on the soup. "Go back to bed awhile. I'll get started on the rooms. Maybe later you can make up a notice about not providin' full board anymore."

"We haven't even discussed what I'm going to pay you..."

"We can do that this evenin', when the men-folks are feelin' more like themselves. Your Cody didn't sleep, either. He was drinkin' coffee in the kitchen when I came downstairs. We talked until I was sure Harold had settled down, an' by then it was time to start breakfast, so Cody ate an' left with his tool belt."

"And when have you got any rest, yourself?" Crystal watched Jolie wiping off the stove, but she was distracted wondering where Cody could have gone so early.

"I slept here and there. I'll sneak off an' take a nap this afternoon." Jolie lowered the flame under the soup.

Crystal thought about eating breakfast, but she felt slightly nauseated from lack of sleep. She decided staying up would just show how contrary she was, and she didn't want to argue with anyone else--she didn't have the stamina for it. She went back upstairs to find Jackson sleeping at the side of her bed, his tail curling like some ragged question mark. Even he seemed to be asking what she was doing with her life.

Crystal tossed her clothes on a chair and pulled her nightshirt over her head before falling onto the bed.

But despite lying still with her eyes closed, sleep eluded her. Her mind kept conjuring up images of her fights with Cody. Even more disturbing were the images of being in his bed and almost making love with him. The fact that he hadn't slept all night comforted her. Maybe he wasn't so shallow after all, she thought, flipping onto her stomach and burying her face in the pillow. Maybe he felt miserable, too.

She tried to sleep for over an hour, but it was hopeless. Despite Jolie's stealth, Crystal heard her making beds, moving furniture to sweep and piling trash into bags in the hallway. Crystal decided she might as well get up and help. But when she tried to put her feet on the floor, Jackson curled his lip.

"Stop it," she said in what she hoped was a stern enough tone. "You've got no business keeping me prisoner. Did Cody put you up to this?"

Jackson yawned, exposing fangs as sharp as rapiers. His long tongue uncurled, curled and slipped back into his mouth as he shut it. His sharp little eyes regarded Crystal from under bushy brows of sandy brown fur.

She tried again to put one foot down. Jackson actually had the audacity to growl.

"You stop that." Crystal remembered hearing dogs didn't like newspaper. Having none available, she took a magazine from her nightstand, rolled it up and shook it at him.

Jackson sighed, closed his eyes and ignored her.

"Hateful animal."

She lay back down. Maybe she could fool him into thinking she was asleep, then sneak out. He napped all the time. In fact, he seemed incapable of keeping awake for more than an hour at a stretch. All she had to do was close her eyes and feign sleep for a while, then crawl over the end of the bed to escape.

She could call Jolie, she thought, but she knew Jackson certainly wouldn't be bossed around by a newcomer, even one with a forceful personality. The thought of asking Jolie to fetch Cody was too demoralizing to entertain. She buried her face back into her pillow and waited, eyes shut, for Jackson to either leave or go back to sleep.

When Crystal opened her eyes again, the sun was high in the sky, its light slanting through her window to strike her full in the face. She rolled onto her side and checked the clock. One-thirty.

Jackson's half-chewed bone lay on the floor beside her bed, but he was nowhere in sight. She swung her legs off the bed and sat up, wriggling her toes. Her nightshirt clung to her, the heat filtering through the window to bake her back. She ran her hands through her tousled hair and wished for a shower.

Unbidden, the memory of Cody's invitation to join him in the creek the night before came back into her mind. Her body tingled in response, and her mind gave her a sensual picture of bare skin and clear, cold water. Her nipples hardened and she shivered with a vision of his hands and mouth on them.

Crystal gave herself a reality check. The mood he'd been in, he'd probably have tried to drown her, not make love to her. But the vision persisted, Cody's mouth leaving her breasts to explore other areas of her body: her stomach, her thighs, her--

A soft knock startled her from her daydream, leaving her breathless and clammy, heart pounding, body quivering.

"Just a minute," she called.

She pulled on her robe. No doubt Jolie was wondering whether her so-called employer was ever going to get up and help her.

But when she opened the door, her palpating heart went into overdrive. Cody stood on the threshold, Jackson at his heels. Crystal groaned inwardly. The sight of him in the flesh was far more stimulating even than in her daydream. His clothes molded his body like loving hands. He looked as tight as a stretched drum skin, and as nervous as she felt.

In a gesture unusual for Cody, he refused to make eye contact. Without asking her, he walked in, the dog trotting over to claim his bone, which he began to gnaw on with great relish.

"Do you have to do that in here, Jackson?" Crystal asked, tightly belting the robe.

One corner of Cody's mouth quirked, but he didn't comment.

"What's up?" she asked.

Crystal wasn't sure if she should try to act casual by sitting on the bed, or tell him to come back later. She opted for the bed, because he didn't look like he was going anywhere. In fact, he'd made himself comfortable in the old rocker facing it.

She sat down and crossed her legs. The robe slid away, exposing one thigh. Cody stopped rocking the chair. Crystal felt heat rise up her neck and spill onto her face when she saw him looking at her leg. She grabbed the offending robe and covered herself.

"I've thought of a way we can make money and get some repairs done." Cody resumed rocking, his worn boots pushing rhythmically against the floor.

Crystal's gaze shifted from his boots to his legs. The denim stretched tightly across his thighs, reminding her of the night before, when she'd seen him bathed in moonlight, as naked as the day he was born. Her inner heat intensified and she tried to surreptitiously wipe away a bead of sweat running down her temple. The traitorous robe slipped again.

"What scheme have you hatched up now?" Damn it, her voice sounded husky.

"I thought we could do a tour of the attic. Show where the skeleton was found, that sort of thing. Tourists love ghost stories. We could invent something. Maybe have one of those..." He paused, apparently searching for the right word. "...You know...those things where people sit around a table an' a gypsy talks to a ghost..." He shifted in the rocker, his eyes drifting from her face back to her legs.

"*Séance*," Crystal said more sharply than she intended. "You're talking about holding a *séance*. Are you out of your mind?"

His attention had slipped from a discussion of his current scheme to a contemplation of her legs, but Crystal's fuzzy state of arousal left with his words. Her sensual thoughts popped like so many bubbles rising to the top of a glass of soda water. The thought of Cactus Station becoming a sideshow appalled her.

"We'll attract all the weirdos in a three state radius."

Cody left the rocker and joined her on the bed. He took her hand, his warm grip bringing back sparks of awareness.

"I know we'll attract some people we wouldn't normally want hangin' around here." He gently rubbed her fingers and looked at her squarely for the first time. She wasn't the only one disturbed by their close proximity--she saw uncertainty in his candid gaze.

"We'll also attract regular tourists," he pointed out. "We need people who spend money, not like Hoyle, who's eatin' us out of house an' home. These prospectors are all desperate to strike it rich because they've sunk everythin' they own into this dig. We're gonna end up losin' more money than we'll ever earn out of this place, unless we make some changes."

"You're the one who keeps feeding Hoyle." She knew she should be pulling her hand away, but the rhythmic stroking from his fingers was too pleasurable.

"I can't see the man starve. Sorry. He can have my rations. I've known Hoyle since I was just a kid."

"But it's not just Hoyle, Cody. We've got a dozen Hoyles around here."

"An' you just brought a couple more on board when you hired Jolie an' Harold." His voice was quiet and even. "She's gonna be a real help to you, but Harold's not gonna be good for anythin' over the next couple of weeks. All he's gonna be doin' is restin' that sprained ankle an' eatin'."

"For which you're responsible," she accused hotly. She ripped her hand out of Cody's grip and shook her finger at him. "If you hadn't planted those nuggets, we would have been able to make rational decisions on what to do with the town instead of being railroaded into becoming host and hostess of the Motel Flophouse."

He stared at her. "What in the hell gave you the idea I planted those nuggets?"

Crystal cringed. She'd have to admit that she'd eavesdropped on him talking to Reed Dalton. "I just know, that's all," she hedged.

His fingers lifted her chin, forcing her to look into his eyes, suddenly filled with suspicion. "How about the truth?"

Crystal decided she didn't like this accusing side of Cody. "That *is* the truth," she tried.

He let go of her chin. "You've never been a good liar."

"You have," she countered, suddenly conscious that her thigh was pressing against his. She tried to slide away, but he was sitting on the end of her robe, effectively holding her prisoner.

"You always turn any conversation we have into a confrontation." He sighed and looked away. "We start out discussin' somethin' and pretty soon you start accusin' me of bein' everythin' from a liar to a lecher."

"I've never accused you of being a lecher." She tugged ineffectively at the robe.

"Havin' problems?" His eyebrows rose, but he didn't move.

"Yes." She folded her arms. "I'd like to get up."

"Fine. Get up. What's stoppin' you?" He grinned suddenly.

"You're impossible." She tugged harder.

"I think I've got you just where I want you at last, Miss Crystal--a captive audience. Let's discuss your problems with me. Ever since we arrived, you've treated me like I've got some bad smell about me. All I wanted was to be friends with you. You started this business between us again."

"*I* did?" Crystal couldn't believe her ears. "You're the one who keeps making passes."

He shrugged. "I admit I made one last night. You didn't seem to be rejectin' me at all though, until the lightnin' struck."

"Yes, well, I made a mistake," she mumbled and looked at her bare knees.

"Are you sure?" His voice was soft, intimate. One of his hands slid up her arm beneath the robe and caressed her elbow. The other hand slid around her waist and pulled her against his lean, hard body.

Crystal was only too aware that her short nightshirt had inched up her thighs, exposing the full length of her leg and even part of her hip on the side that wasn't pressed against him. Cody's hand slipped from her arm to her thigh.

"You take advantage of a situation faster than anyone I've ever met," she protested, wriggling. Her actions only brought the nightshirt higher.

"Is that so?" His hand slid from her hip to cup her buttock.

"Yes." She wished she had more control over her feelings. As he continued to run his hand over her skin, Crystal found herself shifting to a more comfortable position that placed her head on his shoulder and her face level with the opening of his shirt.

She inhaled the scent that was uniquely Cody's--a clean male scent that invited her to place her nose inside his shirt and press her lips against his tanned throat. A slight salt taste tingled against the tip of her tongue as she passed it over her lips and tried to tell herself she shouldn't be capitulating yet again to this renewed intimacy.

He cradled her leg and brought it over his thigh. "Put your arms around my neck, honey," he begged, both hands clasping her buttocks and encouraging her to sit on his thighs.

Crystal couldn't stop herself. She complied, clasping his neck and bringing her mouth to his. Cody's lips opened beneath hers, his tongue lightly rimming her mouth. She found herself moaning softly.

He pushed her legs further apart as his tongue delved deeply into her mouth. Her moans changed to a gasp. One hand remained on her buttocks, but the other had begun to caress her inner thighs beneath the nightshirt that had now risen to her waist.

"Cody," she whispered against his lips. "Don't."

"Don't what?" His fingers continued to explore, found their goal and stroked her until her pulse leaped in her throat.

"Don't do that." Barely able to speak, let alone breathe, Crystal threw her head back to gulp in air and instantly felt the pressure of his lips on her throat.

He found the place on her neck where her pulse throbbed, then the spot behind her ear that had always made her heart pound.

"I only want to please you," he whispered in her ear, his fingers continuing to work their magic. "That's all I've ever wanted." Suddenly his voice cracked and he took her in his arms, holding her tight, his face buried between her neck and her shoulder.

Utterly confused, totally aroused, and with all her nerve endings in an uproar, Crystal clung to him. "I-I don't understand," she stuttered. He lifted his face and pressed her cheek to his, the stubble pressing painfully into her sensitive skin.

"I know you don't. That's what makes this whole situation painful for both of us."

His sigh was so deep, so profound, that she felt pain in her own chest.

"Is there any way I can make it easier?" Her fingers caressed his brow and brushed back his unruly blond hair, shimmering in the sunlight.

"I doubt it, love." He smiled mournfully. "I have a lot of trouble controllin' myself around you, as you can see."

"I do." Her thighs burned against his. She made no attempt to cover herself.

Jackson, forgotten on the floor, stopped his rhythmic chewing to raise his head and growl, ears pricked to attention.

"What's up, guy?" Cody carefully lifted Crystal off his lap and placed her back on the bed.

Jolie called out at the same time she knocked. "The sheriff's on the phone for you, Cody."

"Thanks." He frowned as her footsteps retreated from the door. "How did she know I was here?"

"She knows a lot," Crystal said uncomfortably. She brought her nightshirt down to a respectable level.

Cody went to the door.

"Why is Reed calling you?" she asked.

"About the skeleton. I asked if it could be released back to us, remember?"

"Cody, I don't know why you're persisting in wanting that horrible thing back here." She went over to her dresser and pulled out clean clothes. "Either we need to find some spot in the graveyard and give it a Christian burial, or leave it in Phoenix."

He opened the door. "That's another subject where you an' I differ," he said. "I want the skeleton back here, so we can make some money off it. An' I'm gonna tell Reed just that."

"You always want your own way."

Jackson snarled.

"Oh, shut up," she told the old dog.

He followed Cody into the hallway. Crystal slammed the door on both of them.

CHAPTER THIRTEEN

Harold hobbled down to the kitchen mid-afternoon. After Crystal and Jolie shooed him out from underfoot, he joined Cody outside. With his swollen foot propped up on a box, he kept himself busy first by working on the freezer, and when that started humming, by repairing chairs.

Crystal brought lemonade to the back porch at four o'clock. The heat had settled into a shimmering haze. Many of the prospectors had given up for the day and returned to their rooms to wash up and rest. Crystal's posted notice about reducing the services had led to some grumbling, but most of the guests were too tired after a long morning panning or digging to make too much noise.

"Where's Cody?" she asked as she set Harold's lemonade on a barrel beside him.

"He drove off to get supplies. I think he has plans to put a water-line into the boardin' house an' another wherever those people are plannin' on openin' the convenience store." Harold took a big gulp of lemonade. "Ah, that hits the spot. Thanks."

Crystal snapped her fingers. "I knew I'd forgotten something. The Beckers were supposed to have come out here to find a good location for the store."

"I haven't seen anyone," Harold said. "But then, I haven't been watchin' Main Street the whole time."

"I don't think they would have come without telling me." Crystal turned to go back inside. "I'd better call them."

"Wait a minute." Harold put down his hammer. "I hear a car comin'. Maybe that's them."

"Maybe it's just Cody," Crystal said, but she put the other glass of lemonade down beside Harold's.

Cody's Blazer came into view, a car behind it. Crystal walked to the front of the hotel and recognized the Beckers as they pulled up to the door.

"We got lost," Ruth Becker said through the open car window. "We couldn't come yesterday, and I apologize for not calling you. I should have gotten better directions. We thought it would be easy to find. We drove up and down several dirt roads before we went back to Tortilla Flat. Luckily for us, Cody stopped by the general store there for a soda."

Cody strolled over, hands in pockets. "Cactus Station's kind of hard to find," he said. His unbuttoned shirt flapped against his hips in the fresh breeze that had sprung up.

"There's a sign, but it's easy to miss." He looked up at the sky. "I smell rain."

"It *is* a little humid," Crystal said. "But there was no rain in the forecast." She frowned. After the amount of years Cody had spent outdoors, his weather forecast could very well be more accurate than the one provided by the radio. "If you're right, I hope none of the prospectors are still out." She turned back to the Beckers, who were surveying the clear blue sky. "A gully washer can be dangerous in these parts," she explained.

Arlan Becker grunted. "You're right there. Ruth has never seen what a good rain can do to the Superstitions, but I used to do a little prospecting myself when I was young and foolish." He grinned at his wife, his weathered face lighting up when he looked at her.

Crystal watched their interaction with a pang of something akin to jealousy. They were obviously still in love and as comfortable together as a pair of well-worn slippers. She'd seen it as soon as she and Jolie met them over lunch in their daughter's little café. The Beckers had recently returned to retire in Arizona after Arlan had spent most of his working life in Texas. They'd told Crystal they were bored, passing their days doing nothing but reading newspapers and watching television.

"You want to check out the town?" Cody asked. "I can show you which of the buildings need the least amount of work."

"That sounds like a plan." Arlan clapped Cody companionably on the shoulder. "Lead the way."

He and Cody sauntered off, Crystal falling into step with Ruth a few feet behind them.

"If we really do open up a store here, we're going to have to trade our car in for something more like Cody's Bronco." Ruth picked her way across the boardwalk as though she expected it to collapse. "This is a bit more rustic than I was imagining," she said.

"You found the dirt road a little rough, I guess." Crystal watched Cody's shirt flap again in the wind, exposing a tantalizing view of tanned flesh.

"So, Cody's your partner?" Ruth asked.

Crystal nodded. "Our uncles left Cactus Station to us in their wills."

"They must have wanted you two to get together." Ruth smiled and winked. "I bet that wouldn't be much of a hardship, would it? He's a fine looking man and very personable. Arlan and I liked him immediately."

Crystal's already churning emotions rose quickly to the inadvertent bait. "He's handsome, all right. But all he's really interested in is making a quick buck and leaving most of the management issues to me," she told Ruth as she watched Cody gesturing toward one building after another, his manner already easy with Harlan, who seemed to be hanging on every word Cody uttered. She thought of Jolie's words: "He's a bit of a flimflam man, then."

He was more than a "bit" of a flimflam man, she decided. He was going to bring that skeleton back to Cactus Station, riding roughshod over her objections. He was going to make their inheritance into a three-ringed circus in an effort to turn a profit.

Tension surged through her body until her shoulders ached. She allowed her innermost fear to surface--the one Cody had already given her once before. If she allowed herself to fall under his spell again, he'd use her and the town until he'd made enough money to leave them behind. He'd never stuck around anywhere more than a few months at a time. He'd never change.

She wandered distractedly behind Cody and the Beckers as they viewed one dilapidated building after another. Ruth had left her behind after she had bad-mouthed Cody and questioned his intentions. Both the Beckers had evidently been persuaded to leave their reservations behind as they both voiced approval of Cactus Station's possibilities. They met with a few of the prospectors, and Cody gave them tours of both the hotel and the boarding house. He sold the town in the same way he had always sold the uncles' mining exploits.

At the end of an hour, the Beckers had chosen a location for their store and were making plans with Cody for the remodeling. The site was on Crystal's side of the street, four buildings away from the hotel. Cody had never attempted to sway their choice to his own side, Crystal grudgingly admitted. He had steered the Beckers to the best location and the biggest building that would need the least amount of work. So, maybe he was a flimflam man with a conscience, she thought.

Arlan and Ruth started talking about coercing their daughter and son-in-law into opening a café. Cody led them into the parlor at the hotel and started talking up the tourist angle and his plans for expansion over glasses of lemonade.

Crystal came down to earth with a profound thump when she heard him telling the Beckers about the skeleton and his ideas for turning the attic into a tourist trap. They went for the plan lock, stock and barrel, with visions of turning their general store and their daughter's café into their own version of a gold mine. Arlan even went as far as saying there was no reason not to think about building a second larger hotel and attracting one of the big chains to open up a grocery store with a pharmacy and general store attached, just like in Phoenix or Scottsdale.

"You can't be serious," Crystal said. "Did I really hear you say you wanted to display the skeleton in the front lobby?"

Cody grinned sheepishly. "If I can figure out a way to keep Jackson from takin' the bones an' buryin' them."

Arlan Becker's hearty laugh sounded like a low drum roll. He slapped his thigh. "That's a hoot," he told Cody. He aimed a slap at Cody's back right as Cody took a drink of lemonade.

Somehow, Cody managed to swallow the mouthful, but he had a lot of trouble getting his breath for a couple of minutes.

"Well, I don't think it's anything but disrespectful," Crystal said.

CHAPTER FOURTEEN

The following day a black hearse arrived, bearing the mortal remains of whoever had been wrapped in a blanket and stored inside the attic closet. The investigation into the skeleton's identity still continued, but it had been concluded that the remains had been stored in that closet at least a year.

"That may be Jake Carver?" Crystal pointed to the hearse and its occupant, less than tastefully encased in the cheapest casket the Eternal Peace Mortuary and Funeral Home could provide.

Cody scuffed his feet. "Yeah." He was afraid to say anything else. Crystal looked as though she was about to bust a gut.

"He's...it's...that's not staying here." She shook her finger at Cody. "You tell Billy Ride to take that casket somewhere else." She waved in the general direction of Phoenix. "Maybe he can throw Jake out into the desert on the way back."

"Crystal." Cody didn't know whether to laugh or take her seriously. "I never thought I'd hear you talk about dumpin' a man's bones in the middle of the desert."

"You said that may be Jake Carver." She walked over to look out the door. The rain that Cody had forecast began to spatter the tin and wood shingled roofs of Cactus Station. "He was the meanest man I ever met. I refuse to have him anywhere near me, even if he's dead."

"Aw, come on, Crystal. Be charitable." Cody tried to put his arm around her, but she ducked away. "Jake wouldn't mind where we put him, as long as he's close to the Superstitions. He might even like the idea of bein' kept in the lobby of the Gold Rush Hotel."

Crystal snorted with disgust.

"These mountains are the only thing he ever loved in his whole life," Cody said.

"I don't care what you think he loved. I won't have that man's remains in the middle of the hotel or anywhere else in town, for that matter." She glared at the hearse, as though she could make it disappear just by sheer will power.

Billy Ride came sauntering in from the kitchen, his hat pushed back on his wiry gray hair. "Now Crystal, you should know I can't just take Jake's body an' dump him in the desert," he said, thumbs hooked into the belt loops of his black pants. "Cody's the closest Jake had to a family, far as we know, an' the sheriff's released the body to him. Cody's gonna have to be the one to decide how to take care of Jake's burial."

"You said you don't even know if it *is* Jake," Crystal countered.

"Chances are, it is. The lab's just waitin' on the dental records for confirmation," Billy said.

"Well, regardless of that, Cody's not planning on interring anyone. He's planning on exhibiting the skeleton in the lobby and selling tickets to see the closet I found it in. If that's not sacrilegious, I don't know what is. I'll talk to Sheriff Dalton myself. He can't release the body--ah--remains into Cody's care. That's immoral and unjust. In fact, it's just plain sick."

"I don't care anythin' about that, Miss Crystal," Billy said, chewing heavily on a toothpick. "All I care about is unloadin' that casket and gettin' on my way before I get rained in here. The gullies are already awash. Soon there'll be some darn flash-flood down the creek, and I'll be stuck here 'til it all passes over."

"You are not...do you hear me, Billy Ride?" Crystal stamped her foot. "You are not taking that casket out of that hearse until I've talked to

Sheriff Dalton. I don't care if Noah comes floating past the hotel in his ark. Is that perfectly clear?"

Billy nodded, his eyes big and round. He took the toothpick out of his mouth.

Crystal stepped forward and poked him in the chest with her finger. "And don't you dare start calling me Miss Crystal. Cody's got everyone around here doing that." She lifted the hinged counter at the corner of the desk and let it drop behind her with a resounding crash. "I hate that name." She grabbed the phone and punched numbers.

"A mite p.o.'d, ain't she?" Billy said out the corner of his mouth.

"That's an understatement." Cody fought a desire to laugh. Crystal in a blue snit always seemed to bring out an inappropriate response in him. "Come on, Billy, I'll take the responsibility. Let's unload that casket so you can be on your way. The rain's gettin' worse."

"That it is," Billy agreed. They stepped out of the hotel onto the porch and stood side by side watching the driving sheets of rain pelting the street. "I don't rightly know if I want to go back out in that, though," Billy said. "I believe I'll wait right here for it to pass."

"You'll get stuck here," Cody said.

"At least I'll be in one piece. I don't aim to be one of those death statistics for the Superstitions this year. Particularly not while drivin' a hearse."

"Well, at least let's unload the casket," Cody suggested.

Billy shrugged. "As soon as Miss Crystal's finished her call. She can be mightily persuasive when she wants to be." He stopped speaking and listened with his head cocked to one side. "Besides, she's screamin' her head off at Sheriff Dalton. He might get just enough of an earful to go along with her wishes."

Cody grimaced. The quicker he got the casket into the hotel lobby, the better. He'd already put up handbills all over Apache Junction about the gruesome find in the Gold Rush Hotel's attic closet. He'd called the Arizona Republic, who planned to send out a reporter the following morning. A local television station had voiced an interest in seeing the skeleton.

He had a lot of work to do, what with finding a suitable location for Jake's remains and fabricating a suitably horrific tale of ghosts and ghouls tramping the hallways of the hotel after sundown. He hoped he might be able to stage one of the happenings that night and convince at least one guest that Jake was walking through the Gold Rush in search of his lost treasure.

If everything went well, Cody had dreams of taking tour groups to see Jake's various digs, including a couple of the old mines that honey-combed under Cactus Station. Jake and the uncles, along with various other prospectors, had hacked their way through the bedrock. Most of the old tunnels were unsafe, but tourists would be thrilled just to see the sites and visualize what lay behind the boarded up or collapsed entrances.

Crystal slammed down the phone. Cody saw her pink cheeks and angry eyes.

"He won't listen to me." She pushed open the screen door and joined them, her hair blowing in the wind. She took the scarf from around her neck and used it to pull her hair back from her face. "He said he doesn't want anything more to do with Jake Carver's remains, and he couldn't care less what you do with them." The look she shot at Cody told him just what she thought of him and Reed Dalton, too. "I won't have that casket in this hotel."

"Listen, we need it," Cody reasoned. "That skeleton will give this town a shot in the arm."

"You're insane." Crystal stomped back inside and headed for the kitchen.

Cody thought about following her and trying to explain, but he figured he'd just get another earful of complaints for his trouble.

Jackson came running through the lobby, tail tucked between his legs and his half- chewed bone gripped firmly between his teeth.

"...and stay out!" Crystal yelled before the kitchen door slammed back into place.

"Whoa, Jackson." Cody put out his arm as Jackson started to dive through the half-open front door. "You can't go out in that rain."

Jackson stopped long enough to reproach Cody with a whine before squeezing through the gap and taking off down the boardwalk, his feet flying.

"Well, I'll be damned." Billy whistled through his teeth. "I didn't take that mutt for a coward."

"He isn't." Cody watched Jackson disappear into the boarding house. "Crystal's got her dander up and no mistake. Let's get that casket inside, Billy. No use procrastinatin' any longer. I'll lend you a slicker."

"Fair enough." Billy threw the toothpick out the door. "I'll take the slicker. I'm gonna have to stay here tonight, and I'm not gonna sit around in my underwear while my clothes are dryin'."

"Yeah, you might scare off the guests worse than Jake Carver or Jackson."

Cody easily avoided Billy's good-natured swat.

CHAPTER FIFTEEN

"I think Cody's got a plan," Harold said.

Jolie took her hands out of the dishwater and tossed him a cloth. "You'd better start dryin' and stop thinkin' too much," she warned. "If you step in the middle of Cody and Crystal's affairs, they're both gonna dump on you plenty, hon. You'd best keep your ideas to yourself."

"I'm not actin' dumb for you or anybody," Harold grumbled as he dried the pot she handed him. "Crystal already told me I'm a klutz."

"You don't have to be a smart mouth, neither." Jolie plunged her arms back up to the elbows in soapy water and pulled out a plate. "I like both of them, Harold, an' I wouldn't mind settlin' down in Cactus Station for a while. Fixin' meals an' makin' beds is somethin' I understand."

"I thought you were happy in Port Arthur?" Harold stopped polishing the pot and looked at her, his brow furrowed.

"Never. I love the country. I hate big towns 'n freeways."

Harold put the pot on the table and grabbed her belt, pulling her over to sit on his lap. "I'm sorry, baby." He kissed her lightly. "You should've told me."

Crystal sank down further into the shadows of the back porch. Going outside to cool her burning cheeks and calm her temper had seemed like a good idea after supper was over, but she'd only been there a few minutes when Jolie and Harold had settled into the kitchen. Neither of them noticed her sitting on the old chair with her feet on the railing.

Now she was stuck out there while Jolie and Harold looked like they were about to start making out big time. The rain still poured off the tin roof over the back porch, striking the metal like buckshot being thrown into a tin bucket. Crystal bit her lip. Should she make a dash for the front of the building or stay where she was, hoping neither Jolie nor Harold saw her?

"Psst."

Crystal looked around.

"Psst."

Cody stood at the bottom of the steps, a rain slicker covering him from head to foot, another held over one arm. He beckoned, a rivulet of water cascading from his hood in a direct line in front of his face.

Crystal got up carefully and tiptoed over. He handed her the slicker, which she threw over her head and shoulders.

He leaned in close. "Watch the boards," he told her, his voice barely detectable over the noise from the roof. "They're kind of loose." He offered her his hand.

Crystal gratefully accepted his help, and they dashed hand in hand through the puddles. The first thing she saw when they rounded the building was the hearse still parked where it had been before supper.

"Thanks," she said as she took off the slicker. "Were you looking for me?"

"No, Jackson, but I found you instead." Cody smiled.

"You were going to wrap Jackson in a slicker?" She returned the smile. "You rescued me from an embarrassing moment back there. I got trapped."

"So I saw." Cody chuckled. He shook out both slickers and hung them up on hooks inside the lobby. "I was goin' to get a drink from the kitchen and saw Jolie sittin' on Harold's knee. I was backin' out the door when I saw movement on the back porch. I figured it was you, coolin' off."

Crystal thought there might be some hope for him after all. He had shown perception, for goodness sake, right when she thought he had none. "They'd probably have thought I was eavesdropping," she said.

She turned around and almost fell over the casket, sitting in the middle of the rug she had helped Jolie bring down from the attic late that afternoon. A group of guests had gathered in the lobby, a couple of the men using the casket for a table, their beers and a used ashtray sitting on the lid.

"What are you thinking?" Crystal couldn't believe her eyes. She whipped around to face Cody again. "I told you I wouldn't have that thing in here."

"You were over-ruled. I own half this place, in case you've forgotten. I'm claimin' half the lobby, and my half is displayin' the casket."

"We'll see about that." Crystal's anger boiled right back up to its previous level. "If you insist on doing this, Cody Blye, I'm declaring war. You'll see just what I'm capable of."

"Oh, come off it, Crystal. Long after you've tired of Cactus Station and gone back to civilization, I'll still be here, livin' in this town an' keepin' it goin' in memory of Uncle Willy and Uncle Dock. Jake, too," he added. "He has more right to be here than either of us."

"You're out of your mind," Crystal said.

"You already told me that."

They glared at each other.

"I plan to be in Cactus Station longer than you," she said.

"I wouldn't lay bets on that, Miss Crystal."

"You want to make a bet?" She felt like slapping him, right in front of all the guests who were staring at both of them.

"I wouldn't want you to waste your money." He glanced at the audience. "I tell you what. I'll bet you my half of the town that you give up first."

"You'll sign over all rights to Cactus Station if I win?"

"That's right."

"You'll shake on it? Right in front of all these witnesses?" She waved at the staring prospectors.

"You betcha. This is one bet I'm gonna win, Crystal. You'll be back in Phoenix inside a month."

"Shake." She thrust out her hand.

He closed his over it. For a moment, she felt a pang of remorse for forcing the issue. Cody wasn't going to win the bet they'd so hastily made. He'd sign away all rights to Cactus Station and leave her with a

decaying town and no way to repair it, unless she took on another partner. She'd never see him again.

Unexpectedly, her heart contracted painfully. In the midst of all the
sparring, she'd felt they were growing closer, not only physically, but
mentally as well. She'd seen momentary flashes of maturity in Cody that
she hadn't seen before; flashes of compassion and sincerity in the midst
of all the blustering and bravado.

"I'll lay two to one odds on Cody." Clayton Fisher, one of the men
with a beer on the casket's lid waved money in the air.

"I'll take you up on that." Hoyle Bixby shouldered his way through
the little gathering. He winked broadly at Crystal, as though they shared
some secret.

She groaned inwardly. The last thing she needed was the guests
taking sides. The very *last* thing she needed was Hoyle Bixby thinking
she and he were on the same side. Hoyle had always had the biggest
crush on her, ever since she had come back to Cactus Station. He'd taken
a liking to her when he worked for the uncles the summer she had spent
in the Superstitions. That fatal summer she'd fallen for Cody, she
reminded herself.

Her heart contracted again. What a mistake. If divine providence
hadn't interrupted them two days in a row, she might have given herself
to Cody freely yet again. She had to shore up her defenses now. He'd
shown his true colors tonight--conniving, selfish and shallow.

Turning her back on all of them, she went upstairs to her room, where
she locked the door and buried her face and her problems in her lumpy,
uncomfortable pillow...

She awoke with a start. The sound of a horn rent the air and she jumped
up. Groggy with sleep, she dashed cold water over her face from the
bowl on her dresser. Still fully dressed from the night before, she pulled
open her door and headed for the stairs.

A crowd of people fought each other to gain entrance to the lobby.
She saw vans from several television stations parked outside, and men
pointed cameras at her as she raced downstairs. Cody stood on the front

porch. She heard him trying to give a statement, but his voice became lost in the rising clamor.

"My God," Crystal said. "Where did all these people come from?"

"Word travels fast these days," Jolie said from behind her. "I called the Beckers. They're bringin' their daughter and son-in-law with them an' as many supplies as they can load into a truck in an hour. They're gettin' some friend to deliver used coolers by noon, along with two more generators. They're gonna be rich by the end of the day if'n they only sell drinks, chips, candy bars an' hot dogs."

"I can't believe he did this." Crystal tried to shake the cobwebs out of her brain. "He knew I didn't want this place turned into a three-ring circus. I told him."

"He knew, hon, but he decided he'd better risk your anger to save the town."

"That's a bunch of nonsense. We could have attracted artists, crafts people and a couple of restaurant owners. Then we'd have been fine."

"I don't think so." Jolie squeezed Crystal's arm compassionately. "I know you didn't want commercialism to play a part in your dream, but I think Cody's right. Harold does, too.

You never would have had the money to make the necessary repairs an' pretty soon some buildin' inspector would have come here from Phoenix and condemned the whole town. Then where would you be?"

"No worse off than now. What do you think that same building inspector's going to do, and much quicker, once the publicity puts Cactus Station on the map?"

"Cody'll take care of it, Crystal. He'll look after you the way Harold looks after me."

"I don't need *anyone* taking care of me," Crystal said, darkness rising all around her and threatening to stifle her. "I've taken care of myself for years. My father was a day laborer and my mother ran off with another man when I was twelve. Apart from Uncle Dock's occasional interventions, I've been self-sufficient for the better part of my life. I don't need a swindler like Cody Blye messing up my independence or ruining my inheritance. I came here because I have wonderful memories of Cactus Station, and I want to keep those memories alive."

"Don't those memories include Cody?" Jolie asked softly.

Crystal couldn't believe her ears. "Did he open his big mouth and tell you about us?" she demanded, her blood pounding in her head. "Did he?"

Jolie nodded. "He meant no harm, Crystal. He was so depressed the night Harold got hurt. He'd had a couple too many beers an' he confided in me. I swear I'll never tell another livin' soul. I haven't even told Harold. Your secrets are safe with me."

"Cody didn't know that. He had no right." Mortified, Crystal didn't know how she was going to keep facing Jolie day after day, knowing what Cody had said. "All it takes is a couple of beers and he spills all my secrets. How dare he? How could he ever think I'd trust him again? I'm going to win that bet, so I can run him right out of this town and out of my life."

She left Jolie standing in the middle of the kitchen and took the back stairs up to her room, where she sat on the bed and pulled the blanket over her head in an effort to shut out the commotion downstairs and close her mind to Cody's betrayal.

CHAPTER SIXTEEN

Cody showed the media Billy Ride's hearse, still parked in front of the hotel. He led the way into the hotel lobby to show off the casket. The one thing he forgot was Jackson.

Hackles raised to alarming proportions, the dog growled in a continuous low rumble reminiscent of an approaching locomotive.

"If you'll just wait a minute, ladies and gentlemen, I'll put the dog in the kitchen," Cody promised as the crowd abruptly retreated, followed by Jackson with his belly almost scraping the floor.

The closest reporter grabbed Cody and used him as a human shield against the menacing canine, who began circling the floor and diving at the legs of anyone foolish enough to remain in the lobby. Most of the crowd retreated back outside, where they pressed against the windows and screen door as they waited to see what would happen next.

A couple of cameras flashed, and then a storm of lights went off, catching Cody imprisoned by the panic-stricken reporter behind him. Cameras whirred as Babs Hewett, one of the local television news personalities, scrambled around on the hotel desk, her skirt hitched up to her thighs, exposing a froth of lace petticoat and tanned legs while she gave the men outside a view they had never anticipated. The cameraman cowered on a side-table, his camcorder abandoned on the floor.

Cody wrenched himself free of the reporter. "Don't move," he commanded. "As long as you stay still, he won't bite you." *I hope,* Cody thought to himself, making placating noises at Jackson while trying to herd him toward the kitchen door.

Jolie opened the door and whistled, waving a large dog biscuit. "Come on, Jackson," she purred. "I'm makin' pot pies...with chicken."

Jackson's ears pricked up as though he understood her. To Cody's utter amazement, the dog stuck his cracked nose in the air and trotted into the kitchen as though he'd meant to do that all along and had merely been playing some little game with the media hounds.

As the door shut, Cody felt and heard a collective sigh of relief. When his heart retreated back down his throat and his pulse slowed, embarrassment took over. Jackson had made him look like a complete and utter fool. Not only had he been unable to control the damn dog, but Jolie, who had only been on the job two days, had calmed the savage beast with nothing more than a dog biscuit and the promise of chicken.

A nervous titter from the anchorwoman was picked up by her coworker on the table.

Red-faced with embarrassment, he jumped to the floor and hurried over to help her down from the desk. The reporter who had grabbed Cody hastened to retrieve his notepad and pen, both of which he had flung wildly into the air. The pen was on the floor, but the notepad lay balanced on the edge of Jake's open casket. The reporter took one look inside and turned white, crumpling to the floor in a dead faint.

A ripple of laughter broke through the waiting crowd, swelling until it became a deafening roar. People poured through the open door of the Gold Rush, taking pictures of the prone reporter and the contents of the casket. Cody desperately tried to shield the man from the crush.

"Get back and give him air!" he shouted fruitlessly into the hubbub. He grabbed the notepad and tried fanning the man, whose still, white face scared Cody more than he wanted to admit even to himself. Suppose the guy died of shock. What would happen then?

Never in his wildest nightmares had Cody imagined the ensuing melee. He should have asked Reed Dalton to come over. If they didn't stop pushing and shoving, he'd have a riot on his hands.

Other people joined the throng already filling the lobby. Tourists with everything from high end digitals to cheap disposable cameras began taking pictures and pushing forward in an attempt to see the fainting man and the casket.

"Stop it, I tell you!" Despite shouting at the top of his lungs, no one listened to Cody. He began to panic. The man was beginning to stir, but the throng at the back was pressing the mob at the front, pushing them closer and closer to the tiny open space Cody had maintained.

A man operating a camcorder lost his balance and staggered to regain it, kicking the collapsed reporter in the head.

"For God's sake." Cody shoved the cameraman back.

The man fell, taking several others with him. A ripping sound rent the air and a set of heavy velvet curtains that had divided the lobby from the dining room came cascading down, covering those below them.

Shouting and screaming joined the laughter still reverberating throughout the room. Somewhere in the middle, a fight started between two people who had fallen on the floor. Fists flew and anger surged through the mob.

A sharp report brought everything to a grinding halt. Cody looked up to find Crystal standing on the stairs, a rifle held firmly in her hands, her face grim as he'd never seen it.

"Get out," she said, her voice raised only slightly above her normal tone, but hard as steel. "All of you get outside. If you want to see anything, you'll form an orderly line or I'll start shooting at something other than the woodwork."

The crowd backed slowly through the door, their eyes glued to Crystal's slight figure and the rifle cradled in her arms.

"Have you lost your mind?" Cody asked, helping the now-conscious reporter onto a chair.

Jolie bustled in with a bottle of brandy and a glass of water. "Who wants what?" she demanded.

"Give this guy the water and give me the brandy," Cody said, waving in the direction of the man sprawled in the chair beside him.

"What's your name?" Jolie demanded as she shoved the water into the man's hand and loosened his tie.

"Who cares what his name is?" Crystal strode down the stairs. "He's not staying around long enough for any of us to worry about introductions."

"I asked you what you think you're doing," Cody demanded. He wanted to grab her and take the gun away from her, but he wasn't entirely sure she wouldn't shoot him in the foot or some other, more strategic part of his anatomy. "I think you've lost your mind."

"On the contrary, Cody Blye. I'm the only one around here who's kept any brain function at all. You obviously lost what little bit of sense you had when you brought these people here. You've got the audacity to ask me what I'm doing when there's a mob in my lobby? I didn't see you doing anything constructive to defuse the situation." She looked hard at him. "You called all these reporters out here, didn't you?"

"Well..." Cody couldn't look her in the eye. "...I may have called a couple of people, but I swear I didn't send for all of them."

"The wire services," said the guy on the chair. He still looked about as steady as Hoyle Bixby after a couple of six-packs on an empty stomach, but at least color was creeping back into his cheeks. "Once the wire services get hold of a story, everyone knows about it. This week's been real slow for news, so your skeleton in the closet sounded like something bizarre enough to get a good story out of."

"Great." Crystal slumped into the chair next to his. She laid the rifle across her lap. "Are you okay?" she asked. "I'm sorry I was so rude to you just now. I'm not usually like that."

"Don't believe her," Cody said. "She's usually worse. You're seein' Crystal on one of her better days."

"You're Cody Blye and this is Crystal Penney?" The man looked from one of them to the other, the crease between his eyes sharpening his boyish features.

"That's right." Cody nodded. "How do you know that?"

"A little research before I came out here. You two are going to be famous, you know. Can I get an exclusive?" He managed a grin. "I think I deserve it. I made a complete fool of myself and my face is going to be all over the country within a few hours. I bet I made a perfect picture laid out beside that casket." He shuddered. "I've never been good around death. I shouldn't have come here, but I'm a junior reporter, and I had to get a good story somehow."

"As far as I'm concerned, hon, you can have an exclusive to anythin'," Jolie said, smiling coquettishly at him.

"Jolie!"

They all turned around to see Harold standing in the hallway, his tall frame supported precariously on crutches.

"Oh, keep your hair on." Jolie dropped the brandy bottle into the baby-faced reporter's hands. "I thought you were supposed to be keepin' an eye on Jackson's shenanigans."

"Jackson." Cody took off at light-speed toward the kitchen. "He knows how to get out the kitchen door."

"What?" Crystal jumped up and followed Cody.

"Who's Jackson?" the reporter asked.

"The dog," Cody tossed over his shoulder as he bounced off Harold and pushed open the swinging door.

The first thing he saw was Jackson's rear end heading for the back porch. The second thing he saw was a sea of humanity charging back up the alleyway in the direction of Main Street. Cody took a flying leap and grabbed Jackson's tail. He tried not to think about the fact that the dog would probably bite him. Crystal landed right on top of him and their combined efforts brought Jackson back into the kitchen.

Cody ignored the snarls, his arms wrapped around his pet's neck. "It's okay, Jackson," he soothed. "It's all right, boy."

Crystal rolled off both of them and lay on her back, panting. "The next time you get some hair-brained scheme to make money, would you just stop a minute to consider your partner?" She pushed her hair out of her eyes.

"I made a mistake," Cody conceded. "I'm sorry about that, but think what the publicity will do for us. We'll have more business than we know what to do with. I'll be able to pay someone else to do a lot of the work, instead of burnin' my back out in that hot sun every day while I'm actin' like some maintenance man. I'm sick of fixin' plumbing and doing carpentry. I'm a prospector, not Mr. Fix-it."

She looked up at him, her expression for once understanding instead of accusing. "I realize that. I told you I'm a geologist, not an inn-keeper. But neither of us was having too much luck with what we were doing before, so maybe it was time for a change, anyway."

"I thought you loved your job?" Cody ruffled Jackson's untidy coat and the snarling subsided to a dull rumble.

"So did I." Crystal sat up and straightened her clothes. "I ran into some...trouble." She gazed across the kitchen in the direction of the stove, as though there was something really important over there that she had missed.

Cody sensed they were at the edge of some sort of breakthrough in their relationship. Crystal was finally going to tell him why she'd come back to Cactus Station.

"What kind of trouble? You didn't get into financial problems, did you?" He couldn't imagine Crystal in any sort of trouble. She was too straight-arrow for that.

"I...I..."

The door flew open and Jolie burst in. "You gotta come quick," she said. "Them reporters're bustin'up the place agin, tryin' to get pichers." Her Texas drawl had taken off into the stratosphere.

Cody swore under his breath. Finally, he and Crystal had seemed to be getting past the superficial nit-picking stuff and into the real meat of their problems. Why couldn't Jolie, who had managed everything else put in her path, tackle a few news people and tourists?

"Jolie...," he said.

"You gotta come *now.*" She grabbed his arm and jerked him to his feet.

Cody hoped he'd never have to confront Jolie if she was in the mood for physical combat. He had no doubt she'd be able to deck him quite easily.

"Can't you do something yourself?" he grumbled.

"You're the boss. Act like one." She shoved him in the direction of the lobby.

"What about me?" Crystal had made a recovery.

"If'n you feel like it, you can grab your firearm agin." Jolie shooed them both out of the kitchen. "I'll take care of Jackson," she said when they both looked back at her.

"I hope you do a better job than you did last time," Cody shot before opening the door.

"That weren't my fault; it was Harold's." Jolie folded her arms across her chest and glared.

Cody decided to let that brewing argument slide. He had enough to contend with on the other side of the kitchen door. The media was back in full force. People were milling around the lobby again, taking sporadic photos of the skeleton and generally creating mayhem.

All the furniture had been pushed aside and Crystal's one big potted philodendron had been knocked over and trampled, dirt tracking all over the lobby and being ground into the carpet. Cody put a restraining hand on Crystal. He knew she was about to get out of control again, and he didn't think either he or the media was ready to duck more flying bullets.

"Ladies and gentlemen," he shouted. "I have to ask you to leave. You've done enough damage for one day."

"What about an interview?" Babs Hewett had recovered from her loss of dignity. Apart from an inch of torn lace that hung beneath the hem of her skirt, she looked back in control, her bright pink lipstick moist on pouting lips and her platinum blonde hair immaculate. She thrust a microphone under Cody's nose.

"I promised an exclusive interview to..." Cody looked around.

"To me." The reporter who had fainted elbowed his way to the front of the crowd.

"Well, how about you?" Babs asked, thrusting her microphone at Crystal.

"I'm attending Cody's exclusive to make sure he doesn't say things he'll live to regret later." Crystal glared balefully in Cody's direction.

He felt the force of that glare like the burst from an acetylene welding torch.

"I'll let the rest of you know when I'm ready to give another interview," Cody said. "Until then, I'll have to ask you to leave the hotel."

"What if we don't *want* to leave?" One of the men sidled up and thrust his face into Cody's. He was at least three inches taller and looked like he worked out in a gym.

Cody wondered if Crystal had asked some unlucky star to sit over his head. He watched the man's fists clench. Although Cody knew he could take care of himself, he didn't relish a fist fight after the way the day had already gone.

"I wouldn't advise you to press things." Reed Dalton walked into the lobby as though nothing more were amiss than some petty fender-bender instead of a potential riot. "If you'll respect Cody and Miss Crystal's wishes and move along, all of us'll be quite content. If you want to disagree, then you'll have to deal with me, and I *love* to put people in my jail." He hitched up his belt and elbowed his way to the front of the crowd.

The man who wanted a face-off with Cody backed away. "I'll see you later about this," he warned.

"Try it," Cody said. He'd had just about enough of the media for one day. He wished he'd tried to make Cactus Station's skeleton into a tourist attraction, not a media event.

"Ladies and gentlemen, no one's going to see anyone at any time about this." Reed inserted a wad of gum into his mouth. He chewed unhurriedly, surveying the crowd with a deceptively mild expression.

Cody watched Reed's fingers tighten on his belt and slide toward his gun.

"If you've got any beefs, I suggest you swallow 'em and take 'em back to Phoenix with you." Reed smacked the gum and the crowd seemed to hold its collective breath. "If you want to talk to Cody and Miss Crystal in a civilized manner, then you can hang around outside for a while. I believe the Becker family has refreshments a-plenty for all of you, and at reasonable prices. Go cool off and calm down."

Although several people looked on the verge of mutiny, evidently no one wanted to end up spending the night in Sheriff Dalton's pokey. They all began to file out.

"My name's Brent Hardacre." The baby-faced reporter held out his hand.

Cody mechanically shook the proffered hand. He still wanted to turn tail and run for the hills. Crowds had never been his thing, especially when they were all grouped around him and wanting something he didn't think he could deliver.

Jolie opened the kitchen door. "I've got lunch and refreshments in here," she offered. "Jackson's already eaten and is on his best behavior."

"He may be now, but don't think he'll keep that up if the mob comes back." Cody felt old and tired beyond his years. Lunch and something to drink sounded good after the way the morning had gone.

Reed nodded. "That's right nice of you Ma'am." He looked at Jolie. "I don't think we've met."

"Jolie Webster." She held out her hand.

Reed walked with her into the kitchen, smiling at Jolie like she was a queen who had graced the Gold Rush with her presence.

"Poor Harold," Cody whispered to Crystal.

She smiled. "Jolie's some force to be reckoned with, isn't she?"

"Damn right." Cody wondered why he didn't want to flirt with Jolie, like all the other men did. He guessed he was addle-brained from spending too much time in the Arizona sun. The only woman he had eyes for was Crystal, and she had made it abundantly clear that although she felt a great deal of physical attraction to him, she had no intentions of carrying that attraction any further than some making out. He felt about as frustrated as a gelded bull.

Crystal was offended. Cody had as much as shoved her out of the room while he gave his "exclusive" interview to Brent Hardacre. She couldn't imagine what she could possibly have said to cast a different light on the finding of the skeleton or its identity.

She walked into the lobby, where Jolie was cleaning up. Jackson prowled the perimeter of the room, pausing occasionally to look balefully through the windows. Although a remarkably high number of people were still hanging around, a lot of them had left, including Babs Hewett and other news-team members from the local television stations.

Crystal felt glad they didn't have a television set in Cactus Station. She had no wish to see the mortifying spectacle that had been at the Gold Rush Hotel that day.

Although she had slammed the lid on the casket, Cody had still refused to have it removed to a more suitable place prior to finding permanent accommodations for Jake in the tiny cemetery on the outskirts of town.

She watched the crowd undulating like the surface of an ocean as it moved from one side of the street to the other. The Beckers had run out of food around three o'clock, convincing many of the tourists to leave in search of a late lunch or early dinner.

Crystal was afraid they would all return the following morning. Many of them had spoken with guests of the hotel or boarding house. Talk of gold ran rampant and she could tell that the bug had probably bitten many of those who heard the stories and now envisioned untold riches waiting to be dug up or panned from the creek.

She thought people were too gullible. They listened to what they wanted to hear, not what common sense told them. She was a prime example herself, she decided. If she'd been less trusting and more shrewd, she wouldn't be looking at spending the rest of her life in Cactus Station.

"What's up, Crystal? A penny for your thoughts." Cody came up behind her.

"Very funny," she said. "You always did like to make puns about my name."

"Well, whoever heard of a crystal penny?" he asked with a chuckle.

"That wasn't what my parents had in mind when they named me." Crystal wished he would stop taunting her. She'd taken enough comments all through her school years.

"I know, I know." He put up his hands in mock surrender. "You were conceived in Las Vegas and they named you for the Strip."

"No, they didn't. They named me for the beautiful chandeliers inside the casinos on the Strip."

"I don't think I'd proudly spread that around," he told her. "It makes it sound like either your parents were gamblers or they had no life, naming you after a light fixture."

"You're cruel, Cody Blye." She aimed a punch at his arm, but missed when he neatly sidestepped. "At least I was named for a joyful event. You don't even know why you got the name you did."

"I do, too. I was named after my father's gun."

"Your middle name's Colt Forty-five?"

Cody rolled his eyes. "You're very annoying when you try. My middle name's Winchester, remember?"

She laughed at his grimace. "You deserve all I can give you and more besides. What in the world were you thinking when you started this publicity stunt?"

"I was thinking income. Financial security. I like the sound of those words. I don't like the sound of the word bankruptcy."

She shivered, his remark striking a nerve. "I don't like that word, either. I didn't think we were anywhere close to that, though. I thought we were making money."

"With all the repairs I've had to make and all the supplies you've bought? We're close to the red side of the book, not the black."

She walked away, unwilling to listen. Without thinking, she walked right into the casket and bruised her shins.

"I can't stay in the same building with this thing." She limped over to a chair and flopped down beside a pile of used paper plates, discarded Styrofoam cups and wadded-up napkins.

"Why not? You slept only one floor from Jake's remains for the last month. The only difference was that you didn't know it at the time." Cody sank into a chair on the other side of the garbage.

"It's creepy, knowing he's lying there in that box."

"He's not gonna get up and climb into bed with you."

Cody's eyes were guileless, but Crystal had a funny feeling in the pit of her stomach. "Why won't you put the casket into the funeral parlor?" she asked as she rubbed her shins.

"Because someone could come along in the night and steal the skeleton."

She shrugged. "Why should we care?"

"Because Jake Carver's an oddity that will attract tourists," Cody pointed out with a trace of impatience. "I've told you that a dozen times, but you won't listen."

"That's because I don't want this horrible thing and its contents in the middle of my lobby." She leaned her head back against the wall and drew in a deep breath. He was hopeless after all, she decided. Stubborn, near-sighted...

"*Our* lobby," he fired back. "Don't you conveniently forget I own fifty percent of this place, even if it *is* on your side of the street."

"The funeral parlor's on your side. Take him there."

"I don't want the funeral parlor in working order, thanks. If you want one, then open it on *your* side. I want to turn the parlor into something else."

"Like what?"

"Like a bar."

"A *bar?*" Crystal jumped up, this time knocking her knees on the coffee table. "Are you crazy? We'll not only have the likes of Hoyle Bixby hanging around, there'll also be drunken Hoyle Bixby wannabees staggering all over town."

"You're the one who's crazy."

His exasperated sigh sent her already frayed nerves into over-drive.

"This town needs attractions. You're not gonna get that with some little convenience store an' a down-home-cookin'-type restaurant," he said.

"The Beckers and their daughter and son-in-law will be ideal additions to this town." Crystal stamped her foot. Pretty childish, she thought, but she was past caring. How dare he belittle the only normal, sane people who had come into town in days?

"Ha! The Beckers of Cactus Station. Sounds like the Beverly Hillbillies." Cody rested his feet on the coffee table and gazed coolly back at her.

Crystal wanted to stuff him inside the casket with Jake Carver. He needed it--was asking for it--should get what he deserved. She fought the urge to try.

"Maybe they do," she said through teeth clenched so hard her jaw ached. "But they're bringing revenue into town. The only thing you can say about the types you've brought in is that they destroyed the lobby." She grabbed a paper sack and began stuffing trash into it.

"They also bought all the Beckers' food," he pointed out.

"I realize that." Crystal was sick of him stating the obvious. Why couldn't he see that the skeleton would bring them nothing but trouble?

"If you even try to open a bar, I'll...I'll..." She searched for a suitable punishment.

"You'll withhold your favors from me?"

"Ooh. You...you cretin." She threw the paper bag and its disgusting contents at him.

Cody avoided the missile. "What's a cretin?" he demanded.

She ignored him and left.

CHAPTER SEVENTEEN

Crystal popped awake in the darkness, her heart pounding. Her digital clock read three A.M. She wondered if she'd had a nightmare, but didn't remember anything disturbing. Yet something had snapped her out of a deep sleep.

She lay still, ears straining to catch every little sound. Nothing. Shrugging, she plumped up her pillow, closed her eyes and rolled onto her stomach.

A thud overhead made her flip onto her back. Someone walked over the creaking attic floor and passed down the staircase that bit into her ceiling. Sick panic fluttered around her insides. She felt under her bed for her rifle and came up empty-handed.

Someone had taken it. She distinctly remembered picking it up from the lobby and taking it back upstairs after her argument with Cody. Who would have had the nerve to go into her room and remove her rifle while she slept?

Cody, she decided. The sickness passed, replaced with waves of anger. Jolie and Harold wouldn't creep around her room. Neither would any of the other guests, with the possible exception of Brent Hardacre, the reporter. He had elected to spend the night on a couch in the upstairs hallway rather than attempt to drive the dirt road back to Phoenix at dusk. Crystal tried to picture him crawling across her floor on his hands and knees.

"No," she muttered. No way.

She left her light off. Wishing the moon was still shining through her window, she felt around for her clothes. After a couple of minutes of frustration, she managed to locate jeans and tennis shoes on the floor.

Footsteps stopped outside her door. Her heart started pounding again. Crystal wondered what she could find in her room to hit the intruder.

Someone knocked quietly. "Crystal." The voice, although faint, definitely belonged to Jolie.

"I'm awake." Relieved, she opened the door.

Jolie stepped inside and closed the door behind her. "What's goin' on?" she asked. "I heard someone walkin' around the attic."

"I think Cody's playing a prank. Someone sneaked in and took my rifle so I wouldn't blow the supposed ghost's head off. He's the only one who would do that."

Jolie clicked her tongue. "If'n it is Cody, I'll brain him myself. I got the scare of my life when I heard that noise overhead. My first thought was that ole Jake was goin' back to his closet."

"I'm going to catch him out of his room and get him for this." Crystal walked into the hallway.

She and Jolie weren't the only ones out of bed. Prospectors and tourists, some in nightclothes, others half-dressed, stood in their doorways. One of the first people Crystal noticed was Mrs. Bloomford, an enormous lady who had taken the last room in the hotel with her skinny little husband, a man half her size. She bullied him out into the hot sun on a daily basis, loaded down with shovels, pickaxes, ropes, buckets and pans. Every evening he returned hot, sweaty and with nothing to show for his efforts but dust and a sunburn. Crystal always felt sorry for him.

Mrs. Bloomford invariably spent the first part of the evening screaming at the poor man, after which she made her grand entrance into the dining room. Mr. Bloomford followed meekly behind his wife, whose brilliant red hair was teased and sprayed into a bouffant coiffure reminiscent of the sixties at their worst, her rotund body encased in some hideously bright muumuu covered with spangles.

At that moment, Mrs. Bloomford wore a full head of rollers, an orange nightshirt that rivaled her hair for brilliance and a facial mask of some green goop that made her look like a refugee from a Halloween party.

Crystal shuddered and tried to avoid staring at her gigantic guest. "I'm sure there's some reasonable explanation for this," she said to no one in particular as she headed straight for Cody's room.

Without bothering to knock, she threw open the door and snapped on the overhead light only to find him seemingly asleep, stretched out naked on top of his covers. The crowd behind her made collective noises, including "oohs" from Jolie and Mrs. Bloomford.

Crystal hurriedly slammed the door in their faces.

"All right," she told Cody. "You can stop faking and cover yourself, for goodness sake. Half the guests just saw you."

Cody blinked at her in the harsh light of the bulb dangling from the ceiling. He yawned.

"What are you doin' here? Did you decide you couldn't live without me after all? Come here, darlin'." He moved over and patted the space beside him.

She grabbed a pair of jeans off the back of a chair and tossed them at him. "Put those on and explain to me why you're trying to frighten everyone in the hotel."

"Me?" His eyes opened wide in amazement. "What am I supposed to have done now?"

"Put the damned jeans on." Crystal sank deeply into the worn brocade chair beside his bed. She felt totally exhausted from playing non-stop silly games with him.

He shrugged and pulled on the jeans. "Okay, but I'm not goin' anywhere. I don't know why you thought the rest of the guests needed to see what you're insistin' on doin' without. What did you do--throw my door open to the world?"

"Just about." She hadn't meant to do that. "I'm sorry, Cody. Jolie and Mrs. Bloomford got a good look, as well as about half a dozen of the men."

He groaned and fell backward onto his pillow. "Mrs. Bloomford?" he asked faintly, rubbing his face with both hands.

"And Jolie," she added.

"I bet Harold was ticked off."

"Luckily, he wasn't there. Unless your nakedness is a hot topic of conversation tomorrow, we're safe."

"What's this 'we' business? You're the one who saw fit to invade my privacy and expose me to all the guests."

"Why can't you sleep in a pair of underwear at least?"

"Hon, I've never slept in anythin'; you know that well enough."

"That was then. It was different."

"Why? Because we made love half the night?" He took his hands away from his face and looked at her, his eyes dark blue and infinitely deep in the white light.

He always had to come back to that, she thought. She shifted uncomfortably. One leg of the ancient chair creaked ominously.

"I don't want to get into a discussion of our long-ago affair." She sat on her hands to hide the slight tremor that always came with memories of lying in his arms.

"Makes you uncomfortable, doesn't it?" Unhurriedly, he stood and zipped up his jeans.

Hating herself but unable to stop ogling, she watched. His zipper went up slower than anything he'd ever done, including repairing the generator.

"I suppose you think you're being sexy," she accused.

"I suppose you're gonna say I'm not, even though you watched my zipper every inch of the way." His smirk mocked her.

"You're impossible."

"And you're a hypocrite."

He put on a shirt and shoes while Crystal tried to think of a suitable retort instead of resorting to violence.

"So." He flopped back onto his hammocky bed. "What was important enough for you to get me up in the middle of the night? This had better be good."

Did he really think she'd fall for the oldest trick in the book? "You know very well why I got you up."

"If I did, then I wouldn't be sittin' here waiting for explanations, would I?"

"Yes, you would. You're playing stupid games again, Cody, and they're going to backfire on you."

"What games?" He looked genuinely confused.

Crystal refused to provide him with the excuse that she'd told him all about the footsteps. Instead of discussing things any further, she would let the scared residents of the Gold Rush prove to him that his prank had misfired.

She leaned forward. "You need to talk to the guests," she said.

The chair leg gave way. Suddenly, she found herself at eye level with Cody's knees. Crystal fought her way out of the chair's depths as dust rose all around her. Cody looked dangerously close to laughter, a suspicious twitch at the corner of his mouth. His sexy mouth. Crystal hated herself for thinking the way she did, but she couldn't help it. Even in the midst of her anger, she found him attractive. Highly annoying, but attractive.

"Something frightened them," she said. Drawing herself up, she looked down at him. "I'm not going to take care of it for you."

Leaving rude Cody and his collapsing furniture behind, she threw open the door and flounced out into an empty corridor. As the door swung shut behind her, she heard him laughing.

CHAPTER EIGHTEEN

Where had they all gone? Crystal spotted Brent Hardacre's empty couch, his rumpled bedclothes and jacket bunched at the end of it. A horrible thought came to her. Suppose he had taken the opportunity to explore the attic while everyone was asleep? Suppose she had unjustly accused Cody.

She swallowed with difficulty. Cody had never been completely angry with her. He'd always taken the line of least resistance and walked off his irritation. What would he do if he found she'd awakened him for no reason except her unfounded accusations as well as exposing him to half the guests, including Mrs. Bloomford of all people?

The huge, repulsive lady had the biggest crush on him. Crystal shrank from the thought of Mrs. Bloomford making increasingly obvious passes at Cody. And what about Jolie, whom he might have a great deal of difficulty facing in the morning?

Going back to sleep was impossible after all that had happened. She tramped downstairs to find Jolie and Brent waiting for coffee to perk.

"I told the guests Brent was explorin'," Jolie said. "He didn't mean to scare anyone, did you?" She quirked her brows at him.

Brent shrugged self-consciously. "I didn't realize I was going to make so much noise," he admitted.

Crystal was in no mood to hear that Brent had been skulking around instead of Cody. "Did you take my rifle?" she asked.

"No way." Brent looked horrified. "I wouldn't dare come in your room. The first thing I heard this afternoon when I woke up from passing out was you shooting."

Crystal was back to making Cody the culprit. But why would he steal it? He knew she kept it for protection. She'd shown it to him when she first arrived. After all, she'd had no idea what to expect in Cactus Station.

Cody strolled in. "I smelled coffee," he said.

"Did you take my rifle?" Crystal asked.

He held up his hands. "I don't think I can take any more of this, Crystal. This is the second thing you've accused me of in the last ten minutes. No, I did not take your rifle. I've never liked firearms and never carried one. I stay as far away from guns as I possibly can."

Crystal knew she was going to have to apologize for accusing him of trying to scare everyone in the hotel. Now he was going to chalk up one more thing on his list of points against her. He was batting a thousand, and she had a whole box of eggs on her face.

Jolie sat watching him from across the table. Crystal saw her checking Cody out from head to foot. No doubt she was envisioning him as she'd seen him before Crystal slammed the door in her face. Crystal winced. She'd done enough to hurt Cody that evening, and she felt increasingly ashamed of herself.

"I didn't realize I'd make so much noise checking out the attic," Brent said. "It was so hot, dark and dusty up there. I tried to be as quiet as possible, but I knocked over a pile of books. They made one heck of a thump when they hit the floor."

"That's what must have woken me up," Crystal said.

"You, me an' half the guests on the first floor," Jolie added. She got up and groped for the pot on the stove while she watched Cody.

He straddled a chair at the end of the table and looked pointedly at Crystal. "Some of us were still tryin' to sleep, but we weren't allowed to. Some of us were dragged out of bed and accused of creatin' a nuisance of ourselves."

Crystal flushed scarlet. "Can I talk to you outside for a moment?"

His fingers drummed the table. Tightness around his mouth warned her he was very angry. Her irrational behavior that evening had pushed him to the edge of his long-suffering endurance, and for that she was genuinely sorry. She had to clarify a few things with him, or the situation between them would only continue to worsen.

"Please?" She asked again, when he didn't answer.

"Okay." He got up, his movements quick and choppy, instead of fluid and pleasing to the eye.

"Do you mind if we take a walk?" she asked when they reached the back porch. "I really don't want anyone overhearing us."

"That's a change for you." Cody didn't look receptive, but he shoved his hands in his pockets and followed her down the steps into the alleyway.

"I'm sorry about tonight," she said.

"Is that right?"

She waited, but he didn't elaborate further. The alleyway ran into a track that led to the desert. Moonlight bathed the landscape with a silver glow, illuminating the Saguaro cacti and contrasting with the shadows of the Superstitions.

"I've been acting irrationally," she said.

"You have." His footsteps made no sound as they walked side by side toward the hills.

"Cody, you're not making this easy for me."

For some reason, tears clouded her vision. Since arriving in Cactus Station, she'd longed to have a conversation that allowed her to air her views without any interruptions from him. Now, perversely, she missed his comments.

"I didn't see it written anywhere that I had to be your doormat every time something goes wrong," he said.

She tried to blink the tears away. "I never meant that."

He snorted. "Then putting people down comes second nature to you."

She'd hurt him deeply, intentionally or not. She remembered only too well the comment he had made about barely passing seventh grade while she went on to college. The time he had told her he was dumb. She laid her hand on his arm. Beneath her fingers, his muscles tightened to the consistency of steel cables.

"I said I'm sorry." The tears rolled down her cheeks and she made no attempt to hide them.

"You never touch me unless you want something," he said, and he pulled her hand off his arm.

"I don't want to fight with you. If only you'd stop being so difficult." She almost choked on her words.

"Me, difficult?"

His icy tone sent a chill through her.

"Honey." His blue eyes were colder than the night air. "You haven't *seen* 'difficult' yet. All those threats you made about what you'd do if I showed the skeleton and made this place into a tourist attraction are going to have to be made good. You got the better half of the town because of some misguided plan the uncles cooked up. I'm the one who should have inherited the whole place. You never loved the Superstitions the way I do."

"That's not true." She grabbed his arm again and hung on despite his efforts to shake her off. "I've always loved it here. That summer I stayed here was the most special of my whole life."

She'd admitted the one thing she'd sworn she never would, and she didn't care anymore.

"You're lyin'." His voice rang of hurt, not anger. "You couldn't wait to leave me behind an' go on to college."

"And you never tried to stop me."

"No, an' I'm not tryin' now, either. Go back to Phoenix, where you belong." He pried her fingers none too gently from his arm. "I'm sick of playin' cat 'n mouse with you."

"But you don't mind making passes at me on a daily basis. Is that any way to treat *me?*"

"I care a lot about you," he said. "Always did. Always will. Trouble is, I don't *like* you a whole hell of a lot." He stepped off the track and turned on his heel. "I need to get some rest before facing Mrs. Bloomford in the mornin'. Thanks to what you did earlier, I'm sure she'll be followin' me around all day."

He left her standing in the stark beauty of the moon-bathed desert, her heart heavier than it had been since he had left her behind all those years before.

CHAPTER NINETEEN

Over the next few days, Crystal suffered the intrusion of the skeleton and its casket, telling herself she had to do something to placate Cody.

He avoided her judiciously, as though she had some contagious disease. Every time she came into a room, he found an excuse to leave it. She tried knocking on his door after everyone retired, but it remained firmly bolted against her. She followed him around on his repairs only to find him driving out of town on some errand or another.

On one occasion, she even tried following him into the Superstitions, but he soon out- distanced her. After getting lost on the way back and spending most of the morning aimlessly wandering down one dead-end trail after another, she finally managed to get back to Cactus Station. Frightened, she didn't repeat the experience.

She had been gone too long from the mountains to remember anything but the largest landmarks, such as the far-off Weaver's Needle. Cody, on the other hand, knew every nook and cranny. He unerringly found his way on and off the beaten trails, whereas she realized she could not, and if she was totally truthful with herself, never did. He had taken her everywhere, and watched out for her safety when she had visited that fateful summer.

The publicity generated by the media had attracted so many sight-

seers, psychics and weirdoes that the town turned away from its unprof-
itable status and headed firmly into the black. Selling tickets to see the
skeleton and the closet kept the crowds orderly and the dollar bills
rolling in. Harold's sprained ankle turned out to be more of a blessing
than a curse. He kept order and took tickets with his crutches close-by.
Any unruliness resulted in him waving one of those crutches with
instant results. Crystal had a feeling his long black hair, leather vest and
tattoos didn't hurt, either.

Three weeks passed and the crowds swelled rather than diminished.
The Beckers made good money out of their convenience store while their
daughter and son-in-law worked tirelessly in the continually crowded
restaurant. A pair of retirement-age tourists decided to lease Diamond
Della's House of Splendors and turn it into a gift shop. They sold a lot of
cheap Korean and Japanese imports until Crystal put them in touch with
genuine crafters and artisans in the area. After that, their merchandise
became classier, attracting tourists with more than a few dollars to spend
at the end of their visit.

A month to the day after the discovery of the skeleton, Crystal arose
early to find Cody had yet again left the hotel before dawn.

"You gotta get up mighty early to catch him these days," Jolie told
Crystal as she handed over a mug of coffee.

"He does it purposely." Crystal took the coffee over to the table and
sat down, resting her chin on her hands. Cody still wasn't what could
really be classed as talking to her, and he shied away from any attempts
at discussing the situation on the rare occasions she managed to catch up
with him.

"Sure he avoids you on purpose, hon." Jolie set a coffee cake on the
table and sat facing Crystal. She smiled, dimples appearing on her
cheeks. "He's tryin' to make you understand what you're missin'." She
deftly cut the cake and offered a slice.

Crystal shook her head, her stomach already tying itself into a string
of knots. "I'm not missing anything," she protested, but a little voice at
the back of her mind mocked her.

She missed Cody's searing kisses and his hard, sinewy body. Much as
she hated herself for wanting him the way she did, she had to admit her
attraction to him burned brighter with every passing day.

"You need to shake him up." Jolie stabbed her cake with a fork and popped a large piece of cinnamon and apple confection into her mouth.

Crystal took a sip of burning hot coffee. The resulting pain drove home Jolie's comments. Maybe shaking Cody up wasn't such a bad idea. She was tired of the crowds and sick of having Jake exhibited in the hotel. What would happen if she put up 'No Parking' signs all along her side of the street?

Cody's side had more ruts on Main Street and fewer alleyways, cutting down the available parking spaces. If more people had to leave their vehicles on the edge of town and walk, maybe they'd get angry and leave.

She spent half the morning making signs, which she then hung from every available post on her side of town. The signs continued all the way past the cemetery, until the desert spread out before her, and the only places to hang any more cardboard would be on the Saguaros dotting the landscape.

Her one fear was that either the signs would be ignored, or Cody would go behind her back and tear them down. But when Sheriff Dalton heard about her scheme, he rubbed his hands together.

"I'll be happy to come out and enforce your signs, Miss Crystal. I'll even send one of my deputies out on a daily basis to write tickets," he said over a late lunch.

"I'm so glad I called you." Crystal offered him another sandwich thick with left-over turkey and tomatoes.

Cody came stomping in through the back door. "What's goin' on?" He tossed his hat onto the counter and his eyes narrowed when he saw Reed. "Are you tryin' to wreck things?" he asked Crystal.

"I'm tired of the crowds and the dust." She ignored his scowl. "I don't want to spend my whole life cleaning up after them and taking tickets."

"You don't do much ticket takin', an' you know it." He took a soda from the refrigerator and popped the tab. Two spots of color appeared high on his cheeks. "I usually do all the tours an' Harold takes the tickets. The only time you spell me is if I need a couple of minutes to get somethin' to eat or drink. Now Harold's ankle's about healed, he can even do that, or I'll ask Jolie."

"I want Cactus Station to be a dignified little town again," she said.

"It'll be a ghost town again if we don't have somethin' like this show goin' on." Cody laid the cold can against his forehead. "We *need* these folk, Crystal. I've told you that 'til I'm blue in the face."

"You may need them. I don't." She got up to stack the dishes in the sink.

Reed took a toothpick out of his top pocket and began whittling the spaces between his teeth. He let out a loud, long belch. Crystal tried to give visual signals behind his back for Cody to stop shooting off his mouth in front of the sheriff, but apparently he was too angry and ignored her.

"You think you're too good for all this, don't you?" He strode across the kitchen and grabbed her wrist.

She shook him off and turned on the faucet. "That's not why I put up the signs."

"You think just because you went to college an' got some fancy education, you're above workin' here."

"Stop it, Cody." She squirted dish soap into the water. "You're talking nonsense."

"Quit messin' with the damn dishes and look at me." He grabbed her by the arm and whirled her around to face him.

Reed belched again, louder than the first time. "Better do as the lady says, unless you want to risk spending time in the slammer again," he said.

Crystal stared at him, then at Cody. "You did time in jail?"

He let go of her. "Was that necessary?" he asked Reed.

"I thought so." The sheriff let his belt out a notch.

"What did you do?" Crystal watched the conflicting emotions on Cody's face: anger, embarrassment.

"Ask Reed. I've got better things to do than waste time on the past." Cody headed for the back door.

"You always did run from confrontations," she said.

He hesitated briefly before he pushed the screen door open with a vicious jab and left.

"He gets a mite testy when jail's mentioned." Reed pulled out his cigarettes and lighter.

"I'd appreciate you not smoking in here." Crystal didn't know when she'd ever been angrier with Reed Dalton.

"Ooh. Now you're getting a little hostile, too." Reed grinned. "I brought up Cody's brush with the law because it's in your best interests to know everything."

"Maybe not." Crystal grabbed a dish towel to dry her hands and arms. "What in the world did he do--rob a bank?"

Dalton chuckled. "Nah. Nothing that grand. He used some questionable methods of soliciting funds for the uncles one time. When the mine didn't pan out, people wanted your partner's hide. Cody got off with a year's probation. He was pretty peeved with Willy and Dock. They kind of let him take the fall alone and went on about their business. After the year was up, he went north. I heard he went to Colorado."

"How come I never heard any of this before?"

Crystal felt conflicted. Uncle Dock and Uncle Willy hadn't backed up Cody or helped him out? That sounded so unlike them, yet she'd had so little contact with them after she went to graduate school, perhaps her view of their lives was a little too sugar-coated.

"Who was going to tell you?" Reed tapped his cigarette pack on the table. "After Cody left, the uncles had a big fight and weren't speakin' for a while. They patched it up, of course, an' the next thing, they were in that mining accident. That's when both you and Cody came back."

Crystal bit her lip. "I have to find Cody and talk to him about this."

"You think you'll have any success if he doesn't want to be found?" Reed shook his head. "You'll waste your time and risk heatstroke. He'll come to you when he's good an' ready."

"The way I've been acting, that day may be a long way off." Crystal threw the dish towel onto the table. She couldn't just hang around the hotel until Cody came back. "I'll talk to you later, Sheriff."

She walked through the lobby and out onto Main Street. She had no idea how she was going to find Cody. The line to view the skeleton and the closet had grown steadily, until it serpentined down the block. Crystal wondered what would happen if she told all of them that the tour was off for the day.

"Jolie and I can take care of the tourists," Harold said.

Crystal jumped. Where had he come from? She turned to face him.

Harold had abandoned his crutches. He held a large roll of tickets in one hand and a bucket for the stubs in the other.

"I didn't mean to scare you, but I overheard y'all shoutin' at each other, then I heard the screen door slam and just the sheriff an' you finishin' your conversation. Sounds like you an' Cody have a few problems to clear up. I can manage here, and Jolie'll show the tourists the attic."

"Well..." Crystal didn't know if Cody would like Harold and Jolie operating his business.

"We've both listened to Cody's tale so much, we can recite it in our sleep," Harold assured her. "You can rest easy."

"Oh, all right." She hoped she'd made the right decision, but the alternative was even less workable. Cody had voiced some misgivings about Jolie and Harold being so involved in the everyday operations of Cactus Station, but what choice did she have? The crowd was getting restless and the day sure wasn't getting any cooler.

Harold limped over to the door and started taking tickets. He took a group of twenty into the front lobby and started the customary monologue; word for word the same one Cody gave every day. He explained they were going to see Jake Carver's gruesome remains and the attic closet where he had been found. He told tales of floating specters and cruel deeds in the mines around and under Cactus Station. He opened the casket lid slowly, the suspense building. As the group gathered around the casket and looked inside, he promised them Jolie would scare the dickens out of them in the attic and a collective shiver of anticipation rippled through them.

Crystal decided to check for Cody in town. She doubted she would find him, but anything was better than waiting in that hot kitchen. She decided he might be making more repairs at the convenience store. He had several projects pending for the Beckers, who complained about the delay on a daily basis.

The roar of an engine and a resounding crash sent her running for Cody's side of the street, instead. A plume of dust rose into the air where the mercantile had stood. The building was nothing more than a pile of rubble. What if he was inside when it collapsed?

CHAPTER TWENTY

"Cody!"

Crystal looked in horror at the pile of rubble. She was afraid to step on it even to start searching. What if she inadvertently stepped on him?

"Harold!" she screamed. "Somebody. Anybody!"

"You spend more time screamin' than anyone else I've ever met," Cody said. He stood casually resting one arm on the enormous wheel of a bulldozer.

She stared at him in total disbelief. "I thought the building collapsed on you."

"That would have made your day, wouldn't it?"

The twinkle in his eyes and the smirk that mocked her panic should have infuriated her. Instead, she felt so relieved she could have hugged him.

"No, it wouldn't." The hand she laid on his arm shook uncontrollably.

Cody raised his eyebrows. "Don't tell me you were worried about me." He grinned. "Maybe I should scare you a little more often."

"I don't recommend it." Her pounding heart slowed. She pointed at the bulldozer. "When did this arrive?"

"Yesterday, when you were in Apache Junction." He ran his hand over the wheel cover. "Nice, useful piece of machinery."

"What are you doing?" A pulse still throbbed painfully in her head. She couldn't quite believe he was standing so serenely in front of the ruined mercantile.

His mouth quirked in the annoying way he used all too often around her. "What does it look like? I'm demolishin'."

"Why?"

She couldn't imagine why he'd chosen that particular building. When they both first arrived in Cactus Station, they had discussed which ones needed leveling and decided on the old dental office, two small stores at the end of the street closest to the cemetery, and two houses, one on her side, the other on his. Nothing else, and certainly not the mercantile.

"I need the space." He unwrapped a piece of gum and popped it into his mouth.

Crystal watched his unhurried movements. "We never agreed to demolish this building," she said.

"We never agreed to you puttin' up 'No Parkin' signs, either." He leaned back against the bulldozer, his blue eyes piercing in their intensity. "I had to make some quick decisions about where to put the new parkin' lot."

She gaped, unable to control herself. He was incorrigible. He'd destroyed the best preserved, largest building on his side of the town in order to make room for tourists' cars.

"I'd talk more with you, but I'm kind of busy right now." He opened the door of the cab and stepped up into it.

"Since when have you been able to operate a bulldozer?" She caught hold of the door before he could close it.

"I learned while I was on probation. I had to stick around Phoenix for a year, and a man has to eat--even me." He looked at her fingers. "Do you mind?"

His voice was so cold and detached, goose bumps rose on Crystal's arms, despite the heat. She let go and watched him swing the door closed. He started up the engine.

"You're not going to take down anything else, are you?" she shouted over the noise.

"Maybe. Maybe not. I'll see how I feel." He put the bulldozer into gear and began pushing debris toward the back of the lot.

The buildings on either side of the rubble swayed with the vibrations. Crystal was afraid the whole town would come crashing down around her ears. She couldn't watch the sacrilege, and she understood she had precipitated the destruction of the town as well as any chance at a reasonable solution with Cody.

Cody and the bulldozer toiled for two days. He leveled the space left by the mercantile's demise and removed the other buildings they had previously agreed to tear down. He piled all the debris on one side of the cemetery, where it was picked through by tourists and prospectors alike. Crystal saw the signs from outside the mercantile and the dentist's office change hands several times, for increasing amounts of money.

Cody's parking lot soon filled to capacity. Sheriff Dalton policed the 'No Parking' areas and ticketed violators. Residents and visitors alike wised up and advised newcomers not to risk a fine.

Crystal decided to open a tea-room. She had toyed with the idea ever since she saw the little house nestling between the blacksmith's shop and the chapel. She felt it would make a perfect spot for afternoon tea, coffee, and pastries. Working on the venture appealed to her. Anything to get her mind off the unfulfilling mess her life had become; anything to get her mind off Cody. She was tired of seeing his shirtless bronzed body parading in and out of the hotel kitchen when he came inside for drinks or meals. They hadn't spoken since the day the bulldozer started operations.

Crystal cleaned and scrubbed the little house, Harold repaired the floor and the roof, then brought barrels and boxes from around town to turn into tables. He found enough lumber from the demolished buildings to fashion into benches and quaint stools. Jolie made cafe curtains, tablecloths and cushions out of material purchased from a remnant store in Apache Junction and Crystal bought all the supplies out of her half of the ticket proceeds.

She opened for business ten days later. Freshly ground coffee in five different flavors vied for attention with herbal teas and fresh pastries supplied daily from Phoenix, delivered to Tortilla Flat, and picked up by her as dawn rose over the mountains. The pastries were an expense she doubted she would be able to continue, but they made a statement for the first few days of the tea-room's opening.

From across the street, Cody watched the foot traffic enter her establishment, his brow furrowed and one foot tapping impatiently as he sat outside the assay office. All the commerce was on her side. The only money-making operation he owned was the parking lot, which although always full, was limited in scope as far as increasing revenue.

Crystal allowed herself the luxury of gloating, waving to him with a pleasant, self-satisfied smile. He may have defaced Cactus Station with his money-grabbing and lack of control, but she would have the last laugh. While he sat on the sidelines and watched her rise to economic security, she'd get rich out of this feud. Then she would have the means to either buy him out or leave Cactus Station and Cody Do-Nothing Blye behind.

CHAPTER TWENTY-ONE

Crystal started going to the creek at the end of each day. She found peace in its babbling depths. Despite all odds, including heat, dust and prospectors armed with pans and pickaxes, the water kept flowing from its niche in the rocks to splash its way down the mountainside.

Secure in her solitude, she allowed herself to acknowledge Cody wasn't the only one with a few skeletons in his closet. Her fight to claim her inheritance had been triggered by the collapse of her business. She had been blackballed after being implicated in a fraudulent land deal.

Crystal agonized over whether she should share her misfortunes with Cody, who might understand her situation better than anyone else. But her tattered pride kept preventing her from telling him the truth. Cody was difficult enough when he felt at a slight disadvantage. It was entirely possible he would seize the opportunity to destroy her fragile self-confidence in an effort to prove he was the one capable of turning Cactus Station into a successful venture.

In time, perhaps the scandal would be forgotten, and she could return to Phoenix with an expectation that her phone would be ringing off the hook with prospective clients clamoring for her services. Those daydreams did not include Cody's presence in any shape or form, but they were also dreams which she controlled.

By night, she often awakened drenched with sweat after Cody came to her in her dreams, his lean, tanned body covered only with his habitually tight hip-molding jeans. His bare chest glistened with droplets of water from the creek, where he had been washing away the dust and heat from his skin. Water would drip from his body as he leaned over to kiss her lips, the moisture from the droplets dampening her peasant blouse and brightly colored, billowing skirt.

A soft breeze would blow up, rippling the folds of her skirt and teasing her legs with its light touch. Crystal would feel Cody's lips on hers, the sensation of his mouth trailing down her neck to her shoulder. When he pulled the wide neckline of her blouse aside to expose her breasts, she would arch up to meet his tantalizing touch.

At that moment, the dream would disintegrate. Awakening to find herself alone, unsatisfied and breathless in the darkness, she always felt tears on her cheeks and a hollowness in her heart. Regardless of the way Cody had turned the serenity of the old ghost town into the booming sideshow she loathed, Crystal found she still wanted him with a fierceness and passion that never abated.

After enduring a week of the dreams, Crystal decided she had to try to make peace with Cody before she became an insomniac. But Cody had decided to implement another money-making scheme that would prove more disastrous to their relationship than he could ever have imagined. He started work on the Branch Water Bar.

CHAPTER TWENTY-TWO

Jolie stood at the bottom of the ladder in the assay office. "Can't you see what this will do to Crystal?" she asked.

Cody shrugged, his mouth full of nails.

"She'll never forgive you," Jolie predicted.

Cody stopped hammering and spat the nails into his hand. "Damn it, Jolie. Why don't you go back to your job at the tearoom or the hotel or somethin'? Did I ask for your opinion?"

Ever since he'd arrived, Crystal had been bossing him around and refusing any overtures of friendship. He was tired of being a scapegoat. He wanted respect and recognition for the man he had become, not for the stupid young man he had been the summer he had committed the worst mistake of his life.

If only he had listened to his heart and his conscience, instead of to the uncles. He should have asked her to marry him and hang the consequences. Maybe with Crystal's support, he would even have finished high school and made something of himself, instead of being an odd-jobber, sometime gold prospector and master of nothing in particular.

"I don't see what me openin' a bar on my own side of Cactus Station has to do with Crystal," he explained with as much patience as he could scrape up on short notice.

Jolie made an exasperated noise. "She told me her father used to drink too much and couldn't hold down a job for more than a couple of days at a stretch. She hates liquor an' anythin' to do with it."

"She doesn't have to come anywhere near this place. She's got her tearoom an' all the rent from the convenience store an' the restaurant. I don't have anythin' close to that." He shifted impatiently and the ladder swayed.

Jolie grabbed the ladder in an effort to steady it. "Can't you discuss that with Crystal, hon? I'm sure she'd be happy to help you find a better source of income than this bar..."

Cody wanted to tell her to get the hell out of there, but he was afraid if she left, the ladder would fall. "Look." He backed down a couple of rungs. "We pay you and Harold to work, not act as counselors. Why don't you go take care of your own job and leave me be, unless you want to get fired?"

Jolie drew herself up to her full height. Even though Cody was on the ladder, her eyes came disconcertingly close to his. "Crystal hired us; she can fire us."

"We're partners," Cody pointed out.

"Fine. If you're partners, then how come you're in competition with each other and fightin' all the time? You should both be workin' toward settin' Cactus Station up as a town you both like livin' in, 'stead of you makin' it into a tourist trap Crystal hates and then arguin' over the fact that she's got a better head for business than you do."

Cody slammed the hammer down on top of the ladder. The nails cascaded onto the floor.

"Damn it, Jolie. Crystal likes to ram all that down my throat every time I turn around. Now's she's got you doin' it. Next thing, I'll have to listen to Harold." He climbed down. "Crystal's got more education than I do. I'll be the first to admit that, but there are things I do better, like attractin' a money-makin' crowd. If Crystal had her way, we'd be broke an' the town would still be fallin' to pieces." He brushed Jolie aside and headed for the door.

"Crystal's right, you know," she called after him. "You always run away from confrontation."

When he looked back, she stood watching him with her arms folded.

"Crystal does the same thing," she continued. "That's why y'all don't resolve anythin'. You just yell and leave."

"That's our way. You're not gonna change either of us." He walked out, his throat dry and his temper frayed. At that moment, he'd like to take a lit match to Cactus Station and burn it to the ground.

He grabbed his shirt from the hitching post out front. Dust and particles of plaster coated his body, and he ached from spending too many hours with his arms lifted above his head. He'd almost finished installing the sheetrock, but it had been an uphill struggle.

After seeing Harold helping Crystal with the tearoom, Cody had refused to ask for the biker's assistance. Cody felt betrayed by Harold, who should understand the complicated issues of male ego and pride.

Cody needed to cool off, and fast. He headed for the creek. A dozen yards or so below the spring was a pool large enough to bathe in. He had often used it in the past, but he'd taken to washing down at the back of the hotel since the crowds had arrived in town.

He'd installed a shower stall that the rest of the guests had to pay to use. Water conservation was always an issue, and the tank wouldn't hold enough to accommodate baths for everyone in town.

The sun headed toward the horizon, elongating the shadows of the Saguaros and sagebrush. He had been working too long in the bar. His head pounded and he felt lightheaded. Perhaps that would at least partially justify his outburst to Jolie. Maybe not.

At the pool, he stripped off his clothes and plunged into the water, sinking to the bottom before lying with only his head above the surface. His mood calmed as he watched the ripples subside, his shoulders against the warm rocks. He raised his head to watch crimson streaks illuminate the cobalt blue sky. A circling hawk caught wind currents under his wings and swayed wildly before dipping down behind the hills.

Silence reigned above the soft burble of water from the spring's source. Although his normally laid-back nature had been pushed beyond its limits of late, he knew a quiet spell in the mountains always eased the troubles from his mind and the strain from his body. His aching shoulders felt better already. He moved them experimentally and winced. Maybe not *that* much better.

Soft footfalls warned him of someone's approach. He swore under his breath. So much for peace and quiet. So much for privacy. He was about to call out and alert the other person to his presence, but something familiar about the footsteps made him sink down to his chin in the water and wait.

Crystal appeared, walking carefully over the rocks, her attention on her feet and the ground ahead. She wore a loose white blouse that slipped off one smooth shoulder as she climbed down from the trail above. Her bare legs were tanned and shapely beneath a pair of cutoffs. Cody looked at the bare shoulder and drew in his breath.

She was a natural beauty. Devoid of any makeup, her hair cut shoulder length and never styled, she spent very little time on her looks. Any time she had overslept and he'd had to knock on her door to wake her up, she'd arrived downstairs within fifteen minutes, her skin glowing from a quick wash in the basin she kept in her room, her hair shimmering in the early morning sunlight.

He watched her find a spot beside the stream a little further up from the pool, take off her shoes and dip her feet into the water. She held her face up to the sky, eyes closed.

Cody was afraid to move. If he let her know he was there, she might be angry that he hadn't said anything when she first arrived. Instead, he elected to enjoy the view. She drew the hair off her neck and fastened it at the nape with a clip she took from a pocket in her cutoffs. Then she pulled both sides of the blouse off her shoulders, exposing a wide expanse of slightly pink-tinged skin.

From where he lay, he could see the swell of her breasts above the neckline of the blouse. The water in which he sat became colder as the sun faded behind the horizon. He started to shiver and knew he needed to get out, but the sight of Crystal relaxed and beautiful made him linger. When she lay back on the rocks, eyes still closed, he carefully stepped out and retrieved his clothes.

He should leave her, he thought, but after he pulled on his jeans, his feet turned toward her instead of away. Carrying his boots and shirt in his hand, he trod carefully across the rocks at the side of the stream.

Crystal lay motionless, her cheeks pink, her breasts rising and falling enticingly. He stepped out of the water beside her, afraid to speak, yet afraid not to do so. Her eyes opened as he stood over her and widened when they saw him.

"I didn't mean to frighten you," he said, lowering himself down beside her. Droplets of water from his skin dripped onto her blouse. The material became transparent. Cody realized she wore nothing beneath.

"You didn't frighten me." Her voice was a soft caress. She smiled. "I guess you'll think I'm crazy, but I've sort of been expecting you to come like this."

"Is that right?" He returned her smile and stretched out, propping himself on one elbow. "I've made you wet." He brushed a drop of water from her chin, then one from her shoulder.

"I don't mind. The cold water feels good. You've been in the creek." She reached out and touched the water still on his chest. "Mmm, you're cold. You feel good." Her hand splayed across his chest.

Cody could hardly breathe. She was touching him of her own free will, and he had initiated nothing except the first contact. "My hands are cold," he said, placing one on her shoulder.

Crystal shivered, then giggled. "How long were you in the water?"

"A while. Before you came." He slid the blouse further down her arm and lightly brushed his fingers across the neckline, passing over the swelling globes of her breasts. Crystal sighed, but didn't object. Her own hand languidly caressed his chest, her palm passing across his nipples, then pausing while she circled one, then the other.

He lowered the blouse again, completely exposing her breasts. "You're beautiful," he told her. He covered her lips with his own while his hands cupped her breasts and his fingers teased the stiff peaks.

"Am I?" She looked up at him, her eyelids fluttering.

"Yes." He took his lips from hers and lowered his mouth to her breast, suckling gently.

He wanted to tell her he still loved her, but he was afraid she wouldn't believe him, and he'd spoil the moment. She had unfastened his jeans and was trying to get her hand inside, but he had swelled so much, so quickly, her efforts were futile.

He helped her pull the jeans off. "I'm not going to stop this time," he told her before she could take him in her hand.

"I don't want you to."

She stood and shed her clothes, her face glowing in the diffuse light that still covered the western sky. He looked at her, naked and beautiful, standing before him as she had all those years before. It seemed right that they had returned to the Superstitions and were about to make love in the open, as they had so many times in the past.

Her hips were more rounded, her breasts fuller than he remembered. He hoped his body would please her. There wasn't an ounce of spare flesh on him anywhere. He was fully erect and completely ready without any help from her, but she settled down beside him and sent him to the edge of insanity with her lips and her hands.

"You don't need to do any more, sweetheart," he assured her, drawing air into his lungs with great, gulping breaths.

"Let me," she whispered against his mouth. "I've waited too long for this. Those other times, I did nothing for you. Now it's my turn."

He lay impervious to the rocks biting into his back while she kissed and caressed every inch of him. Finally, unable to take any more, he grasped her firmly and lowered her onto him. He thought he might die willingly when he felt her surround him, but dying wasn't an option when she began to move, rising above him, a sweet smile on her face when she saw his pleasure.

His thrusts increased rapidly in tempo, his body quivering. When his release came, he held her hips tightly against his until her eyes glazed and her body stiffened in her own climax.

Afterward, he kept her close, reluctant to release her even to get his breath. He caressed her back and her buttocks, ran his hands down the side of her breasts. Kissed her eyelids, her temples, her cheeks, her lips. He never wanted to let her go again. All the arguments, the fights and the anger seemed irrelevant with Crystal's body against his.

In only a few minutes, he felt himself stir to life again. Unsure whether she'd be pleased or appalled, he set her gently away from him, placing her on top of their discarded clothing.

"Ready again?" She laughed, her laughter clear and musical. "Did you think I wouldn't notice, just because it's dark?"

"I'll always be ready for you." He covered her mouth with his and brought his hand to the junction of her thighs, which she quickly parted for him.

"The feeling's mutual," she said, taking his hips and guiding him into her. He accepted the invitation gladly as she opened herself fully to him, her breasts crushed against his chest, her fingers clutching his back, encouraging him to plunge ever deeper until they both reached fulfillment.

Cody lifted his gaze to the star-kissed sky and wished the happiness of that moment could last for the rest of their lives.

CHAPTER TWENTY-THREE

They bathed in the pool before heading back. Cody thought he'd never kiss Crystal enough to make up for the years they'd been apart. He felt as though he had just stepped into the light after a long journey through a very dark tunnel.

"We'd better get back," she said. "Everyone will know what we've been doing."

"They will when they see my expression." He captured her face in his hands and gave her one last kiss before helping her out of the pool.

He used his shirt to dry her, lingering over the swells and valleys of her body, longing to tell her how he felt, yet afraid to do so, because his mouth had gotten him into so much trouble before.

Although they were so compatible physically, how could they ever be together in the real world? Even in Cactus Station, where they started as equals, she had already made a success of her inheritance, while all he had to show for himself was a tacky tour, a parking lot and a half-finished bar.

His heart plummeted at the thought of the bar. Jolie was right-- Crystal would never forgive him if he continued with the project. He had to get back and stop the gears he had already set in motion. Big Ed Calloway, a sometime acquaintance of Cody's from his days in Phoenix, had agreed to apply for a liquor license and run the bar after he found how many people came through Cactus Station on a daily basis. Cody knew he had to give Big Ed a call before any more damage was done.

"What's wrong, Cody?" She finished pulling her damp hair into the clip and placed her hand on his arm.

"Nothin'." He couldn't look at her with the lie on his lips and in his eyes. "Why don't you leave your hair loose? I like it that way."

She smiled. "Okay." She took out the clip and shook her head, her hair settling back onto her shoulders. "Better?"

"Much."

He made a big deal of shaking out his shirt while he pushed the guilt away. He'd take care of things as soon as they got back. She slipped her hand into his and they walked slowly down the trail while he struggled with his conscience.

"You're so quiet," she said when they reached the edge of town. "Something's wrong. What is it?"

He kept his face in the shadows. "I'm just tired and overwhelmed, I guess. I never thought we'd be together again. Never in a million years the way things were goin'."

"I know. We've had so many fights." She pulled his head down and planted a kiss on his lips, her mouth curving into a wry smile. "I guess we still have a lot of differences," she said against his mouth. "I hope we can work them out. I want to..." She paused as though searching for words. "I...I..."

"We need to get back." He tore himself away, taking her hand and almost dragging her along the path, his heart hammering like thunder in his ears.

She'd been about to tell him she loved him. He knew it. And he couldn't let her do that, not with the issue of the bar and his shortcomings standing between them. He didn't deserve Crystal, even though he'd let his body over-rule his common sense that evening.

His thoughts were so scrambled. Once, he'd thought if only he could make love to her, everything would magically be resolved. Now it had happened, he knew nothing was that easy.

"We need to go slower," he told her. His body rebelled, remembering only too clearly how incredible he had felt when she was in his arms.

"Slower?" Her voice was no more than a hurt whisper. She pulled her hand away from his. "We haven't been together in eight years. How much slower do you want to go?"

He heard the emotion in her voice and hated himself. "I'm afraid we'll rush into something we'll both end up regretting." He struggled to find the right words. "I haven't been very successful. In fact..." He took a deep breath. "I've been a complete failure. The only things I had to show for the last few years were two small nuggets, and I gave those away when I planted them to start the gold rush that got people into this town."

He turned away as the bitter knowledge washed over him. If he'd kept the nuggets, at least he would have had something tangible to show her he wasn't a complete deadbeat.

She slipped her arms around him. "Why do you always make so much trouble for yourself?"

"It comes naturally, I guess." He stared at the moon rising white and cold above the darkened peaks. "I'm pretty much a fool, Crystal. Always have been; always will be."

Silvered by the moonlight, her features were soft and breathtaking. "I'm going to tell you something. I don't want you to be angry with me. Will you promise?"

How could he refuse? "Sure."

"I overheard Sheriff Dalton threatening you the night I found the skeleton. He said if he found out you'd planted those nuggets, you were going to be in a lot of trouble."

"Criminal fraud. If I get charged again, I'll do time." He voiced his innermost fear. "You wouldn't turn me in, would you?"

The shock on her face made him sorry he'd even asked.

"How could you even suggest anything so terrible?" Instead of being angry, she started crying.

He held her against him, his face in her still-damp hair, sweet-smelling from the spring water. "I shouldn't have asked. I'm sorry. I'm so scared of losing you again."

"You won't unless you keep holding things back from me, or doing things in that underhanded way I hate so much. I don't even know why you keep doing that."

"It's like I can't help myself." He gently took her arms from around him. "Come on, let's walk."

Crystal sighed deeply. "I wish you'd open up and be completely honest with me. That's always been your biggest problem." She tried to match her shorter strides with his long ones.

"Talkin' about myself doesn't come easy to me." He grabbed her elbow when she tripped. "Careful."

"You're the only person I know who can find his way around here in the dark." She slipped her arm around his waist again and held him tightly. "I bet you could find the Lost Dutchman Mine if you really tried."

He laughed. "What makes you think I haven't already?"

"Because you wouldn't be fooling around doing maintenance on Cactus Station if you had. You'd be living it up, instead of being here with me."

"If I'd had money, Crystal, I swear I'd have come to you sooner. I'd have found out where you were and pestered you until you gave in an' came away with me."

"Oh?" She gave him a squeeze. "And where would you take me?"

"Wherever you wanted to go. Paris, Rome, Hawaii or somethin'."

"Maybe I wouldn't want to be anywhere else but here with you."

"I doubt that. You were made for better things than the likes of me an' Cactus Station."

"Why do you always put yourself down?" The concern in her voice was genuine. "I don't understand it."

They walked past the cemetery, serene in the moonlight with its handmade wooden crosses and disintegrating picket fence, and stepped from the rough track onto the well-worn dirt road that led to Cactus Station. The town was ablaze with lights. People walked to and fro, in and out of the stores, hotel and boarding house.

"It's funny to see the old town alive again." Cody decided it was time to leave his motives and inadequacies alone. "The day I arrived back here, I had no idea you'd have such an effect on the place."

"Me? Who brought the crowds in the first place?"

He had to smile. "I guess I had something to do with that. But how much is our little secret, isn't it?"

"Absolutely. You're a great salesman, and that's the truth, anyway."

She made him stop and kiss her one last time before they strolled down Main Street, past the blackened interior of the smaller bordello next to the Dry Dust Saloon.

"We need to do somethin' with that place," Cody said. "It's a real eyesore."

"Well, I guarantee it's not going to be running the same business inside that it had before." She giggled.

"Oh, come on, Crystal. These prospectors need a little entertainment sometimes."

"Not that kind. Not in my town...or yours, either." She slipped her hand into the back pocket of his jeans and pinched him.

"Ow! Are you getting physically abusive with me?"

"Not unless you ask me to." Her voice was a low purr.

Cody felt himself harden. "What are you tryin' to do to me?" he demanded in an undertone. He pulled her into the darkness between the buildings. "Don't you know you'll get yourself into trouble, and right beside the town bordello, too?"

"Must be some ghostly influence," she said.

He kissed her, his hand on her breast. Her mouth opened fully under his and her tongue dove into his mouth in a gesture so uncharacteristically aggressive for her, Cody was taken aback.

"Maybe I'll reopen the place myself." She laughed against his mouth as she pulled down the neckline of her blouse.

"As long as I'm your only customer." He pressed her back against the boards, his body molding to hers.

"Cody! Whaddya doin' back here, boy?"

Cody pulled quickly away from Crystal. He would have known that voice anywhere. His heart felt on a level with his boots. Big Ed Calloway, already in Cactus Station and following him into an alleyway. Cody turned, shielding Crystal as she hurriedly pulled up her blouse.

"Big Ed," he said. "How did you find me?"

"I was standin' on the hotel porch when I saw you an' the young lady duck into the alleyway." Ed laughed. "Figured you was havin' a little fun and wondered if you'd like to share the action."

Cody felt Crystal stiffen. He'd forgotten how coarse Ed could be. He wanted to get her away as quickly as possible.

"Ed Calloway, this is my partner, Crystal Penney. Crystal, this is Big Ed, someone I know from Phoenix. I thought he might be interested in openin' up a business here. Ed, you lay so much as a hand on Crystal and I guarantee you'll go into the Superstitions and never come out. You hear me?"

"Sure, Cody. I get you. Personal Property, huh?" He winked and dug his elbow into Cody's side.

"Personal property?" Crystal stalked out of her hiding place. "I'm no one's property, Mr. Calloway. Cody and I are good friends. No more. No less. We were trying to decide whether this building's salvageable. We've been so busy lately; time tends to get away from us." She looked at Cody. "I'll see you back at the hotel." Then she stalked away, passing Big Ed without so much as a glance in his direction.

"Whew-ee!" Ed whistled between his teeth. "That's some fine, classy little lady there. Bit of a spitfire too, heh?" His teeth flashed white in the gloom. "So, let's get down to business. I've seen the progress you've made on the bar. When's it going to be ready for business?"

Cody saw Crystal stop at the end of the alleyway, the flinch in her shoulders unmistakable. She turned back. "Excuse me. Did you say bar?"

"That's right, little lady. I guess Cody here forgot to mention it, you bein' so busy an' all." The tone of his voice made a wink unnecessary.

"Cody, can I speak to you in private for a moment?" she asked.

Oh, Lord, Cody thought. *Now I'm in big trouble.*

"Sure," he said. He shoved his hands in his pockets and sauntered over to where she waited.

She just about pulled him over, leading him away from Big Ed and the alleyway. "I thought you'd decided *not* to open a bar."

Cody was glad it was too dark to see her face. "I was mad at you, and I brought Big Ed out here to talk about it. That's all."

"You know how I feel about alcohol. How could you? Mad at me? Oooh." She stamped her foot on the boardwalk. "And to think I just made love with you--twice."

"You were about to make it a threesome," he pointed out, unable to stop himself.

He wanted to laugh, which wasn't the reaction she was looking for, he knew. He still felt like he was walking ten feet off the ground, after the way they'd spent the last few hours. He wasn't ready for a serious discussion.

The slap caught him off guard. Her aim wasn't too good, but her palm connected with his nose and her fingers jabbed him in the eye.

"What the hell is the matter with you?" He held his smarting nose.

"You're hateful. You're a two-faced, lying hypocrite."

"And what do you think you are?" How could she change so quickly from the love of his life into some annoying, pissy little woman he'd like to fling into the nearest canyon?

"I'm sure you'd enjoy laughing and making colorful jokes with your friend, Ed, but I'm not going to hang around here while you do it. I'm going back to the hotel. Don't you dare try coming to my room tonight or any other night. As far as I'm concerned, this afternoon was a mistake I'm never repeating again."

"Suits me."

He watched her run off. She was narrow-minded and domineering. It was always her way or the highway. They'd never find a middle ground, and he was through trying. He went back to join Ed.

The Branch Water bar opened with a lot of free beer the following Friday night. Everyone in town went with the notable exception of Crystal, who sat in her room and tried to shut out the noise with a pair of headphones and country music.

Sleep eluded her, whatever she tried that night. At two in the morning she wandered down to the kitchen, where she found Cody sitting at the table, his head in his hands.

"Hangover?" she asked snidely.

"No. Nightmares." He rubbed a hand over his face. "I keep getting visits from ole Jake in the middle of the night. He comes in an' stands over my bed. I swear, even when I wake up he's still there. I'm gettin' pretty spooked. Maybe I should try movin' to another room."

"What other room? The hotel's full. Do you really think anyone's going to trade with you when you tell them why?" She took the jug of lemonade out of the refrigerator. "Want some?"

"I guess." He took the glass she handed him and sipped.

He looked terrible--big bags under his eyes and his hair sticking up all over his head. Crystal couldn't help feeling sorry for him. "Maybe you should bury Jake's remains. He's probably trying to tell you he's sick of being on show."

"Maybe you're right." Cody drained his glass. "I'm thinking of cuttin' out. Want to buy my half of the town? You can probably afford it by now."

Crystal toyed with her glass. The thought of buying out Cody had occurred to her countless times in the past, but now the opportunity had arrived, she wasn't so sure she wanted to see the last of him. The memory of their time together at the spring was still too fresh in her mind. Maybe they didn't belong together, but she knew neither of them had given their relationship a chance. Giving Cody an easy way out of his predicament wasn't going to solve anything for either of them.

"Let me think about it," she said. "In the meantime, I'll swap rooms with you, at least for tonight."

"That's real generous, but not a very good idea. If anyone saw me goin' in and out of your room right now, there'd be gossip all over town."

"That's never worried you before."

"Well, it does now. Leave it be."

"How about the end room with the big hole in the roof? You and Harold could patch that in a day. There's lots of space and a good view of the mountains."

He rubbed the stubble on his chin. "That's an idea."

"And please bury Jake."

"Okay. The tour crowds are beginnin' to thin out, anyway."

"That's because the skeleton smells, Cody. And the heat coming down from the attic is making the whole first floor hotter, too."

"I know." He pushed back his chair. "I'm bushed. I think I'll try sleepin' again. Maybe Jake won't come to haunt me if he knows I'm sendin' him to the cemetery."

"Maybe."

She wanted to smooth the furrows from his brow and tell him everything would be okay, but she knew it wouldn't. She wasn't about to tell him she couldn't sleep anymore, either. When she lay in bed, her mind conjured up memories of their lovemaking. Cody's techniques had improved a lot in the intervening years. A tingle ran up her spine. He stood up, and her eyes strayed all of their own accord to his zipper.

Crystal swallowed hard. She remembered only too clearly taking down that zipper and pushing her hands inside his pants. She looked up to find him studying her, creases visible at the corners of his eyes. Beneath her thin cotton shirt, her nipples had become erect and stood out in stiff peaks. She got up quickly and took the glasses to the sink.

"Crystal, about the other night..."

"I don't want to discuss it."

"Your body does."

He came up behind her and she felt his breath on the back of her neck. Her eyes closed. She forced them open and ran water into the sink. Cold water. It splashed her and she jumped back, running straight into Cody's warmth and hardness.

He didn't reach out. He didn't need to. His mere presence was enough to ignite a flame as hot as heat lightning. She moved away and scrubbed the glasses so hard, she wondered why they didn't shatter.

Mercifully, a scratching at the back door broke the spell. Cody went over to let Jackson in, and Crystal started breathing again. She willed her body to relax, but the tingling persisted.

"What's up, Jackson?" Cody bent over to scratch the old dog behind the ears.

Crystal watched. He wore his habitual tight jeans and an equally tight t-shirt. She wanted to put her hands all over him.

Why did he have to look so sexy in the middle of the night? By rights she should be wanting to climb alone into her bed and sleep, not wanting to sink into it with Cody on top of her. Why couldn't she control her urges, even when common sense told her she had to if she wanted to keep her sanity?

"What have you got?" Cody asked his pet.

Jackson whined and deposited something in Cody's hand. "What's this?"

Crystal dried her hands. "What did he find now--another piece of bone?"

"No. Some kind of coin. Look." Cody dropped it into her hand.

Crystal turned the coin over a couple of times, her heart beginning to race. It wasn't possible. "It looks like a gold doubloon," she said. "I've never actually seen one outside of a museum. There have always been rumors of Coronado's gold being hidden around the Superstitions."

"Or Montezuma's treasure." Cody touched the coin reverently with one finger. "A memento from the Conquistadors. Do you think it's real?"

"It looks authentic," Crystal said. "It's a bit discolored, but I can see markings. I know a couple of people in Phoenix who'd be able to tell for sure."

"You know, I've got something similar to this on my window sill," Cody said. "But it's really dirty. Jackson brought it in that day Hoyle ate half the food you had made for supper. You were so mad; I put it into my pants pocket and forgot it. Jolie dug it out when she went to the laundromat and put it on the sill. I was so busy and tired, I forgot about it. I'll go get it." He took off up the stairs as she stood cradling the coin in her hand.

Crystal looked at Jackson. Where had the old mutt gone to find doubloons, if they were in fact real? Was this another of Cody's underhanded schemes? She couldn't believe he would have left a gold doubloon sitting on his window sill for weeks. He was too smart for that, and too desperate. He needed money, and if this coin was real, it was worth something in the region of eight hundred dollars, at a conservative estimate.

Cody came back into the room and placed the other coin in her hand. He was right-- filthy and covered with some white, crusty substance, it didn't look at all like it was worth anything.

"I thought Jackson had dug up some prospector's lucky coin," Cody said. He took the other one out of her palm and held it up to the light. "If it looked like this, I'd have been runnin' into Phoenix myself to get it checked out."

"I still don't see how you could have forgotten it," Crystal said.

"That was the night you brought the whole hotel to my room to see me naked. I was a bit distracted and damn tired."

"Oh." Crystal felt color creep up her neck and spill onto her cheeks.

"I might never forgive you for Mrs. Bloomford, you know. She still uses every opportunity she can to push me into the wall when she passes by." He gave her a weak smile.

"I can see how that might be reason enough for you to forget something..." Crystal began.

"What's goin' on?"

Crystal saw the look of dismay on Cody's face. Big Ed stood on the threshold.

"Nothing." She wanted to pocket the coins, but she was only wearing a thin nightshirt.

"What did I hear about Montezuma?" Resplendent in a pair of garish Hawaiian print cutoffs and a black t-shirt emblazoned with the words *Branch Water Bar* in gold letters, Big Ed marched into the room. "What were you two looking at?"

"She told you. Nothin'." Cody started to push Crystal behind him.

Ed ignored the bad vibes and swooped in with amazing speed for someone so large. He grabbed the doubloons out of her hand before she could close her fingers and examined them, his thin, greasy grey hair falling over his prominent forehead. "Damnation, people. Do you know what these are?"

Cody sighed. "Yes, Ed. We know what they may be."

"Where in tarnation did they come from?"

"Jackson found them." Crystal motioned for Cody to snatch the doubloons back from Ed's enormous hand.

"Who the hell is Jackson?" Ed bit down on one of the coins.

"The dog," Crystal and Cody chorused, making a simultaneous dive for the doubloons.

Big Ed closed his fist, effectively defeating their rescue attempt. "Hell n' damnation," he thundered. "The mutt's found buried treasure."

Before they could stop him, Big Ed ran for the lobby.

"Gold!" he screamed. "Buried treasure!"

The gold rush was on with a vengeance.

CHAPTER TWENTY-FOUR

"It's all your fault," Crystal accused as she stood over Cody.

"Again?" He pushed aside his half-finished eggs and toast. "Why is it always my fault? Where were you while Big Ed was running around the lobby with the doubloons?"

"Well..." He had her there.

"That's no excuse. You knew about the first doubloon for weeks before you told me."

"I said I didn't think it was anythin' more than some prospector's lucky piece. Besides, I had other things to occupy my mind."

"Like the bar." She walked over to the window and looked out. "Now there are more pressing issues. They're beginning to dig under the hotel."

"What?" In his haste to get up, Cody knocked over his chair. He joined her at the window. "What the hell is the matter with these folk?" He threw open the door and hollered at the top of his voice: "Stop that!"

Crystal watched him run down the steps and chase people out from under the porch. They scattered left and right. She massaged her throbbing temples. Gold rush--ha!

She'd never seen so many people in her entire life.

$\sim$

Hundreds jammed the streets from daybreak to sundown. Some of them had even tried to dig at night with the aid of lanterns or generator-powered arc lights, until they were stopped first by Cody, and then by Reed Dalton.

With the amount of holes peppering its surface, Main Street would never be navigable again, Crystal thought as she grabbed a quick cup of coffee before going wherever she was needed most--the convenience store, the restaurant or the tea-room. Big Ed opened the bar at the crack of dawn and served until the last straggler left at two A.M.

Crystal wished with all her heart that Jackson had never discovered those doubloons, whose authenticity had been verified by her friend in Phoenix. Despite Cody's cajoling, Jackson wouldn't take him to the cache so the commotion outside would grind to a halt.

So much for coming to Cactus Station for the peace and quiet. Instead, Crystal found herself at the center of a comedy of errors over which she had no control. Every time she thought she was getting on top of the situation, something else happened.

"Hi, hon." Jolie walked in with a basketful of clean, folded laundry.

"Oh, hi." Crystal poured more coffee. "Don't tell me you've been to the laundromat already."

"Nah. This is left over from yesterday's trip. Harold forgot to unload the back of the cab. I realized we were missin' a few items when I came up with only one pair of clean panties an' he was out of shirts." She set the basket on a corner of the table. "I'm gonna grab some more coffee, too."

"Can you believe this crowd?" Crystal sat at the table and decided to finish the toast Cody had left untouched. "People were digging under the hotel a few minutes ago. Cody chased them off."

"They'll be back. I guarantee it." Jolie offered Crystal more coffee.

"No, thanks. I'm jittery enough as it is. I didn't sleep well last night. I kept hearing noises."

"Me, too." Jolie took a piece of toast still in the toaster and spread jam on it. She pointed to the plate in the middle of the table. "Whose eggs?"

"Cody's."

"I doubt he'll be back for the rest of the day. I'd better give them to Jackson. Cody's tryin' to keep some law an' order out there."

"Cody? That's a laugh."

"He's good at it, hon. People listen to him. If Cody tells 'em there's no diggin' in the graveyard, they leave it alone. You said yourself he chased people away from the hotel."

"That's true. I guess he does have his uses."

Jolie gave Crystal a look filled with disapproval.

"Don't you go preaching to me, Jolie Webster," Crystal warned. "You have no idea what Cody's really like. He's only shown you his good side."

"Hon, he's shown me every side he's got durin' the past few weeks, includin' the one you gave me access to the night you busted into his room." Jolie grinned and waggled her eyebrows. "I can't see why you don't overlook a few faults in order to get the benefits."

Crystal blushed. "That night was a mistake. I've been hearing about it ever since from you, Cody and Mrs. Bloomford."

"I thought you two were gonna smooth over your differences at one point. What happened?"

"The bar happened. Cody lied to me again. I can't handle that. I only want the truth."

"Like you've been givin' him?"

"What do you mean?" Crystal put down the half-eaten toast.

"I met someone the other day, when I was at the laundromat. Said she knows you."

Crystal's stomach knotted. "Who?"

"Evelyn Waters. Said she was an administrative assistant or some such fancy title in the offices you used to work out of."

The toast Crystal tried to swallow stuck in her throat. She almost choked and finished the glass of orange juice Cody had left behind. "You met Evelyn Waters? She doesn't live anywhere near Apache Junction."

"She does now." Jolie put more bread in the toaster. "She married some guy with a home there. Evelyn said you'd been in some trouble with the law."

"That's not accurate. I was implicated in a scam that was going on without my knowledge. I surveyed the property, but they changed my findings and then forged my signature on the documents. People lost a lot of money investing in worthless land."

"Kind of like Cody's circumstances, huh?"

Crystal looked at her hands, clasped firmly in her lap. "Not exactly," she said.

"How come, sugar? He didn't know the mine was worthless at the time he asked those people to invest."

"He told them the uncles had found the Lost Dutchman Mine. Reed Dalton told me the whole story over coffee the other day."

"Trust Cody." Jolie laughed. "He's a bad son-of-a-gun sometimes."

"You think it's funny." Crystal got up and put all the dirty dishes in the sink.

"Not doin' time, I don't. Poor Cody. He escaped jail, but he sure messed up his life. He did the same thing you got accused of."

"My name was cleared, not that it's done me much good. No one would hire me again. That's why I jumped at the chance to come to Cactus Station. I was so close to bankruptcy, it wasn't funny."

"You should tell Cody. He understands you better'n anyone else, an' he's so smart. Much smarter than he gives himself credit for. He'd feel a lot better if'n he knew you were a little vulnerable, too. He thinks you walk on water while he's steppin' in hog doo."

"I know." Crystal sighed. "But he's such a liar."

"He made a mistake. You got him angry an' Cody goes with his mood. He needs to learn to cope with his anger instead of doin' the first mean thing that comes to mind." Jolie scraped the remains of the eggs into Jackson's bowl. "You could help him with that, an' he could teach you to be more open with your feelins'."

Crystal started washing the dishes. "I'll think about it."

"You do that. You'll never find a man who loves you more than Cody."

Crystal dropped a plate back into the suds and almost broke everything in the sink. "He told you that?"

Jolie bustled over and firmly waved her away. "I'll do that, hon," she said. "You're a mite fumble-fingered this morning.'"

"Cody told you he loves me?" Crystal pursued. She couldn't believe he'd confide in Jolie.

"No way." Jolie smiled. "But I can tell. So could you, if you'd just give him a chance."

Crystal wondered not only if she'd ever feel she could give Cody even one more chance, but whether he felt the same way about her.

CHAPTER TWENTY-FIVE

That night, noises awakened Crystal again. Above her head, footsteps creaked on the stairs, then walked across her ceiling. Subdued scraping sounded like furniture being moved around.

She'd never found her rifle. She took up a stout piece of lumber she'd salvaged from the debris of the mercantile and went to investigate.

The thought of going up into the attic intimidated her and brought on the beginnings of a panic attack. She thought about waking Cody up, but after telling him he was never to come near her door again, she figured the least she could do was reciprocate. Besides, the fact that she always ran to him with every little problem was humiliating. She'd better wake Jolie instead.

A sleepy Jolie answered Crystal's soft knock by cracking open the door a few moments later. "What's up?" she asked.

"I can hear someone moving around the attic again. Will you come up there with me?"

Jolie pushed her hair out of her eyes. "Sure, if you've got another gun. I ain't goin' to disturb no ghost or burglar without a firearm for protection."

"I've got a big piece of wood. Is that enough?" Crystal showed her the two by four and shook it for emphasis.

"Wood won't stop much. You gotta get in too close before you can do any damage. Besides, it might be the person who stole your rifle." Jolie wrapped her arms around herself. "I'm cold. Let me put on a robe."

"What are you doin' at that door in the middle of the night?" Harold grumbled from the bed.

"Crystal heard noises in the attic. She wants me to go up with her to check on things."

"I think you two are crazy," Harold said.

Crystal heard him get out of bed, followed by the rustle of clothing. He opened the door wide, his shirt unbuttoned, his hair wild and no shoes on his feet.

"Well? Don't stand around after you've gotten me up." He pulled on his boots. "Let's get goin', girls. I'm sick of both of you complainin' about intruders."

They headed for the attic. Harold produced a knife adequate for gutting a ten-point buck, and Crystal wondered if she had underestimated him in thinking he was a mild man who depended on Jolie to be the force in their marriage. He refused to let her put on the upgraded lights he and Cody had installed. They were forced to feel their way up the stairs.

Crystal's heart hammered and her breath caught in her throat. She should have brought Cody's flashlight, but he probably kept it in his room with all his other tools. She tried to will the claustrophobia away, but the higher they climbed, the more the feeling of being enclosed increased to frightening proportions. Beads of sweat broke out on her forehead and ran down her face.

Any minute, her panic would overwhelm her and force her to abandon the all-encompassing darkness. Stars danced in front of her eyes as she mounted the last stair. She ran straight into Jolie's back.

"Hush!" Jolie put a restraining hand on her arm.

The reassurance of that warm grip brought the symptoms down a notch and Crystal drew in gulps of musty air. She ran her tongue over her dry lips and tried to concentrate on evening out her breathing. In--out--in--out...

Creaking broke the silence. Not ahead of them, but behind. She stood quivering in her nightgown and flimsy robe in the airless blackness and waited, for what, she didn't know. The pounding of her heart deafened her, and the stars already dancing in front of her eyes increased to the proportions of a full constellation. Something brushed her legs and she screamed, stumbling into Jolie and sending them both tumbling to the floor.

"Jeezus!" Harold found the light switch and flipped it, the attic illuminating like a Christmas celebration.

Jackson leaned over Crystal and made grunting noises. He licked her face, his fetid breath unexpectedly a comfort.

"Ghost or intruder, huh?" Harold chuckled, his laughter sounding more like relief than mirth. He helped them both up. "No broken bones, I hope?" He chuckled again. "Jackson's one hell of a specter." His laughter died in his throat when he tried to dust Jolie down and saw her white face. "You look like you saw the devil," he said, putting his arm around her. "What's wrong with you, gal?"

"I felt somethin'. Right as I fell. It brushed past me, headin' for the stairs," she said. She clutched Harold tightly. "Hon, I'm frightened."

~

"It's all in your imagination," Cody said when Crystal, Jolie and Harold confronted him the next morning.

"I don't have an imagination, sugar," Jolie said. "I know if what I felt was real...or not." She clasped her hands around her coffee mug.

"What I want to know is how you slept right through all the ruckus." Harold's eyes narrowed as he looked at Cody, calmly eating a left-over cinnamon roll he had found in the refrigerator.

"Easy." Cody used the fork to saw through the stale roll. "I was exhausted. Crystal knows I haven't been sleepin' much lately. I slept good last night, for the first time in about a week."

She figured Jake had stopped tormenting Cody's dreams, but maybe he hadn't been asleep at all. Maybe he was the one searching the attic at night, and maybe it was for the rest of those doubloons.

"I don't think I can stay another night here," Jolie said. "That skeleton's givin' me the willies. Can't you take it out an' bury it, Cody? We don't need it no more, anyway.

There's a treasure hunt goin' on now, an' no one wants to look at some moldy ole remains." She looked toward the lobby. "Sorry, Jake," she called out. "I don't mean no disrespect."

Cody admitted defeat apparently, both in abandoning his attempts to eat the stale pastry and keeping Jake out of the ground. "All right," he said. "I'll take him to the cemetery an' bury him this mornin'. Will that make you feel better?"

"It'll be a good start," Crystal said.

In the past two days, they had barely netted twenty dollars from the tour. After the screaming and falling last night, rumors were flying and some guests already packing to leave town. Mrs. Bloomford was the first to go, dragging her husband in her ample wake at six o'clock that morning.

Several other long-term guests and prospectors had followed the Bloomfords' lead. Tired of digging up nothing but rocks and dust, angry with Cody for chasing them out of buildings and Reed Dalton for issuing citations when he caught them digging in town, a steady stream of them had settled up and headed for their vehicles. The vacated rooms remained empty. Even those who had pitched tents on the outskirts of town no longer wanted to stay at the haunted Gold Rush Hotel.

"I think Harold and me are gonna be leavin'," Jolie said. "We're gonna be out of jobs, anyway, by tomorrow by the looks of it. An' we both think there's no more gold to be had." She looked at Cody. "I know what you're capable of doin', Cody, an' I think you planted them nuggets to get folks riled up about a gold rush. Now the tour's sourin', I think you brought out these doubloons to get things goin' again."

"There's no way I had doubloons hidden up," Cody protested. "I didn't even know what the first one was when Jackson brought it in. You saw it. It was in my pocket, and it stayed where you put it on the window sill until Jackson brought the other one to Crystal." He got up and threw the rest of his roll into the trash before dumping his dirty plate on the counter. "Harold, can you give me a hand with the casket? I'll get Hoyle an' Big Ed. We can load it into the back of Big Ed's truck."

"Sure." Harold followed him out, Jackson at their heels.

Crystal wasn't sure she believed Cody's explanation, but she wanted to--she was as sick of blaming him for everything as she knew he was of being accused. And she knew in her heart he would never do anything to place her in danger. She'd been so close to the top of the stairs last night, one wrong step would have sent her down them.

No, someone else was on the hunt for a cache of doubloons. And if it wasn't one of the guests, then it had to be someone like Brent Hardacre, back to get a scoop that would propel his mediocre career into the spotlight, or someone else who knew where they must be hidden.

She left the dishes and walked over to look at that casket still resting in the front lobby. The uncles were definitely dead. If she took Cody out of the equation, then the only logical, missing piece of the original group prospecting and speculating in the shanty town that had become Cactus Station was Jake Carver. Crystal wondered whether there had been some mix-up in the identification of that skeleton. Jake was too mean and too savvy to wander out into the Superstitions and die. She also doubted he would end up stuffed into the attic closet of the Gold Rush Hotel.

Maybe burying him wasn't the best thing after all. She called Reed Dalton. "Do you think it's possible Jake's alive and we don't have his remains here?" she asked.

"We got the reports from the dental office, Crystal, an' they show the skeleton missing two eye teeth, just like Jake's X-Rays. I don't think there's any doubt."

He listened while she told him about the search going on in the attic.

"I think your imagination's working overtime," he said. "If anyone was up there, it was probably just one of those folk Cody chased out of the other buildings. People have gone crazy up there lately. They all think they're gonna find buried treasure. Maybe they're right, maybe they're wrong. The Superstitions have always attracted crackpots. That's what keeps me busy--chasing down missing persons, hauling in trespassers and trying to patrol a huge area of sand an' rock to stop people doing things they shouldn't."

Crystal heard the pickup truck arrive outside. "Thanks, Reed," she said, frustrated by his lack of enthusiasm for pursuing another identity for Cactus Station's skeleton.

"Any time."

She walked over to the casket and stared down at the skull lying against a white satin pillow. The mouth looked like it was grinning at her.

CHAPTER TWENTY-SIX

With Jake interred in the cemetery, Cody hoped the noises and hysteria would stop, as well as his nightmares. He thought it ironic he had once fabricated a ghostly presence in the hotel. His doubts about the uncles' tales of hauntings were jelling into a solid belief. After all, the Native Americans believed, and they were closer to understanding the unexplainable than anyone else in and around the desert, he reasoned. Who was he to remain a skeptic?

Unfortunately, the crashes, scrapings and footsteps continued. Cody convinced Harold and Jolie to wait things out, despite Jolie's fears. He and Harold tried staking out the attic to catch the perpetrator, but their midnight vigils netted nothing but frustration. If they sat upstairs, the noises started on the ground floor.

More guests moved out. Cody and Crystal actually came to a mutual agreement and offered to lower the rent on the hotel rooms. None of the departing guests decided that was enticing enough to stay. They continued to leave at an alarming rate, many reporting sightings of a silent ghostly figure in their rooms.

Cody couldn't come up with any other schemes, for once in his life. All his dreams were tumbling down with the rest of Cactus Station. Crystal still wasn't really warming back up to him, and both Harold and

Jolie went about their business, but kept their distances. He knew if one more thing went wrong, or Jolie got scared again, they would be gone. Big Ed's bar was still operating, but with reduced hours. Cody spent most of his day hanging out there, because repairing the rest of town wasn't necessary, or a financially sound proposition.

He could have kicked himself for not coming clean to Crystal about the bar and everything else. He'd mismanaged every aspect of their relationship, just as he had mismanaged Cactus Station's boom until it had become a bust.

"You're a jackass," he told his reflection in the cracked mirror above his washstand. He finished shaving and wiped off his face.

If he hurried, he could get breakfast started before anyone else got downstairs. Perhaps he'd make a few slim brownie points for helping out, instead of lounging around in the *Branch Water Bar* all day. The agony of being close to Crystal without touching her felt like too much for him to handle, but he figured if he didn't do something to mend the breach between them, it would soon be too late. Cactus Station would be empty, and they would have to leave before they starved to death. Neither of them could buy each other out, and no one else would be willing to buy a useless piece of real estate.

The only thing that would salvage their dreams and maybe their relationship would be if he found the source of the doubloons. Maybe there would be more than two, and he'd have financial stability to offer Crystal as well as his flawed self. He could prove to her that he was reliable and trustworthy.

He walked out of his room only to see Crystal heading for the stairs. He swore under his breath. Another plan had backfired. He was going to have to get up in the middle of the night to make it into the kitchen before she did. The best he could hope for was talking her into letting him make breakfast while she drank coffee on the porch. He quickened his pace.

Crystal was already on the lower flight of stairs. She heard him and looked up. Her foot landed squarely in the middle of the next step and to Cody's horror, went right through. With a scream she crashed up to her hip in the broken stair, only to scream even louder as the entire bottom section of the staircase collapsed.

Cody didn't know if the section he was running down would collapse, too, but he didn't stop to consider an alternative plan. He plunged down to the landing, tested the outside banister and found it loose. Keeping close to the wall instead, he inched toward Crystal, clinging to the loose banister.

"Don't move." He tested each step before placing his weight on it. "The more you do, the more the banister's loosening."

"I'm going to fall!" Her voice filled with blind panic as the banister came further out of the wall.

"You're gonna be okay," he assured her, although he had no idea how he was going to save her, even if he managed to reach her in time.

She sobbed and clung to her precarious lifeline. "I'm going to break my neck and die."

"No, you're not. Calm down. I'm comin'. Just hold on for a couple more seconds, honey." He tried to speed up, but he was afraid, too. If he fell through, he'd probably take the rest of the stairs, and her, with him.

"What the hell?" Harold stood at the top of the staircase. "What can I do?"

"Keep back," Cody warned. "Any more weight on this, an' it'll collapse for sure."

He slid more than walked down three more steps until he was right above her. Only two more steps to go. Two full, intact stairs, hopefully. He grasped the banister attached to the wall and pulled on it. It held.

"I'm gonna slide down as close as I can get to you," he said in what he hoped was a reasonably calm voice. "When I'm close enough for you to grab, I want you to hold onto me. I'll pull us back up."

She nodded, her eyes wide with terror. He edged toward her, one arm wrapped around the banister, his palms slick with sweat.

"Grab me," he said when he was hanging over the hole.

Crystal shook her head. "I can't. I'm too scared." She looked down. "Oh, God."

"You have to trust me. Please, honey. I can't hang out here much longer."

"I have to let go of the banister. I could miss and fall." Her voice trembled.

"Then give me one of your legs."

"You're not dangling me head down over this hole, Cody Blye."

Her terror had receded a notch, at least. He welcomed her sarcasm, and wondered if he dared lean closer to her. The stair on which his hips rested sank down as he tested it with more of his weight. Not much, but already too much. He abandoned that idea.

"What's happenin'?" Hoyle Bixby stood behind Harold. "You want me to go get help?"

"Some rescue this is." Crystal looked up at all of them. "I'll try to use the railing to climb up closer to you."

"I don't think that's a good idea," Cody warned as she started to pull herself up by her arms.

"Oh, shut up, Cody. You don't seem to have any better suggestions, and my arms are getting tired."

There was no other way. He slid down another couple of inches and made a grab for her, his clutching fingers coming up with a handful of her shirt, which promptly ripped.

"What are you trying to do--save me or tear my clothes off?" She glowered at him, panting, one side of her shirt in shreds.

"Shut up yourself," he told her, clenching his teeth and stretching.

That time he managed to grab the waistband of her jeans. With a yank, he pulled her away from the banister, which promptly fell to the lobby below, landing with a resounding crash.

Crystal screamed again, flailing her arms and almost dislodging Cody's grip.

"Stop screaming and hold onto me," he told her.

His barked orders jolted her into action. She flung her arms around his waist and held on tight, her face against his belt buckle. Cody's arm bit into the unforgiving wood of the railing and he gritted his teeth while he dragged them both onto the unstable but still intact section of stair treads and struggled for something, anything to brace his feet against. Crystal's body weighed him down and his upper body strained until every sinew felt like it was ripping.

"Give me your hand," Harold said. "I'll pull you both up."

"I...don't...think...you can hold..." Cody's thrashing arm connected with two vice-grips.

Harold and Hoyle hauled them both up by Cody's straining arm.

When they all lay in a heap on the landing, a white-faced Jolie waded in, helping them to their feet. "What happened?" she demanded.

Crystal pulled the tattered edges of her shirt together and tied them in a knot. Her hands were bleeding, as was a long scratch on her cheek. "I don't know. One minute I was running down the stairs. The next thing I knew, they just weren't there anymore." She sat on a bench against the wall. "I thought you reinforced them," she said to Cody.

"I did." He massaged his aching shoulders. What was she implying--that he'd sabotaged them himself?

"You didn't do a very good job, then." Crystal examined the cuts on her hands. "I'm going back to my room to get cleaned up."

"I'll go with you, hon." Jolie slipped her arm companionably through Crystal's. "Harold, why don't you get breakfast started? We could all do with somethin' to eat after this."

"You'd better get cleaned up, too, Cody," Harold said.

Cody looked down at his tattered, filthy clothes. "I guess so." He ached in every joint of his body, and his heart still hadn't slowed down to a normal pace.

Harold clapped Hoyle on the back. "Come on, little guy. You can help me. You did good there."

"I did?" Hoyle stuck out his meager chest and hitched up his pants.

Crystal stopped and turned back. "Thanks, all of you," she said, and then she disappeared into her room with Jolie and the door closed.

Cody went back to his own room. Crystal had all but accused him of weakening the stairs instead of reinforcing them. After he had gotten himself cleaned up, he had a little investigating to do. One thing was certain--no ghost would be able to saw through the supports of a solid wooden staircase. Cactus Station had a living, breathing potential murderer as an unwelcome resident.

CHAPTER TWENTY-SEVEN

Cody stepped out from under the stairs. Someone had definitely tampered with the supports, which had been partially sawn through. This tangible evidence made him acutely aware first that they were all in danger, and secondly, that everyone was suspect.

Even Jolie and Harold. Even Hoyle Bixby. They may have come to Crystal's rescue, but perhaps she wasn't meant to be the victim. A chill ran up Cody's back. Maybe he was the one supposed to die.

But neither he nor Crystal used the front stairs on a regular basis. They both used the servants' stairs into the kitchen. He ducked out from under the remains of the staircase and headed for the back of the hotel. He'd better check things out there before someone else had a potentially fatal accident.

Harold was already ahead of him. "I'm makin' sure we all don't fall through these," he said. "What did you find out front?"

Cody checked the staircase out himself, using his flashlight.

"You don't trust me," Harold said. He sounded disappointed.

"Sorry. I'm gettin' paranoid," Cody said.

"That's okay. I don't trust you, neither, anymore," Harold said. "Even though you saved Crystal. She might not have been the one you wanted to get rid of."

Cody had to smile. "I had the same thoughts about you, Jolie and even Hoyle. That's why I said I'm gettin' paranoid. Havin' your life flash in front of your eyes does that, I guess."

Harold sighed. "We're all gonna have to leave, you know," he said. "This town's dangerous."

"I know." Cody snapped off the flashlight. "I've got to talk to Crystal, an' then we should have a town meetin' of sorts."

"Jolie's packin'. She doesn't want to leave you guys, but she's frightened. You figure out who messed with the stairs, then we can come back." Harold pulled his bandana further down his forehead. "We want to come back," he said. "We like workin' for you, and Jolie likes it here a lot better than she ever liked Port Arthur."

"I'll remember that." Cody felt a twinge of regret. Harold and Jolie weren't only good workers; they had become great friends and acted as buffers between him and Crystal. Without their common sense mediation, he imagined the fighting would only get worse.

Harold went up to join Jolie and Cody called Reed.

"You know, Crystal had this idea that Jake Carver might be still alive, an' we misidentified that skeleton," Reed said.

"That's a bit far-fetched," Cody said. "But at the time Jake disappeared, I thought it was strange. He knew these mountains better than anyone, even me. Unless he fell an' broke a leg or somethin', he'd have been able to survive an' find his way back out. It was like he *wanted* to disappear."

"I'll check things out," Reed said. "I'll get one of the technicians to come with me. Maybe whoever tampered with the stairs left fingerprints behind or somethin'."

"Yeah, mine." Cody watched a procession of cars passing the windows of the hotel as they headed out of town. "I was under the stairs a couple of days ago, reinforcin' the struts. Crystal would love to hear it if mine were the only fingerprints you found."

"If they are, then I can't do much about that," Reed said. "But maybe we'll get lucky an' someone else's will be there, too. Tell Harold and Jolie to stick around. Hoyle, too. I don't want any of you leavin' town before I get there. I know you said a lot of people are packing up."

"I'll tell them," Cody said. "They won't be happy about it. Jolie's scared to death. Hoyle won't go anywhere. He's got no place else to go." He said goodbye and hung up before going to tell everyone the bad news.

CHAPTER TWENTY-EIGHT

Crystal couldn't handle all the dirt in the front lobby. While they awaited Reed's arrival, she talked Cody, Harold and Hoyle into taking all the rubble outside. Jolie refused to budge from her room, but Crystal had to keep busy. She swept the floor and started polishing the furniture. They might not have a main staircase any more, but at least they could seem to be halfway tidy, she thought.

She looked at all the cuts and scratches on her hands and arms as she put a shine on the coffee table. Without the casket and the staircase, the lobby felt like a chasm. Her footsteps echoed on the boards when she took the cushions out to the front porch and knocked all the dust out of them.

"Let me hold that door for you, Ma'am." A middle-aged man in a straw hat hurried to help her as she struggled to get back inside with the armful of cushions.

"Thank you." Crystal threw the cushions on the couch. "I'm sorry," she said. "The hotel's closed for business right now."

The man looked at the gaping hole where the stairs once stood. "Looks like there was an accident," he said. "I hope no one got hurt."

"No. We're all fine." Crystal hid her hands behind her back.

"Actually, I'm looking for Miss Crystal Penney," he said. He placed an attaché case on the front desk. "Do you know where I might find her?"

"And you are?" Crystal asked, avoiding the question.

"Daniel Hunter, Real Estate Broker." He took a card from his case and handed it to her.

Crystal looked at the embossed black writing on the dove grey card. Very refined. Not at all what she'd expect from someone Cody hung out with, she decided, thinking instantly of Big Ed. The card told her Mr. Hunter specialized in commercial real estate and 'those hard to sell properties.'

"And what do you want with Miss Penney?" She walked around to the opposite side of the desk and set the card down on top of it.

"I wish to make her an offer." He looked around. "Is she here?"

"What sort of offer?" Crystal asked.

"Are you Miss Penney?"

He placed his hands on the counter, his fingers long and tapered, his nails manicured. A turquoise and silver pinkie ring adorned his right hand, while a heavy turquoise and silver watch band encircled his left wrist. His hands were tanned, the backs covered with spidery black hairs.

"We could conclude this business a lot quicker if you would either own up to being Miss Penney or tell me where I can locate her," he said.

"I'm Crystal Penney," she owned. "What sort of offer do you have for me?"

"To buy out your fifty percent of Cactus Station." Hunter opened his attaché case again and handed her a small stack of papers. "A fair offer," he said. "In fact, considering the condition of this place..." He shuddered for effect and grimaced. "...a more than fair offer."

Crystal flipped through the papers. She had to agree. Thirty thousand dollars was more than a fair price, especially the way things had been going lately.

"Are you making my partner the same offer?" she asked.

"No, Miss Penney. I am not."

"May I ask why?"

He closed the attaché case with a snap. "No, you may not. I'm not at liberty to tell you."

Stuffed shirt, Crystal thought. She dropped the papers on top of his attaché case. "Why should I accept this?"

"Why not? Do you wish to spend the rest of your life in a dump like this?" He flicked an invisible piece of lint from the sleeve of his charcoal grey jacket. "This isn't the place for a fine looking young woman such as you." His smile was condescending.

Crystal wanted to boot him right out the door. "What I want to do with the rest of my life is no business of yours." She brought up her nose an inch and tried to look down at him, because he was pretty short and the desk was on a raised platform.

He stopped leaning against the desk and stood up straight. "I didn't mean to imply you shouldn't do what you want," he said. "I just meant..."

"Skip it," Crystal said. "Let me get to the point quickly. Unless you tell me who wants to buy me out, there's no deal."

He shook his head.

"Then we're done here," she said. "You found your own way in; you can find your own way out."

"I'll leave the papers for you to look over." He placed them back on the desk. "And you have my card."

"Yeah, yeah." Crystal waved him away.

She made lemonade and took it onto the back porch. The sun beat down relentlessly on the shabby tin roofs, but the clear blue sky felt like a balm. Crystal sat in the shade and propped her feet on a cooler. Drowsy from lack of sleep, she dozed.

"Crystal?"

She jerked awake. Her lemonade had turned watery, and her watch told her she must have been asleep over an hour.

"Out here," she called. She felt lethargic and out of sorts.

Jolie stepped onto the porch with the morning's mail in her hand. "Here," she said, thrusting several envelopes at Crystal. "I'm gonna look through the junk mail and then throw it out."

"Help yourself. I'm not interested in anything, not even the grocery coupons right now." Crystal saw her name on every one of the envelopes. "Oh, great. Bills."

Jolie retreated. "I'm gonna sit under the fan an' take a rest. It's too hot out here. When do you reckon the sheriff'll get here?"

"Knowing Reed and his procrastination, probably around six o'clock, so he can eat supper while he's here." Crystal took a sip of the watered-down lemonade and grimaced. It was warm.

She thought about going back inside, but she couldn't be bothered to move. Instead, she opened the mail. Three were bills, one was a solicitation from a charity, but the last one with no return address, intrigued her with its block capitals in what looked like a thick-tipped magic marker.

Inside was one sheet of paper, covered with cut out newspaper and magazine words. Her stomach did an ugly flip as she read:

UNLESS YOU TURN OVER THE COINS THE HOTEL WILL BE BLOWN UP

Crystal read through the letter twice, as though she'd missed something. It was unsigned, and except for the envelope, held no clue as to the writer's identity. Whoever wrote it didn't even tell her where she was supposed to leave the doubloons.

"Pretty stupid," she said.

"Who's stupid?" Cody stepped onto the porch, his tool belt slung over one shoulder and a hammer in his hand.

"Oh, no one in particular. I was just talking to myself." Crystal waved the envelopes. "Bills are in."

"My favorite time of the month, especially *this* month." Cody grimaced. "We'll be lucky if we break even with all the guests leavin'". He leaned against the hitching post. "Are you ready to quit an' go back to civilization yet?"

What an odd remark, Crystal thought. Had Cody sent the realtor or written that note? Was this threat yet another of his scare tactics?

"I have no intention of leaving." She tucked the note back in its envelope. "If you're ready, go right ahead. Don't forget to sign over your half of the town and get it notarized, though. Ruth Becker's a notary, so it won't be a big chore."

"Fat chance. If you're stickin' it out, then so am I." Cody deposited the tool belt and hammer on top of the freezer. "Think I'll get some water before I go back an' finish what I started."

"Sawing off the uprights from under the back porch?" she asked.

Cody stopped on the way inside. "What's that supposed to mean?" He sounded miffed.

"Nothing. A bad joke, that's all." Crystal fanned herself with the mail and took another sip of the warm, watery lemonade.

"Any more jokes like that an' Reed Dalton will lock me up. You'd like that, wouldn't you?" He slammed the screen door.

Crystal sighed and threw away the lemonade. She wasn't sure what she'd like to see happen to Cody. Everything was way too complicated, and the arrival of the note had just compounded the problems.

She made oatmeal raisin cookies that afternoon, despite the heat. She found baking therapeutic, and she needed something, anything to lower her stress level.

"Do you have any coffee to go with those cookies, Miss Crystal?" Sheriff Dalton strolled into the kitchen.

"Hi, Reed." She placed the last batch on the wire rack to cool. "There's always coffee around here. The pot's on the stove. Help yourself."

"Thanks. I believe I will." He found a mug, poured coffee and selected two of the largest cookies from the plateful that had already cooled.

"What do you make of that staircase collapsing?" she asked.

"I'm leaving that issue be until the technician's finished checking for prints an' any other evidence you didn't clean up." Reed bit into the cookie and munched like a horse chewing a sugar cube. He swallowed. "Mighty good." He took a sip of coffee.

Crystal waited. She had a feeling he was going to tell her more, but at his own slow pace.

"Why don't you sit down?" he asked. "I have a few questions to put to you."

Crystal put the cookie sheet and spatula into the sink. "What sort of questions?"

"I got the coroner's report on Jake's death. Seems he had a fractured skull. I wondered if Cody had said anything about why Willy 'n Dock didn't report Jake missing?"

"No. He just said Jake disappeared into the Superstitions about a year before the uncles died. I believe Cody was out of the state at the time, and I don't think he was in contact with any of them. Jake liked to wander off; he'd done it before. Probably they didn't think anything of it for a while."

"But he'd never wandered off for over a year, had he?"

"Maybe not, but Uncle Willy and Uncle Dock were always so busy doing one thing or another. They didn't keep track of time very well, except of course when the seasons changed. I'd get a Christmas letter from Uncle Dock some time in spring most years, if at all."

"That sounds a mite flimsy, Crystal." Sheriff Dalton finished his cookies and looked longingly at the rest of them. "I don't like the sound of it, in view of the doubloons that turned up."

More than a little worried about the direction the conversation was heading, Crystal pushed the plate toward him. Any moment now, Reed would make some remark about the doubloon treasure hunt being about as convenient as the gold rush.

"Where were you when Cody found those coins?" Reed managed to ask with a mouthful of cookie.

"I was with him when Jackson brought in the second one. Cody was with Hoyle Bixby when the dog brought the first one in, but Cody said he thought it was just a prospector's lucky piece, so he put it in his pocket."

"Then he showed it to you?"

"No. He told me he forgot it in his pants pocket. Jolie found it when she was sorting laundry, and she put it on his window sill. It stayed there a couple of weeks at least."

"Does that sound realistic to you, that Cody would forget about a gold coin?"

"Well, no, at the time it didn't. But when he showed me, I changed my mind. The coin was so filthy that it didn't look like it was worth anything. And a lot's been going on around here, too. I guess if I was him, I might have forgotten about it, too."

"Really?" Reed looked piercingly at her.

"Well...no. But that's me, not Cody. He operates on a different wavelength from the rest of us half the time. He's like the uncles. You know that."

"Do you think he's kept his nose clean since he got here?"

"I think he always has done. I don't believe he knowingly caused people to invest in a scheme that wasn't going to pan out. I think he trusted the uncles implicitly, but they got carried away in their quest for the Lost Dutchman and pulled him into the middle of it." Crystal sat at the table and took a cookie. She didn't feel much like eating it, but she had to do something to occupy her hands other than twist them around because she was nervous.

Reed noisily slurped coffee while he considered her explanation. "I understand you've had a little trouble yourself, lately."

Crystal felt the blush rise up her neck. "Yes. How did you find out?"

He picked at the cookie crumbs left on the now-empty plate. "I did a little investigating."

"Then you know I wasn't formally indicted."

"I saw there was a move to indict you, but then the charges were dropped." He drained his cup. "I wondered if you coming to Cactus Station had anything to do with the fraud scheme."

Her cheeks flamed. "Don't tell me you think Cody and I are in some scam together."

"It's crossed my mind. Did you know the uncles were going to leave you half the town and the other half to Cody?"

"No, of course not. From what I heard from Cody, they didn't tell him, either." She stopped herself from telling Reed she hadn't thought about Cactus Station for years, because that would be a lie, and she knew Reed would sense it. For a small-town sheriff, he was pretty astute.

He took out a toothpick and stuck it between his teeth. "Maybe Cody knew about the doubloons, but didn't know where they were hidden. That would explain a lot."

Crystal saw the noose tightening around Cody's neck. "You can't possibly think he would risk people's lives by making those stairs unsafe, do you?"

Reed chomped on the toothpick. Crystal couldn't sit looking at him a moment longer. She got up and started making a fresh pot of coffee.

"Do you think the noises you've been hearing at night could be Cody searching for the doubloons?" Reed asked.

"He could, but I can't imagine why he would. He's got as much right to hunt for them in the daylight. More. He owns fifty percent of them if they're found inside the town."

"And he'd own a hundred percent if you died. I checked the terms of the will. He stands to gain the whole town and its contents if you pre-decease him."

Crystal dropped the coffee grounds. They spilled all over the counter, the stove and the floor.

"Oops," Reed said.

Crystal knew her face must have turned from red to white, because he got up quickly.

"Sit down." He pulled a chair over to the sink. "You don't look so good."

Crystal couldn't argue with him. Her legs were shaking too much, anyway. She sat.

"Did he ever talk about the mining accident that killed the uncles?" Reed pulled another chair over and sat facing her.

"No." Crystal shook her head. She felt numb. "We don't discuss our personal lives very much."

"Do you think he'd be angry enough to kill them if he found they were hiding a fortune in gold from him?"

"Never."

The numbness disappeared as quickly as it had arrived. *Cody a murderer? There was no way. Absolutely.* Crystal shook her head.

"If you say Cody could have played some pranks on me, even one that went wrong, in order to get me to give him my half of the town and leave, then I could go along with that idea, much as I hate to admit it," she said. "But I won't listen to you accusing him of trying to kill me, or of engineering some mining accident so the uncles wouldn't be around to sell the doubloons and spend the money. Next thing, you'll be telling me he should be accused of killing Jake Carver, and I don't think that skeleton we had in the lobby even *is* Jake. It looks too tall and too big and heavy. Jake was a wiry little man with a big head and really bad teeth."

"Now don't you get your dander up, Miss Crystal, before you hear the entire scenario." Reed leaned forward, hands on knees. "What if Cody keeps in touch with the uncles an' they tell him they've found some doubloons? Cody knows doubloons are worth a fortune, so he comes back to Cactus Station, but the uncles won't tell him where the coins are stashed."

"I'm telling you, he doesn't know if there are more than the two Jackson found," Crystal insisted.

"I'm not finished," Reed said.

"Fine. Go ahead with your movie plot," she said.

Reed's face flushed. "They go off to the mine and Cody's real mad," he continued, watching Crystal intently. "So he follows them and tries to scare them by setting off a little dynamite. But he detonates too much, an' there's a cave-in that kills the uncles."

"Are you done, yet?" she asked. "This is all very interesting, but it's pure fiction."

"Listen, little lady. I'm the sheriff here, and you could well be an accomplice, so you'd best keep your comments to yourself unless you want to go back with me to Apache Junction, so we can talk at the station."

"Sorry," she said, and she straightened up in her chair. "Go on."

"Unknown to him..." Reed glared at her as though he expected her to interrupt him again, but when she kept silent, he sucked in a deep breath and kept talking: "...the uncles made a will that leaves half the town to you an' half to him. When you arrive, he can't look for the doubloons in front of you, or he'd have to give you half. So he simulates a gold rush that keeps you so busy, you don't have time to see what he's doing. He hopes to run you off with the skeleton an' the crowds, but you won't go, so he rigs the staircase to frighten you."

"That's enough, Sheriff. That's all hearsay and conjecture. It wouldn't stand up in a court of law and you know it." Crystal got up. "I think it's time for you to leave."

"If he already knows where the rest of the doubloons are, he may have to get rid of you."

"Out, Sheriff." Crystal opened the kitchen door and beckoned him. "Time for you to go home and take that crime scene technician with you."

"If you ignore my warning, there's a chance you'll end up dead, like the uncles and Jake Carver."

"Cody would never kill anyone. That's absolutely ridiculous."

Reed continued to make his case. "Cody might have done one more favor for the uncles. He doted on Willy Blye. Jake was a mean son-of-a-bitch. He may have wanted more than his fair share of the take."

"How long has he been dead? Could the coroner tell?"

"About a year. If Cody's to be believed, that's about the same time Jake went missing."

"He could have fallen and fractured his skull."

"And then wrapped himself up like a papoose and locked himself in a closet?"

"Maybe not," Crystal admitted. "But there's no telling who did that--there are so many weirdos and eccentrics living in these parts. The uncles may even have found him and done it themselves. They were busy with their new mining venture. The ground here's mostly solid rock. They probably didn't want to take the time out to bury him right then, so they secured his body the best way they could."

"That's true, and we may never know for sure, but I'm going to keep on investigating, believe me. You can warn Cody, if you like." Reed nodded to the technician, standing beside the front door with his kit in his hand.

The man barely glanced at Crystal before heading outside. The sheriff started to follow.

"I bet you will warn him, too," Reed said over his shoulder. "I think you're still in love with him, Crystal. I don't think you ever stopped."

"Unless you have an official reason to come back here, you should stay away from now on," Crystal said. "We don't need you any more for crowd control, and I'm taking down the 'No Parking' signs right now."

"Those doubloons are going to turn up sometime. An' when they do, I'll be back." Reed walked unhurriedly out the door and over to his squad car.

Crystal waited until the car left before she returned to the kitchen and started cleaning up the coffee grounds. She dropped the broom first, then the dustpan, spilling everything back onto the floor.

She left the mess and retreated to the back porch, where she sat staring into space while the sun went down behind the mountains.

CHAPTER TWENTY-NINE

"More mail." Jolie brought another envelope to the back porch. "It was on the front desk. I must have dropped it somewhere earlier." She looked at Crystal sitting silently on the porch. "How did things go with Sheriff Dalton? He was with you for a long time. A lot longer than any of the rest of us, includin' Cody."

"He was making a nuisance of himself." Crystal took the envelope. She recognized the magic marker at once.

Jolie had her nose in the want ads of the newspaper. "Harold's gonna try to get a maintenance job in Phoenix," she said. "We could manage some apartments or somethin'."

"I'll give you a reference," Crystal said. "It's the least I can do." She got up. "I'm going to lie down for a while."

She hurried upstairs to her room, where she opened the envelope and scanned the contents. Like the other one, the words were cut out of magazines and newspapers. The instructions were more explicit this time:

LEAVE THE GOLD COINS BETWEEN THE UNCLES GRAVES AT MIDNIGHT TONIGHT IF YOU WANT TO AVOID ANY MORE TROUBLE

IGNORE THIS AND YOU'LL SUFFER THE CONSEQUENCES

Crystal sat on her bed. What if she confided in Cody and he turned out to be the one who had sent the notes? But she couldn't keep these threats to herself. If a building collapsed next time, burying people under the rubble, she'd never forgive herself.

Who should she pick? Jolie or Harold? She laughed mirthlessly to herself at the thought of going to Big Ed. She could call Sheriff Dalton, but after she'd just thrown him out, she doubted he'd be too eager to return. If he did, he'd probably just arrest Cody.

After splashing cold water on her face, she went in search of her nemesis. Maybe he had played a few pranks on her to scare her off, but she couldn't believe him capable of anything more malicious. Those notes had to have come from whoever rigged the stairs and tossed the attic.

It took her a half-hour to find him, installing a new wall plug for the freezer at the convenience store while the Beckers grumbled about the lack of foot traffic since the incidents started at the hotel. Ruth Becker in particular was almost rude in her comments about the way Cody and Crystal had handled the crises.

Arlan leaned over the counter and spat tobacco into a plastic trash can. They both looked older and more wizened than they had when they first arrived in Cactus Station; all grey hair and crinkled skin, like a pair of apple dolls. Crystal tuned them out and went out back, finding Cody shirtless and ill-tempered. He told her he had spent most of the morning listening to the Beckers' grievances while he fixed any number of small things in order to keep them at least partially content. Then Reed had stopped him in order to grill him about the staircase, the uncles and Jake.

"After that, I had to come back here and listen to Ruth an' Arlan again. I've just about had enough, Crystal. What do you want from me?" He drove the last screw home with a vicious flick of his wrist and threw his tools back into his battered kit. A fine sheen of sweat covered his bare bronzed chest.

Crystal tried to tune out Cody's enticing chest as well as she had the Beckers, but with much less success. "I'd rather not talk here," she said, trying not to gawk. He really had the most magnificent set of pecs she had seen in far too long. "Can we go somewhere more private?"

"Only if we're not talkin' business."

He must have read her mind, posing with one hand on his hip, the other arm resting on the porch rail. His manner went from peeved to cocky. Crystal tried looking elsewhere, but her eyes kept straying back to him, and she hated herself for her lack of control.

"Dear me, Miss Crystal, you've lowered your standards a whole hell of a lot--I'm filthy and I probably stink after workin' outside in this heat." He leaned toward her, challenging her to push him away.

She tried to ignore his goading. He wanted any excuse to pick a fight, because he needed to vent his anger on someone, and it might as well be her.

"Where would you like to go?" She wondered if she sounded cool, poised and self-confident or as much on edge as she felt.

He picked up his tool kit and shirt. "Is the tea room closed?"

"Yes. Tea's the last thing anyone's going to buy around here." She leaned against the railing and it shifted.

Cody pulled her off it. "Why do you always find new projects for me? Now the Beckers will be yellin' about the railin' bein' loose, an' I'll get to spend more time here listenin' to them gripin'."

"I'm sorry." Crystal heard the unmistakable stomp of an approaching Becker. "Let's get out of here."

They set off up the alleyway at a pace closer to a jog than a walk. They rounded the corner right as Arlan Becker opened the front door.

"Cody!" he shouted.

"Ignore him," Cody whispered. He propelled her into the tea room and locked the door behind them. "Ah," he said. "Peace."

Crystal turned on the fan. "Want some iced tea?" she asked.

"Please." He threw his tool kit and shirt onto one chair and sat in another.

When she brought the glasses of tea, she also brought him a damp towel.

"Thanks," he said. "So, what do you want to talk about?" He wiped his face.

"These." Crystal gave him the notes.

He read carefully, one finger moving word to word like a pointer, a frown of concentration on his face. "What's this?" he asked, indicating the last word in the second note.

"Consequences," Crystal said. "What do you make of them?"

"Whoever wrote them went past seventh grade." He laid them carefully side by side on the table.

Crystal ignored his self-derisive jibe. "What else?"

"Lots of different newsprint. I have no idea if that's a clue, but maybe the police could make something of it." He ran his fingers over the cut out words. "Do you think he's serious?"

"What makes you think it's a 'he'?"

Cody shrugged. "Because there aren't that many women around here."

His brow furrowed. "Jolie wouldn't have any reason to send threatening notes," he said. "She likes it here, apart from the getting scared part. Ruth Becker would never send notes. She'd hunt me down to tell me off and take great pleasure in it. Her daughter's only interested in makin' and servin' meals. She's not into cuttin' up magazines and newspapers."

He ran his fingers over the notes again. "Anyway, apart from Jolie, none of the women around here is tall enough or good enough with tools to saw halfway through the supports of the stairs."

"That's true," Crystal said. "But you keep coming back to Jolie. She's tall and definitely strong. She could certainly climb a ladder, and Harold has access to everything. They could be operating as a team."

"Nah. Harold's a good guy and Jolie's too smart. If she thought she could make money out of us, she'd do it in a more up-front way."

"Maybe they're in debt or something?"

"Possibly. Have you talked to Reed yet about these notes?"

"No." She told him all about Reed's visit.

Cody's face registered first rage, then despair. "He's gonna hang everythin' on me," he said when she finished.

"He can't unless we let him. I told him everything was circumstantial. He's got no proof."

"What's this 'we' business? I thought you hated me."

"I thought I did, too. But when the sheriff started accusing you, I found myself defending you. Cody, I may be a fool, and you may be the one responsible for all the incidents around here, but I can't and won't believe it of you. I think you're innocent and someone who knows you well is trying to frame you."

"So where does that leave us?"

"Allies. You help me, and I'll help you. We need to make a concentrated search for the doubloons. Maybe if we do what this person wants, whoever it is will take the coins and leave."

"That would suit me. Cactus Station is about all I have left in the world."

"Me, too." She looked at his hands, roughened by work, gripping the empty glass. Those hands were so strong, yet could be so gentle when they were touching her. How she missed them. How she missed being close to Cody. If she lost Cactus Station, she would lose far more than her inheritance.

He got up to pour them both more iced tea. "What happened with your job?" he asked, his tone casual. "I thought you were a successful geologist."

"I thought so, too." Crystal avoided his gaze as she struggled with herself. Perhaps she should try trust and candor for a change. "A couple of clients took advantage of me.

They used my name and my specs, only they altered a few details to make it seem like the land was worth a lot more. People bought into it and lost money."

"Sounds familiar."

He wasn't mocking her. He took her hand and held it comfortingly.

"Go on," he encouraged. "Maybe if we get rid of all the secrets between us, whoever's threatenin' us won't have such a hold. We've been played off each other since we got here. Some of it's our own fault, but someone who knows us has been takin' advantage."

"It's hard for me to tell you everything." Crystal thought about withdrawing her hand, but she'd pulled away from him, physically and emotionally, too many times already. "You always make fun of me, and I made such a fool of myself. I ruined my career--no one will use me as a consultant now, even though my name was cleared. For a while, it looked like I was going to be indicted for fraud, but that's all behind me now, at least."

"Hmm." Cody maintained his reassuring grip. "Now I understand why you looked so tired and down when you arrived. The strain must have been too much. You were luckier than me, though. I ended up on probation for somethin' I didn't do."

"Why in the world did that happen?" Crystal asked. "Reed told me the uncles didn't help you out at all."

"They didn't. They just went on with their lives like nothin' had happened. I was so mad, I left Arizona altogether. I guess they left me half of Cactus Station because their consciences were botherin' them." He shook his head. "Uncle Willy wanted to name this damn place Saguaro Station, but he didn't know how to spell it. Ignorance runs in my family, an' I inherited it. I ended up havin' to become a maintenance man because I didn't have trainin' for anythin' else."

"It's only because of you that anything is working around here at all, even if most of it is bandaided together." She smiled. "I'm so sorry. I've been horrible to you, and you don't deserve it. I placed all the blame on you for leaving me all those years ago. I loved you so much."

"The uncles told me to leave you alone. Uncle Willy said you were too good for me, too smart for me, an' he was right. You've got to get out of this place, Crystal. You can get your career back, or try somethin' else. Look how you turned your side of the street into a moneymaker while I was flounderin' around on my side."

"But you brought in all the crowds. I may not have liked the way you did it, but it worked."

"I'm goin' to apologize," he said. "I've been so jealous of your success, both in goin' to college an' then what you did here. I've been so rude, an' I've treated you so badly."

"Oh, Cody."

She wanted to kiss him, but he kept his distance on the other side of the table. She figured he'd been burned too many times already. This time, she'd have to be the one to prove herself to him, instead of the other way around.

"I'm apologizing, too," she said. "I'm so sorry I acted the way I did." Tears blurred her vision and rolled down her cheeks.

He wiped them away with his thumb, the gesture soft and caring. "Apology accepted," he said, his voice as soft as his touch.

She tried to smile. "So you'll help me search for the doubloons?"

"Sure. Anythin' to keep the peace." He grinned when she looked sharply at him. "I mean that. No sarcasm intended."

"Then let's shake on it." She extended her hand.

He took it, his grip firm and comforting.

Maybe she was being foolish all over again, but she felt this was a new beginning for them. A beginning she was determined to nurture.

They started the hunt that night, after deciding that digging around town during the day would only precipitate another treasure hunt by the fanatics who had refused to leave the area.

Cody dug futilely around the foundations of the hotel. They searched Diamond Della's House of Splendors, newly abandoned by the couple who had tried to make the old brothel into a souvenir and crafts store. The site of the old dental office yielded nothing but scorpions, leaving them with the more undesirable locations to search. At the head of that line was the funeral parlor.

"This is going to give me claustrophobia," Crystal warned as she followed Cody into the bowels of the establishment. "I hate these places even in broad daylight. Can't you go in there alone?"

"If I have to be in here, then so do you. I'm not hangin' around this place by myself, especially at night." Cody shone his flashlight around, illuminating a row of decrepit caskets. "Besides, you might accuse me later of findin' the doubloons an' hiding them from you."

"I will not." Something drifted across her face. Crystal brushed it away, feeling the cobweb cling to her hand. "You'll have to use the lantern or I'm running out right now," she warned. She realized she was clutching his waist and abruptly released him.

He had the audacity to chuckle, but he lit the lantern and balanced it on a table, his features chiseled and handsome in the flickering yellow glow. "You'd have made a lousy miner," he observed.

"That's why I did my surveys above ground." She checked her clothing for spiders. "If you're so eager to get on with things, then stop talking to me about my career. My heart's already pounding, so if you don't hurry, you're going to be finishing this search alone."

"Oh, fine. I'll look around the back room while you take care of the caskets."

"That's disgusting." She wrinkled her nose at him, but he only smiled and left her with a room full of cheap caskets and an insipid yellow light.

"Why don't I just go back to Phoenix?" she said as she gingerly lifted the lid on a thankfully-empty casket.

"Because you're stubborn," he said from the other room.

"Smart aleck," she muttered, moving from one casket to the next.

She completed her search right before he rejoined her, his face grimy and his clothes covered in cobwebs.

"We can't keep this up much longer," she said, brushing the dirt from her jeans.

She longed to submerge her aching body in one of those bubble baths she still dreamed about at moments like this. Her watch said two o'clock. She had gone to bed three nights in a row at five A.M., and she felt terrible all day, her head heavy and her sinuses blocked from the dust.

"Do you have any better suggestions?" Cody rubbed his back and grimaced before perching on the edge of a casket.

"Don't sit there." Crystal dragged him back onto his feet.

"Why not? It's empty or you would have started screamin' again."

"It's a horrible seat. I don't want you anywhere near a casket for about fifty years."

"I thought you'd wanted me in one a few times in the past."

"If you keep it up, I'll put you in this one myself." She wagged her finger at him. Cody only laughed softly.

A whine announced Jackson's approach.

"What are you doin' in here?" Cody squatted to scratch Jackson's matted coat. "I haven't seen much of you in the last couple of days."

The old dog's tail waved like its motor was having trouble kicking into gear. He dropped something at Cody's feet and sat down to scratch behind one ear, fur and dust flying.

"Jackson," Crystal protested, stepping back.

"Look, he's brought another one." Cody held up a gold coin, winking at Crystal in the lamplight.

The dog looked at her and panted, his tongue hanging out of his mouth.

Crystal gave him a wide berth and took the coin. "That's another one, all right. Where is he getting them?"

"Beats me." Cody watched Jackson sink to the floor and close his eyes. "I wish you could talk."

Jackson rose up and gave a short bark.

"I mean people talk, not dog talk." Cody smiled indulgently. "I swear this dog understands everythin' I say."

"Then tell him to lead us to the doubloons." Crystal tested a parlor couch for sturdiness and sat. "Life would be a lot simpler if he'd do it."

"I've tried, believe me. He's selectively deaf." Cody flipped the coin in the air.

"Don't do that, you might lose it." Crystal made a dive for the doubloon.

Cody caught it above her outstretched palm. "Sorry, this one's mine."

"We're not starting that again, are we?" She remembered only too clearly Cody's adamant refusal to let her keep the doubloons in a safe deposit box in Phoenix. He had insisted they stow them in the Gold Rush Hotel's antiquated safe.

"I figure you've got the first two under lock an' key. This one's mine to keep. I'd like to look at it once in a while for inspiration."

"Someone will knock you over the head for it, you stubborn fool."

"That's what you really think of me, isn't it?"

"Stubborn? You're denying it?"

"No, a fool." He picked up the lantern and made for the door. "Come on, let's go to bed. We won't get anythin' else done tonight."

"I don't think you're a fool. Misguided, maybe, along with the stubborn, but not a fool. I was speaking..." She fumbled around in her mind for the right word. "Figuratively."

"Figuratively, huh?" Cody opened the door and stepped into the street. "That's one way of weaselin' out of things."

"I am not weaseling out of anything." She trudged after him. "We're just tired. And when we're tired, we start arguing."

"I'm goin' to the creek," Cody said. "Want to join me?"

"I don't think that's a very good idea. Look what happened the last time."

"Afraid you'll do the same thing again, then?" He handed her the lantern.

"No, that's not what I think. You love to put words in my mouth."

"That's not all." He spun on his heel and marched off, clinking the doubloon along with the other articles in his pocket.

Crystal didn't know quite what to say to his last remark, so she shut her open mouth and headed for the hotel.

CHAPTER THIRTY

The following day, lacking a better idea, Crystal tried trailing Jackson around town. She reluctantly followed him to three groups of garbage cans and partway under five buildings, then stood by while he dug two holes for what appeared to be no other reason than for the sheer joy of feeling dirt and rocks flying from between his feet.

"Ugh," she told him, wrinkling her nose as he passed her by and headed out of town.

Jackson curled his lip and trotted away.

"This is stupid," she said, but she followed him anyway, down to the graveyard.

When he started digging between the headstones, she almost ran over to stop him, but she was afraid he might be digging for the doubloons.

"He's diggin' for bones," Cody said from behind her.

"What?" She looked at Jackson, energetically sniffing the hole he'd made. "He's your dog--stop him. This is a graveyard, for goodness sake. He's being sacrilegious and disgusting."

"I don't know what sacril...whatever you said means, but he's a dog, Crystal. He doesn't know any better." Cody sat down on a mound. He looked tired and dispirited.

"What's wrong with you--not enough sleep?" Crystal almost sat beside him. She decided she hadn't yet got to where she would dishonor the dead, even if the headstone beside his elbow said that was the last resting place of Belching Bill Beasley, the town drunk.

"I followed Jackson around all night." Cody rubbed his face. "I think I've had maybe three hours sleep over the last two days. I don't do well without my rest."

"So I see." Crystal looked at his stubble-covered chin and the dirty shirt he must have had on for at least the past two days.

"It's like he knows what we want and isn't going to give it to us," Cody said.

"He probably *does* know. He hates me, so it would give him a great sense of satisfaction to see me upset." Crystal retreated when Jackson resumed his digging with increased gusto after the brief rest.

"You'll be more than upset if we lose this town." Cody yawned and stretched. "Stop it, Jackson."

Jackson ignored his master by digging deeper and faster. Dirt flew, peppering Cody and Crystal with sharp, painful missiles.

"I promise I won't go near Crystal if you stop," Cody said.

Jackson paused momentarily, then resumed excavating.

"I guess that won't do it," Crystal said wryly. "How about some of Jolie's chicken pie?"

The digging ground to a halt. Jackson turned one bloodshot eye toward Crystal.

"Really. Cross my heart," she promised.

He whined and trotted over to lead them from the graveyard.

"He's pretty nasty," she whispered to Cody.

"Why are you whisperin'? I thought you didn't believe he understood everythin' said around him." Cody shoved his hands in his pockets and kept his distance from her.

"I've changed my mind. I think it's entirely possible the hotel has a ghost and that Jackson speaks English."

Cody shook his head, a half-smile lighting his tired eyes. "Wonders will never cease. Maybe you'll start likin' me next."

"Maybe. Miracles *can* happen." She took his arm. "We've been good partners the last few days, haven't we?"

"The truce is barely two days old, Crystal. We've got plenty of time for a relapse."

They strolled back into town, the atmosphere between them less charged than usual, Crystal thought with a glimmer of hope. Cody had been so distant since they shook hands and sealed their pact.

When they arrived on the outskirts of town, the first thing Crystal noticed was a clump of people standing in front of the boarding house. Harold spotted them and loped over.

"What's up?" Cody asked.

"The upstairs porch collapsed. Half of it's in the street." Harold pointed at the rubble.

Crystal gasped. "Anyone hurt?"

"No. Luckily. The place was pretty deserted because it was lunch time an' everyone was out somewhere eatin'."

Crystal looked at Cody. "You think it was an accident?"

"I doubt it, the way things have been goin' lately."

A cry interrupted them.

"That came from the convenience store," Harold said. He took off, Cody right behind him.

Crystal followed them into the Beckers' store. Arlan lay flat on his stomach in the middle of the floor with half the counter and its contents resting on his back. When he saw them, Arlan yelled even louder than he had before.

"Are you hurt?" Cody squatted down beside the prone man.

"My back!" Arlan flailed his arms and legs like a beached turtle. "I've broken my back. I can't feel my legs. I'm paralyzed."

"We'll have you out of there in a minute." Harold threw things left and right: gum, cigarettes, plastic roses, pens and pencils whizzed past Crystal.

"He's paralyzed." Ruth Becker wrung her hands, tears pouring down her apple doll cheeks as she watched her husband struggling.

"If he was, then he wouldn't be moving his arms and legs." Crystal forced herself to put her arm around Ruth's shoulders. The Beckers had proved to have a real flair for drama, and Crystal was sick of listening to them.

Ruth dabbed her eyes with a tissue. "Stop kicking, Arlan," she ordered. "You'll only hurt yourself worse."

Harold and Cody took both sides of the heavy marble-topped counter that Arlan had insisted on having installed. They lifted the section and slid it off him.

"Careful," Ruth warned. "You'll break that marble in half." She rushed forward, not to check on Arlan, but to examine the marble. After running her hands over the surface, she breathed a sigh of relief. "We can get this repaired without too much trouble."

Arlan sat upright with help from Cody and Harold. "What about me?" he complained. He rubbed his back. "You don't seem to care if *I* can be fixed or not."

"If you were really hurt, you'd still be hollering," Ruth said. She stooped to gather up the lottery tickets, then moved on to the other counter paraphernalia.

Jolie ran in and beckoned wildly. "Come quick."

Cody, Crystal and Harold left the Beckers to their own devices and hurried out of the store.

Jolie pointed. "Look."

The entire top floor of Diamond Della's leaned at a drunken angle, the roof sliding toward the street. As they watched, the building toppled and fell with a grinding crash. Cody grabbed Crystal and held her face to his chest as the resulting dust storm blew over them. His chest felt so good against her cheek, her arms slid around his waist of their own accord. Her eyelids fluttered closed, her rebellious mind wishing a couple of other buildings would collapse, too, giving her a chance to hold him longer.

"It's clear now." He gently disengaged himself.

Crystal felt the emptiness in her heart as well as her arms. She had pushed him away one time too many, and he no longer wanted her, she thought with a pang.

Cody was already crossing the street to inspect the damage. She lingered behind, her desolation complete. He had held her as impersonally as he would have held Ruth Becker. As Cactus Station tumbled around Crystal, so her future with Cody tumbled, too. The writing was on every dilapidated wall. The little intimacy she had sensed in the graveyard had been no more than wishful thinking on her part.

"What's up, hon?" Jolie put her arm around her friend's shoulders. "You look down in the dumps, an' I don't think it's got anythin' to do with the town fallin' down."

"I've been such a fool," Crystal said, watching Cody talking with Harold and Big Ed.

"Yeah, you have." Evidently Jolie had no trouble realizing what Crystal had been a fool about. The longing must have shown on her face.

Crystal started walking toward the bordello. "I don't know if I can fix the damage."

"I don't know that, either. If you want any happiness in your life, I suggest you try. You'd do best if you started tellin' him what you just told me." Jolie linked arms with her and they stepped off the street into the shade of a porch.

Crystal swallowed hard. Admitting fault was the hardest thing for her. She had striven to achieve perfection in every area of her life and achieved it nowhere. Her messy, passionate relationship with Cody defied being neatly pigeonholed, and she had fought it until she had destroyed it.

"I don't even know if he'll listen after all the things I've said and done," she said, more to herself than to Jolie. "When it comes right down to it, I'm not sure which one of us has the most hang-ups."

"Me neither." Jolie squeezed her shoulder. "I think both of you need to eat a little crow before you can make up, don't you?"

Crystal managed a weak smile. "I guess so." She patted Jolie's hand. "I'd better get over there and see if this was yet another staged accident. Cactus Station's becoming a very unsafe place to be."

A creaking groan above their heads alerted them to jump right before the porch collapsed on top of them.

CHAPTER THIRTY-ONE

Cody and Crystal stood side by side in front of the hotel. They had just hugged Jolie and Harold before watching them leave on the motorcycle, bound for Phoenix.

Crystal waved the Beckers' car and Big Ed's truck out of town. "Well, that's the last of them," she said.

"Yeah." Cody leaned on the porch rail and studied her profile. He didn't like the determination he saw in the tilt of her chin. "You aren't leavin', are you?"

"Not without those doubloons." Crystal shielded her eyes with her hand.

"Pretty stubborn," Cody said. *Didn't Crystal give up on anything but him?*

"Mad as fire." She kicked a rotten board with the toe of her boot. "I'm going to give them to whoever is willing to kill for them, so he leaves town."

"What's left of it." Cody looked around. The piles of rubble made Cactus Station look more like a war zone than a ghost town. "You an' Jolie were lucky yesterday."

"I'm glad you finally talked everyone into leaving, at least for now." She smiled at him. "See, your glib tongue continues to have its uses."

He shrugged. "You an' your fancy talk, Crystal. I think you just gave me a compliment, but I'm not sure."

She laughed. "I'm done with snide comments. We called a truce, remember?"

"Yeah, we did."

Since the day they had shaken hands, Cody had seen a shift in Crystal's manner. She'd been more responsive, much kinder. But he knew a lasting relationship that went past friendship was impossible. They were fire and water, never able to meet on common ground for more than a brief time. He inadvertently sighed at the thought of never holding her in his arms again.

"What's the matter?" she asked. Her wrinkled clothing and dirty boots told a story of fatigue and frustration. She stifled a yawn.

Cody sighed again. "Everythin'. Nothin'. I tried my best to make this town come back to life, an' now it's empty again an' half the buildings have either collapsed or been damaged so badly they're not worth savin'. We've got nothin' left."

"We've still got the land and plenty of lumber. And don't forget, somewhere there's a cache of doubloons. I'd say we've got plenty. Why don't I make us some lunch and then we'll go hunting with Jackson again?"

"Sounds like a plan. I've got nothin' better to offer." Cody followed her inside.

She made sandwiches while he set two places at the kitchen table. After the chaos of the last few weeks, the place was so quiet he could hear the wind blowing down the alleyway and sand skittering across the back porch.

"It's weird here without all the guests," he said into the silence.

Crystal put the sandwiches on the table. "I kind of like it. I haven't had a chance to breathe since I arrived here. It's peaceful right now. Restful." She looked at him with those cornflower blue eyes he loved so much.

Cody had never heard her associate him with being restful. He liked the quiet peace between them after all the tension. "You've put in a lot of work," he said.

"You, too," she said as they sat down and started eating.

Crystal's food always tasted good. He enjoyed her company, too, when they weren't fighting.

"I made your favorite," she said.

"Chicken salad. It's great, Crystal." He poured them both a glass of lemonade. No sense in spoiling a pleasant meal by getting a beer out of the refrigerator and subjecting himself to one of her disapproving looks.

"I thought you didn't like lemonade." She watched his face pucker.

"I'm tryin' to turn over a new leaf."

She smiled. "Honestly, Cody, you don't have to overdo things. At least have a soda. I think there's still a six-pack on the bottom shelf, at the back."

He returned her smile and fetched the soda. "I hope we have more luck with Jackson this afternoon."

It was Crystal's turn to sigh. "Me, too. We can't live here indefinitely on what we've got put by in the hotel safe. Even if we sell those three doubloons, we'll only have enough to keep us going a couple of months. And if we do sell the doubloons, we might be putting ourselves in more danger than we are now."

"If we don't find the coins, you can go back to Phoenix 'n try startin' up your business again. You said your name's been cleared."

"I guess." She didn't sound at all convinced that was a good idea. "What will you do?"

"What I do best--disappear into the mountains an' do some prospectin'. If that's not successful, I can get construction work or some-thin' in Apache Junction or Phoenix. Maybe even head back up to Utah or Colorado again."

She propped her chin on her hands. In the sunlight filtering through the windows, her hair shone like the spun sugar Jolie had told him was on top of one of the pastries he liked from the tea room. Cody thought Crystal had never looked more beautiful, despite the blue smudges of fatigue below her eyes.

"Why didn't you finish school?" she asked, regarding him candidly. "It's not too late. You could get your GED and then train for a better job."

Discussing his lack of education wasn't one of his favorite topics. "Schoolin' was never a priority with Uncle Willy," he said when she continued patiently waiting for an answer. "He was too interested in spinnin' tales about findin' clues to the location of the Lost Dutchman Mine. He kept talkin' up how much gold there was, an' how easy it would be to get it, long as we had the supplies and the equipment to go into the Superstitions an' stay there until we found it." He toyed with his empty plate, reluctant to look at her. "I was a good talker. We made a good team. He taught me about gold minin' an' I raised funds for his projects. "

"And yet Uncle Dock and Uncle Willy both encouraged me to get a degree. They had a skewed perception of what was right and what was wrong. There they were, telling you that you weren't good enough for me, but they were using you to further their own schemes." Crystal looked angry. "That was so unfair. If only I'd known, I would have told them."

"Oh, I've done okay, Crystal," Cody said. "I never was a good student. I couldn't sit in a classroom all day while Miss Grandy talked about things I had no interest in. Then she retired, an' the teacher that replaced her ran off with some prospector to the White Mountains, an' school was permanently out. That was right after those three people were found murdered about a mile away, an' no other teacher would come here."

"Murdered? Really?" Crystal's eyes opened wide.

"Yeah. You never heard about that? I must have been slippin'. I could have frightened the life out of you that summer you stayed here."

"You'd have taken great delight in doing it, too." She gave him a fond look that rocked him all the way to his toes.

Cody wanted to reach across the table and take her hand, but he had no emotional reserves left if she rebuffed him. He kept his hands to himself.

"Well," he said. "What say we chase Jackson around some more?" As he stood up, he could have sworn he saw regret on her face, but he knew it must be his imagination.

～

"Watch yourself." Cody guided Crystal away from a wickedly long nail protruding from a stack of rubble.

Crystal's pulse picked up speed from the contact. She shied away from his touch with lightning-quick reactions. When they first arrived in Cactus Station, she had felt only anger toward him. Then they made love again, and everything had changed.

At the thought of the creek and the ability of those hands to arouse her passion, a flush rose onto her cheeks. Cody still had not released her, as though similar emotions were passing through him, too. Crystal turned to face him. She caught an unguarded moment of intense longing on his face before he masked it.

"We'd better get on," he said, his voice low and thick. "Jackson'll disappear if we don't catch up." He strode around her and took off at a fast pace.

Crystal followed, her heart hammering like some adolescent school-girl's. The way his hips moved in those tight jeans should be banned from women's eyes--her's, anyway. She felt tempted to run her hands all over him.

What was she thinking? she asked herself. *Of going to bed with him,* her rebellious mind told her. *Of having him do those things to her body that she needed so badly.*

Stop it, she told herself firmly.

She broke into a run and passed him. She'd much rather he looked at her back view than she was forced to look at his. Spotting Jackson sifting through a pile of debris, she ran over to see what he had found. Nothing except old fast food wrappers from the convenience store. He licked a paper that had once cradled a hot dog. *Revolting,* Crystal thought.

Cody stood still, his nostrils quivering. "Do you smell that?"

Crystal sniffed. "No."

He sniffed again himself, harder. "God, Crystal. I smell smoke." He pointed. "Look. There *is* smoke." He took off at a dead run.

Crystal couldn't keep up. Jackson passed her, catching up easily with Cody and keeping close to his heels. She passed the shacks and ran up the dirt road back into town.

A terrible sight greeted them; one building after another had caught fire in the dry atmosphere and fresh breeze. The hungry flames leapt across alleyways and open spaces, heading for the hotel. Intense crackling accompanied the blaze and smoke spiraled into the air, carried by wind currents.

Crystal stopped, panting. "What are we going to do?" She stared in disbelief.

Cody took off again, straight toward the flames.

"What are you doing? Get back." She wanted to catch him, to grab him and stop him, but he ran so fast, her efforts were as hopeless as her desire to prevent the destruction of Cactus Station.

"I'll detonate the building next to the hotel," he shouted over his shoulder. "You keep away. I don't want to be worryin' about you and dynamite at the same time."

"Where did you get dynamite?" she asked.

"I'm a miner, Crystal. We always have dynamite." He widened the distance between them, despite the fact she was running as fast as she was capable of doing.

Out of breath and choking on smoke and fumes, she arrived at the hotel in time to see Cody heading for the smoldering building with a canvas bag in one hand. Everything in Cactus Station had been built too close together, she thought, watching the flames leap from roof to roof. He'd never make it, and the dynamite would detonate, taking him with it.

"Come back!" She started after him.

"I told you to stay out of the way." He disappeared down the alleyway. He didn't look back, neither did he hesitate.

Crystal stood thinking of unstable dynamite and Cody setting too heavy a charge because he was in a hurry. How many years had it been since he'd even used dynamite? She had to get the doubloons out of the safe. He might blow the hotel clear over Weaver's Needle, the precious gold coins going along for the ride.

Taking a deep breath, and then wishing she hadn't after smoke poured into her lungs, she coughed and choked her way up the steps into the hotel lobby. Inside the safe lay not only the doubloons but all the paperwork pertaining to their inheritance. She looked around. What else could she take in a hurry? The photo of the uncles, posed in black and white above the reception desk, or something more practical, like her purse upstairs in her room?

If she was going to get her purse, then she had about two minutes. Without thinking rationally, because rationality had deserted her, she ran for the back stairs. Smoke drifted along the back wall of the kitchen, where the sink was located. She figured sparks must have fallen onto the wood pile and ignited. Abandoning her quest for her purse, she put her faith in Cody's abilities, ran outside and grabbed a shovel. She had to get that wood off the porch before his efforts were rewarded with nothing but a big pile of burned lumber where the hotel once stood.

She used the shovel to push logs off the porch. It was slower going than she expected, the wood heavy and unwieldy. She had asked Cody to get rid of it all weeks ago, but he'd had other, more pressing chores to attend to, and it had never got done. Her efforts were too late. The wall caught fire. Embers flew in on the wind created by the fire, threatening to set light to her hair and her clothes.

Crystal doused herself with a bowl of water left on the porch for Jackson's use. She shoveled up sand and threw it at the fire in an attempt to smother the flames.

"Fire in the hole!" Cody came charging toward her, his hands over his ears.

Crystal dropped the shovel and ran with him. He dragged her into the shelter of a large boulder butting up against the alleyway and covered her with his body.

Like the roar of a locomotive in a tunnel, the dynamite detonated. Debris rained down and the earth shook. Hidden beneath Cody, Crystal could barely breathe. When the noise subsided, he rose up and peered around the boulder.

"Well?" She sat up. Her blouse had ripped somewhere along the way, one sleeve hanging off her arm. Her knees throbbed and she saw they were both grazed and bleeding.

"Nice to know I haven't lost my touch." He got up and offered her his hand.

Crystal allowed him to pull her to her feet. She saw a neat pile of smoldering rubble where the house had once stood. The blast had put out the flames on the kitchen wall and taken out most of the livery stable two doors down.

"You know, you're really good at this," she said.

"Lots of practice always makes perfect." He grinned. "Boy, you're a mess."

"What do you expect?" She pulled off the torn sleeve. "If Sheriff Dalton saw this blasting job, he'd never again talk about you making mistakes and blowing up the uncles."

"Reed's a hard man to convince of anythin' except his own opinions," Cody said. "You shouldn't wear shorts around here, you know. Look at your knees."

"It's too hot to wear jeans." She used her sleeve to brush the dirt off her scrapes.

"You're too hot for your own good in anythin'." He walked off, leaving her behind.

"I thought you'd given up being rude and sarcastic." She followed, limping slightly.

"Only returnin' the favor," he said.

"When was I last rude to you?"

"When you made love with me and raised all my hopes for nothin'."

He stopped abruptly, and she ran into him.

"Jumpin' me right now isn't gonna help," he told her.

"You're...you're..."

"Irresistible?" He smirked at her. The old Cody. Totally intact.

"More like incorrigible." She started to tell him what that meant, but stopped herself in time. She figured he might just be joking with her. Her immediate and maybe irrational response was to act like a shrew. What was wrong with her? He'd just saved her life. Yet again.

"I should thank you," she said.

"Yes, you should." He held the back door open for her.

The inside of the kitchen looked blackened and ready for demolition. Acrid odors of burned wood and melted plastic hung heavy in the air.

Cody opened the cabinet under the sink. "Better check for sparks," he said. "I think the force of the blast put out the fire, but why take chances?"

He took a crowbar from the tool kit he had left on the end of the counter. As he pried away the shelves, something dropped out.

"What's this?" He pulled out a blackened bag. It split, gold coins cascading across the bottom of the cabinet and spilling onto the floor.

"The doubloons. You found the doubloons!" Crystal threw her arms around his neck and almost pulled him over. "I could kiss you."

"Why don't you?" He tumbled her to the floor, his lips inches from hers, his arms pinning hers to her sides.

"You're holding me down," she protested, stiffening.

"I guess I am. It's the only way I can guarantee gettin' close to you without riskin' a slap." He watched the warring emotions on her face. "So, are you gonna kiss me for findin' the doubloons or not?"

Jackson pushed his face between theirs.

"For God's sake, Jackson." Cody sounded breathless.

Crystal knew why. She'd felt him harden as he lay on top of her.

Jackson waved his tail and panted, his sour breath bathing them.

"I can't take this." Crystal coughed. "His breath's gagging me. Get off, both of you."

"I never get a break." Cody hauled Crystal to her feet. "Let's get these coins to Reed."

"No way." She opened the canvas bag Jolie used to transport the mail from Tortilla Flat and started shoveling coins into it. "I got another note yesterday, with instructions where to leave them. We have to put them in the graveyard. If we don't, whoever wants them may hunt us down and kill us."

Cody ran his hands through his hair. "How can you be sure he won't try to kill us anyway? We've got no guarantees that handing over the gold will satisfy him."

"Don't you think we stand a better chance if we give him what he wants than if we don't?" Crystal shook the blackened bag to make sure it was empty.

Cody sighed. "Okay," he said. "I'll go along with you, but I don't like it."

"Good." She went over to the back door.

He stayed by the sink.

"Well? Are you coming?" She held the door open.

"All right." He sounded rebellious.

Crystal stepped outside. "You're moving like a tortoise," she said.

"I'm comin.' I said I was. How many times do you want to hear me say 'okay'?"

Crystal led the way. She didn't want to admit how heavy the sack was, but the handles bit into her palms and her fingers were going numb. She swung the bag to her other hand. She swore eyes followed them all the way, peeking from inside ruined buildings, peering from behind rocks. Even staring from between the Saguaros that ringed the cemetery. She sped up. Whoever wanted the gold was fanatical about it, and she didn't want that bag in her possession any longer than was necessary.

"Where's the fire?" Cody caught up with her.

"I want to get rid of these things before anything else happens." She broke into a run. The doubloons bounced inside the bag and hit her leg. She stumbled.

Cody took the bag from her. "That's damned heavy," he said. "Why didn't you ask me to carry it in the first place?" He grimaced. "Don't answer that. You probably thought I'd take them an' run off."

"It passed through my mind, I'll admit."

They jogged into the cemetery. "Over there." She pointed. "Between the uncles' graves. That's the place we're supposed to leave them."

"Close to that shack?" Cody sounded slightly winded.

"Yes, the dilapidated thing. I wonder how it's still standing." She picked her way between the headstones to find a box waiting between Uncle Willy's cross and Uncle Dock's headstone.

Cody kicked the box with his foot. "Someone's expectin' us."

"I don't doubt it." Crystal glanced furtively around, but saw no one. "Hurry up and put the bag in the box. Let's get out of here. It's too spooky."

Cody dropped the bag, which landed with a pronounced chinking sound in the quiet air. Without another word to each other, they jogged back the way they had come. At the hotel, Crystal told Cody she was going to clean up the kitchen. He told her he would check the damage on the other buildings.

Crystal loaded a backpack with a couple of bottles of water, a flashlight and a small blanket. She was going to find out who wanted those doubloons, even if she had to sit in that cemetery all night. She let herself out the back door and grabbed the shovel she had used on the woodpile. It made no sense to go back unarmed.

~

Cody hated cemeteries, even in broad daylight. Now he was crouching behind a shack as the sun sank behind the mountains, its last few rays illuminating a row of graves with handmade markers.

He shifted his cramped limbs. Nothing like a graveyard to make you more aware of your own mortality, he decided. In a few years he'd be lying six feet under, too, and without anything more to show for his life than the inhabitants of this godforsaken place.

He eased himself down against the marker on the grave behind him and stretched out his legs, both of which were well on their way to becoming totally numb. When feeling returned, pins and needles made him grit his teeth. Beside him, Jackson made a snuffling sound.

Then he heard it--a soft crunch of footsteps on gravel. Cody got to his feet. Annoyingly, his right knee buckled, not yet ready to take his weight. He staggered and regained his balance, swearing under his breath. Something hit the back of his head and he felt the ground come up to meet him.

The next thing he knew, he was face down in the sand. He didn't remember what had happened, but his head throbbed and Crystal was on his back, screaming her head off as usual.

"Get off me," he said.

"What?" She stopped screaming.

"I asked you to get off me," he mumbled, spitting sand out of his mouth.

"Cody?" Her weight eased off him. She helped him roll onto his back.

"What's goin' on?" He tried to sit up, but dizziness swept over him. "What happened?"

"I'm sorry." She was crying. "I didn't know it was you. You changed your shirt for the first time in days. And where did you get a baseball cap, for goodness sake?"

"I got them both out of my truck. You hit me?" He clutched his head. "What the hell with?"

"A shovel," she said in a small voice.

"Are you nuts? You could have killed me."

"I thought you were the doubloon bandit."

Crystal helped him to his feet. He leaned on her and wondered if he was the crazy one, because suddenly, getting hit on the head wasn't such a bad thing, after all. With Crystal so contrite, he might be able to get some mileage out of playing wounded.

"I'll take care of you," she promised.

She sat him on a grave and left to check the box. He heard her searching around.

"They're gone," she said when she returned.

"They can't be gone. I checked to make sure they were here when I arrived, and I haven't taken my eyes off the box since. At least not until you hit me."

She ignored his glare. "I was here, too," she said. "I hid on the other side of the shack."

His headache returned full force. Those damned coins couldn't be gone. "I don't suppose you thought to bring a flashlight, did you?" he asked.

"Of course I did. Obviously you didn't." She went behind the shed and came back with a beam of light guiding her way.

Cody took the flashlight from her and panned the cemetery. Nothing but graves confronted him. He swore outright.

"That's not going to solve anything." She sounded offended.

"You're to blame for this," he snapped. "If you hadn't interfered, I'd have caught him."

"You?" Her voice quivered with rage. "You made so much noise back there; you probably scared away everything in a ten mile radius."

"You told me you were gonna clean up the kitchen," he said.

"And you told me you were going to check on the buildings," she countered.

Cody sighed. "Arguin' isn't gonna help," he said. "Where's Jackson?"

"How should I know? Why should I care?" She sounded even angrier.

"He was with me when I was hidin' behind the shack. Now he's gone."

Crystal placed her hands on her hips. "Maybe Jackson took the doubloons."

"Maybe he did." Cody didn't like her standing over him like some avenging angel. He shone the light on her. "Jackson didn't like you planting them in the cemetery, either," he told her.

She pushed the light away. "That's a bunch of hogwash, Cody Blye, and you know it."

Cody couldn't see her expression, but he could imagine it--scowling like some dark force.

"Let's go back to the hotel," he suggested. He didn't like thinking about dark forces while he was sitting on a grave. "Unless you have some better idea," he added when she gave a very unladylike snort.

"Maybe I should just hit you over the head with the shovel again."

In spite of her words, she slipped her arm around his waist, and he was able to lean on her while they walked slowly back to town.

Cody still felt unsteady. His head hurt and his bottom lip throbbed. He must have bitten it when she hit him. He licked his lips and tasted blood. What an evening. Certainly not one he wished to repeat ever again.

At the hotel, he made for the back stairs. "I'm gonna lie down," he told her.

"You can't," she said. "You passed out. You have to sit up at least an hour, and then I'm supposed to wake you up throughout the night to make sure you haven't got a concussion." She peered at him. "I've got to make sure your pupils are equal. Let me shine the flashlight in your eyes."

He pushed her away. "Get that thing away from me. I've been knocked out before. I'll be fine."

"At least let me make you an ice pack and give you Tylenol or something," she wheedled.

Cody sighed. He just wanted to lie down and close his eyes. But he had a feeling she wasn't going to leave him in peace until he at least agreed to let her do something for him.

"Okay," he said.

He sat on one of the blackened chairs while she bustled around, fetching him water and painkillers, then an ice pack, which she placed on his head a little too hard.

"Ouch!" Cody jumped. "That hurt."

"Oh, honey, I'm sorry. " She sat beside him. "I didn't *mean* to hurt you."

Cody's mind registered the fact that she'd called him honey. She'd never done that before. She must be really upset.

He took the ice pack out of her hands and held it against his head. Tears glistened on her lashes. Her shirt was partly unbuttoned. He found his headache diminishing as a throb started in his groin. He told himself to ignore everything and downed two painkillers with a glass of water.

"How do you feel?" she asked. "You're not still dizzy, are you?" She touched his brow with cool, gentle fingers.

"I feel lousy," he said. "You pack quite a punch. I've got a lump on my head the size of a goose egg."

"How would you know? You've never even *seen* a goose egg." She smiled, her eyes lighting up in a way he hadn't seen for a long time.

She trailed one finger across his bottom lip. "Was I responsible for this, too?"

"I bit myself when you hit me, yes."

"I'm sorry," she said again. And then her lips touched his.

Despite the discomfort, he returned her kiss. As far as he was concerned, she could hit him repeatedly if she followed that by kissing him the way she was at that moment. She pressed herself against him, her mouth crushing his and her tongue darting into his mouth to perform such passionate acrobatics, he wondered if he felt dizzy from his head wound or her erotic kissing.

"Crystal," he said against her lips. "What are you tryin' to do to me?"

"Something I should have done when I first saw you again," she whispered. Her lips pressed against his cheek, his ear, his temple, his neck--darting here and there-- arousing him with her questing tongue and her nipping teeth.

"If you keep doin' what you're doin', you're gonna end up in bed with me," he warned, unable to stop pulling her shirt out of her shorts and sliding his palms up and down the softness of her back.

"That's what I want." She ran her own hands up his chest.

He unfastened the rest of the buttons on her blouse and shrugged it off her arms. He unclasped her bra and flung it to join her blouse on the floor. Her breasts rose and fell in rhythm with her breathing, the pink tips hard and begging.

Crystal gently took his head in her hands and kissed his lips before guiding his mouth to her breast. Cody wrapped his arms around her and she flung her head back, exposing the length of her throat, the pulse in her neck beating a wild tattoo.

With reverence he claimed first one breast, then the other, marveling at the sensations moving through him. When he kissed the pulse at the base of her neck, she moaned deep in her throat.

"Take me to bed," she said, her voice low and sultry. "Show me how much you care for me." She unzipped her shorts and wriggled out of them, then her bikini panties, leaving herself completely naked.

Cody sucked in his breath. "Dear God, Crystal. Someone might come."

"You don't like what you see?" She raised her arms and her breasts bounced gently, enticingly.

"I'd be a total fool not to."

He picked her up. She wrapped her arms around his neck and her legs around his waist. His headache forgotten, he held her tight against him and mounted the stairs. He took her to the Presidential Suite.

"I'll show you how much I care for you," he said.

He kicked open the door.

Crystal laughed and began to unbutton his shirt.

CHAPTER THIRTY-TWO

Those hours under the canopy in the ornate bed were the happiest of her entire life.

Cody came to her without reservations. He made love to her as though he had never done so before, giving endlessly and seeking so little in return.

Crystal knew she had been a far more selfish participant in the past, and she did all she could to make up for it. She matched caress for caress, kiss for kiss. When he raised above her, she rose up to meet his thrust. When she rolled him onto his back and straddled him, her actions told him how much she loved him. Cody had lost so many dreams in his life. She hoped to replace them with something more permanent and magical than anything he had experienced before.

By giving herself so freely, she unfettered her spirit. She gave of herself in ways she had never dreamed, enjoying the new sensations and Cody's gasps of pleasure.

She discovered new ways to please them both until she could bear no more waiting, no more ever-building sensations. Her release came in an explosion of light that left her depleted of energy but fulfilled in a way she had never experienced before.

Cody lay beside her, his chest heaving and slick with perspiration.

She turned on her side to face him, straddling his hip with one leg, reluctant to break contact even for a moment. Then she touched his skin with her tongue, tasting salt.

"What are you doin', sweetheart? Tryin' to kill me?" He enfolded her in his arms, pulling her head into the crook of his shoulder.

Content for the first time since she had fallen in love with Cody all those years before, Crystal snuggled against him.

"I love you," she said softly.

Beneath her head, she felt his muscles tense. She raised her head and gazed at him. "Why is that so threatening to you?" she asked.

"You and I don't belong together."

His voice held profound regret. His eyes filled with such pain, her breath caught in her throat.

"Pretty soon you'll want to go back to Phoenix, an' I can't fit in there."

"You could fit in anywhere you wanted to," she said.

But she couldn't see Cody cooped up in her sterile apartment while she went back to work. What would he do with himself? His talents lay in prospecting and mining. He'd end up back in construction, spending his days performing meaningless, empty tasks and hating every moment. Soon after that, he'd end up hating her, too.

"You know that's not true," he said. He pulled her face down to kiss her forehead. "Why don't we just enjoy things the way they are, until it's time for us to give up on Cactus Station?"

"I don't want to lose you again." She squeezed her eyes shut, fighting the ready tears, and dropped her head back onto his chest.

"You'll never lose me. You'll always have me close to your heart." His hands were gentle on her body, stroking away the pain. "You know how I feel about you. You can carry that with you wherever you go."

"Do I really know what you feel?" She wished she could see his face, but shadows obscured it, the moon filtered by the heavy drapes at the window. "You've never told me outright. You always avoid the issue, just like you're doing right now."

"I'm not avoidin' anythin'. You always want black n' white, Crystal. I'm not a black n' white kind of guy."

"You could always change. It's never too late for that."

She ran her fingers around his hard, flat nipple and felt his body react with a surge of power. She took the nipple between her teeth and rolled her tongue over its contours. Cody groaned and shifted her on top of him. His fingers stroked the sides of her breasts, then trailed down to clasp her buttocks, grinding her against the part of him that had grown and hardened.

"Do you know what happens when you start somethin', honey? You end up havin' to finish it." His hand slipped between them, finding her dampness and stroking until she cried out.

He entered her with one swift thrust and held her there, motionless, despite the pulsating in his groin. "Tell me you want it, Crystal." His voice was harsh with the effort of holding himself back.

"Yes," she said, barely able to speak. "Yes. I want you. Give me what I want." Her nails sunk into his arms. "Give it to me--now."

He took her with him, onto her back, legs spread wide and arms pinned above her head. Their eyes met in the dim light.

"I'll always give you what you want." His voice quavered around the edges.

"Promise," she said, his bottom lip between her teeth.

He winced and stilled above her, barely breathing.

"Promise," she pursued, biting down oh, so gently as her hips undulated softly against his pelvis.

Cody gasped and shuddered, on the brink of climax. "Dear God, I promise." His voice was a whisper against her mouth. "So help me, I do."

"Good." She clasped him to her as his body rocked and bucked.

CHAPTER THIRTY-THREE

Crystal awakened to the distant sound of pounding. Her head lay on Cody's chest. One of his arms held her close; his leg lay across her hip. She savored the moment, still on the edge of sleep, drowsy and sated.

The pounding continued. Cody stirred. "What's goin' on?" His voice sounded muffled.

"I don't know. Maybe someone at the door?" She disentangled herself from him and kissed his lips. "Stay here. I'll go check."

He pulled both pillows behind his head and the sheet fell around his hips. "What's the time?"

Crystal found her watch on the nightstand. "Eight o'clock."

"Who would be bangin' on the door at this time of the mornin'? You think Jolie and Harold came back?" He rubbed a hand over his face. "Or Big Ed." He threw back the covers. "You're not goin' down there alone."

The sight of him, naked and sleepy, made her feel distinctly like making love again. Whoever was pounding on the door would get a piece of her mind and no mistake. She gathered up her clothes and pulled them on as Cody did the same thing on the other side of the bed.

He placed his hand in the small of his back and grimaced as they walked down the hallway. "I think I pulled somethin' with all our antics last night."

"I'll massage it better as soon as we get rid of whoever's downstairs," she promised. She smiled, happier than she had been in far too long. Waking up next to Cody for the rest of her life was a goal she meant to meet, regardless of what it took to attain it.

He pulled her to him and kissed her before they went downstairs.

"I love you," she told him again, her heart filled to overflowing. Now was the time for revelations, for sharing secrets. Now was the time for him to tell her he loved her, too.

But instead, he looked away. "We'd better find out who's there," he said, all nervous energy, jangling keys in his pocket and staring at the toes of his boots.

Crystal wanted to hold him back and demand to know why he couldn't tell her how he really felt, but she already knew. He couldn't tell her he loved her and then tell her goodbye for a second time in his life.

She ran ahead of him down the back stairs and through the kitchen. "It's the sheriff," she told Cody when she saw Reed's face peering through the glass. "What could he possibly want this early in the morning? He must have set out from Apache Junction before sun-up."

Cody loped past her to unbolt the door. "What's up, Reed?" he asked.

Dalton stepped over the threshold, his face creased into a frown, his eyes wary. "There's a problem."

"What?" A ripple of cold fear ran all the way up Crystal's back. She'd never seen Reed Dalton look so dour. "Did someone die?"

Reed looked at Cody. "Cody Blye, I'm here to arrest you for the murders of Willy Blye and Dock Penney," he said, his voice as grim as his expression. "We have reason to believe you planted dynamite in the mine shaft and detonated it to secure your interests in Cactus Station."

"What?" Cody shook off the hand Crystal placed on his arm. "Is this some sort of bad joke?"

"No joke. I wish it was. We reopened the investigation after Jake's body was identified. Remnants of blasting caps and dynamite were found in the shaft. It wasn't a cave-in, as was originally recorded by the deputy who made out the preliminary report."

Crystal watched Cody's face turn white under his tan. Reed kept talking, and she forced herself to listen.

"We figure you and Jake may have been in cahoots an' you killed him, too, when he got a little too greedy. We don't have enough evidence to charge you with that murder yet, but we're working on it." Reed glanced at Crystal, his eyes sliding over her disheveled hair and clothing.

From the corner of her eye, she saw Cody stealthily backing toward the kitchen door. Despite a mind as numb as any sleepwalker's, she tried to absorb the enormity of Reed's accusations while she stood in the remains of the Gold Rush Hotel, her dreams as charred as the building.

"Give me your wrists, Cody," Reed said. "I'll have to cuff you."

"The hell you will." With a bound, Cody passed the reception desk and was through the kitchen door.

"Oh, damn." Reed drew his gun and started after his escaping would-be prisoner.

"Are you out of your mind?" Crystal made a wild grab for the lawman's arm, caught a handful of sleeve and held on tight.

Reed tried to fight her off as he hit the swinging door. Crystal's head connected with wood and she lost her grip, her head spinning as she fell through the doorway. Dalton was almost at the back door.

Cody's life depended on her slowing the sheriff down, and Crystal didn't care what she had to do to stop him. Lurching forward, her head swimming in protest, she launched herself at Reed's legs, clasping him right below the knees and almost bringing him down.

He staggered, stopped and hung onto the kitchen table. "Get off me."

She wrapped her arms tighter. He tried to pry her off, unsuccessfully.

"I *knew* you were still in love with him." Reed scrambled for the door, dragging Crystal behind him.

She saw Cody running down the alleyway, heading for the hill behind the buildings.

Reed leveled his gun at Cody's flying figure. "Stop!" he bellowed. "Stop or I'll shoot."

Crystal bit Reed's knee. Howling with pain, he squeezed the trigger. A deafening roar echoed around the kitchen. A bullet zinged into a rock a few yards behind Cody.

Abandoning Reed's knee, Crystal made a dive for his gun hand and sunk her teeth into his wrist.

With a yelp, Reed dropped the gun and grabbed his arm.

Crystal ignored the swearing man and watched Cody clear the end of the alleyway and leap between rocks and scrub up the side of the hill.

"Out of my way." Reed pushed her aside. "Damn it." He holstered his gun and glared at Crystal. "He's out of range."

Cody crested the rise and disappeared over the other side, taking Crystal's heart with him. She pressed her cheek against the porch upright and felt tears coursing down her face.

"As far as I'm concerned, you can go to hell with Cody," Reed said. "You know damned well no one will be able to catch him now."

Crystal wiped her tears away. "You need to do some better investigating," she told Reed, whose face had darkened to a color resembling pickled beets. "I'd bet my life Cody had nothing to do with those deaths. He told me he was working in Utah and Colorado. I believe him. I'm sure you'd be able to trace his employers."

"I'll be back," Reed warned. "You can count on that. So can Cody. If he tries to come for you, I'll nail him."

"He won't come for me."

She knew he would stay out of her life forever. Misery cloaked her, and she sat on the porch steps. Even if he did come back, where would they go? What would they do--run over the border to live in Mexico? Cody was a fugitive. If they were caught, they'd both go to jail, and he'd be tried for murder.

Her brief interlude of happiness was over. Her one hope was that Reed wouldn't be able to convince his superiors that capturing Cody was a top priority. Otherwise, the sheriff would be back with reinforcements, including dogs and helicopters with heat-seeking devices onboard.

Cody would spend the rest of his life wandering alone around the Superstitions while she stayed on in Cactus Station until she couldn't bear the loneliness and isolation any longer. Totally demoralized, she allowed herself to wallow in her misery, telling herself she deserved it. They would never be able to resolve their differences now.

A dry, rough nose nudged her bare arm. Crystal looked up to find Jackson staring at her, his rancid breath bathing her face.

"Where did you come from?" she asked, sitting upright.

The dog had been missing since they were all at the cemetery the previous evening. Now he was back, covered with dust. As she watched, he trotted down the steps, looked at her and returned. Again he nudged her elbow with his nose.

"What do you want?" Crystal got up. Jackson enthusiastically wagged his tail. "Don't you want to go in and have dinner?" She opened the screen door.

Jackson barked at her and ran a few yards up the alleyway toward Main Street. There he stood, waiting.

"You want me to go with you?"

He barked again, his raucous voice piercing the still air.

"All right." Crystal followed him as they took a left onto Main Street and headed for the cemetery. "Do you know where Cody is?"

Her hopes rose. Suddenly, she didn't care if she had to live with him in the middle of the Superstitions for the rest of her life. He'd always look after her; always make sure she had shelter, food, and water.

Jackson wagged his tail and increased his pace. Crystal jogged to keep up as they passed the cemetery and headed up a narrow trail into the hills.

Crystal slowed her pace. "Cody went over the hill back there," she protested.

Jackson curled his lip at her.

"Okay, okay. You know best. Lead the way."

Despite being an old dog, he trotted easily between boulders, over hills and into gulleys dotted with Saguaro and Cholla cacti, scrubs of wild sage and tumbleweeds. The Superstitions misted into the distance, and Crystal desperately tried to remember landmarks: Weaver's Needle, Miner's Needle, Bluff Spring Mountain--it had been too long and everything looked the same to her--hill after undulating hill, gulley after hot, dry and dusty gulley. She was becoming too tired and scared to recognize anything.

Sweat formed on her brow and trickled down her face. It ran down her back and into the valley between her breasts, leaving her hot and sticky. Her lovemaking with Cody, followed by the altercation with Reed Dalton had ill-prepared her for a rigorous hike in the wilderness. Every muscle in her body ached; her scraped and bruised knees smarted in protest. And she had brought no water. She licked dry lips with a hot tongue.

"How much further?" she asked Jackson, as though he would answer her.

She scrabbled for a foothold in what appeared to be a smooth ridge of rock. Shale scattered, the resulting hail of gravel breaking the silence. Crystal's fingers hooked into a crevice and she pulled herself onto what looked like solid ground, only to feel it sliding away beneath her tennis shoes. Jackson waited at the summit, crouched down and watched her intently. She lost her footing completely and slammed down onto her sore knees.

"I suppose you think this is funny," she told the panting dog, who looked like he was laughing at her. "Cody had better be at the end of this nightmare hike, otherwise I swear I'll use the last of my remaining strength to skin you and roast you over an open pit.

Uncle Dock showed me how to make fire in the wilderness, so don't think I can't do it."

Jackson had the audacity to snarl.

"Shut up," Crystal said. "I've had enough of your bad temper. If you don't control yourself, I'll be forced to give you what you deserve." She panted her way up the rocks again. "You...need to...show me some...respect. I'm the one who's...been buying...your food...all these weeks."

Jackson lowered his head onto his paws and whined plaintively.

"That's...better."

Hands on hips and heart hammering, Crystal paused to catch her breath before hauling herself onto the wide ledge occupied by the dog. She was at the entrance of a mine shaft. The black hole yawned at her in a silent challenge she had no wish to accept.

Crude steps, fashioned into one side, disappeared into the all-encompassing darkness.

"This is where Cody is?" Her heart sped up again, but not from anticipation. Cody would never expect her to go down into that hole. She couldn't do it. Her claustrophobia reared its head and the pounding started in her chest.

"I'm not going in there," she told Jackson when he nudged her from behind.

He nudged harder. Crystal stepped forward uncertainly, taking the steps down until blue sky and sun shone above, but her feet stood in the black void. "Are you sure this is where Cody's hiding?" Her voice echoed around the cavern.

Jackson blocked the entrance, feet spread in a wide stance, hair bristling along his back. He snarled, fangs fully exposed. Drool slid to the ground between his feet.

Crystal's stomach churned. She couldn't possibly force herself deeper into that shaft, but it was evident Jackson was through playing and wasn't going to let her back out.

She stood paralyzed with fear at either outcome. Suddenly, a hand encircled her wrist. She gasped with relief. "Cody."

But the hand was gnarled and squared off at the fingertips.

"Get goin," a hard, gravely voice told her, and Crystal found herself gazing into the face of Jake Carver.

CHAPTER THIRTY-FOUR

"You're supposed to be dead," she protested faintly as he shoved her deeper into the mine shaft.

"Playin' dead suited me for a time, but I'm done with hidin' out now I have those doubloons." Jake pushed her again. "I had to kill another prospector an' assume his identity. Henry Giddings was his name. I switched his dental records with mine. It was easy--the dentist was sloppy and his assistant was greedy. I gave her a twenty an' sent her out for donuts. Told her I was needin' to use her phone."

"You killed the uncles, too." Crystal felt for the wall and put one foot in front of the other. They'd left daylight far behind and the steps were becoming steeper and harder to find.

"Stop talkin'." Jake shoved her for emphasis.

Crystal clung desperately to the wall. She couldn't stop talking. If she did, the claustrophobia would claim her. She had a feeling she'd find Cody at the end of that tunnel, and it was the only thing keeping her going.

"You're the one who was waking us all up at night while you were trying to find out where the coins were stashed." Her foot slipped and encountered nothing but empty air. Choking back a cry of dismay, she regained her footing and stepped down again.

"I told you to get movin'." This time, he pushed her so hard, she almost fell.

Crystal saw only blackness ahead of her. Jake held the beam of his flashlight close to his own feet while she stumbled along, hitting her head on the low roof with sickening regularity.

"I can't do this." She stopped. "I've got claustrophobia. You've got to remember I suffer from it. I couldn't go into the mine shafts when I stayed here before." She tried to control her breathing, but a great weight was pressing onto her chest.

"I don't care what's wrong with you." This time, he pushed too hard. Crystal pitched forward into space.

As his flashlight swung wildly around, she caught a glimpse of a steeply sloping trail. Down it she slid in a precipitous rush, rocks tearing at her exposed arms and legs.

Down and down into a profound blackness deeper and darker than anything she had ever encountered before, even in her worst nightmares.

After what seemed like an eternity, she crashed onto a flat surface. All the air knocked out of her lungs, she coughed and gagged as she clambered onto her hands and knees. She found herself in a large cavern illuminated by oil lamps winking comfortingly from the walls. Two other tunnels forked out from the end of the main shaft, their entrances dimly visible in the flickering light.

Jake dragged her to her feet.

"Please don't hurt me," Crystal pleaded. "You've got the doubloons. What more do you want?"

Jake's snarl sounded even more threatening than Jackson's. He dragged her along until they reached the far end of the cavern and then threw her. She landed against something hard and warm. Cody lay bound and gagged, tossed into the corner like a discarded pile of laundry.

Relief flooded her when he groaned. She flung her arms around his neck.

The eye closest to her was swollen shut. The other one glittered in the lamplight. He managed to nod, showing her he was okay.

"I tried to get both of you to leave, but you wouldn't do it." Jake waved a rifle at them.

Crystal felt sure it was hers. "You did all of this for money," she said. "I can't believe you would kill three people for a bagful of gold coins." Keeping her body in front of Cody, Crystal tried to loosen the knots on the ropes binding his wrists.

"Damn right. Those coins're worth a fortune, an' the uncles wouldn't give me my fair share. I knew Willy'd found the Dutchman. All that treasure huntin' he'd done had paid off. I caught him showin' Dock one of the doubloons."

Cody was making noises under the gag. Crystal pulled it down. They were deep underground--what was the point of keeping him quiet now she was there, too?

"Uncle Willy never found the Dutchman," Cody said. "He would have told me."

Jake shone the flashlight on Cody's bruised face. "He didn't tell you 'bout the doubloons, did he?"

"Well, no."

Jake pulled Crystal out of the way and kicked Cody, who doubled over, moaning.

"You don't like it when someone else has the upper hand, do you?" Jake kicked him again. "You Blyes are all alike: liars and cheats."

"What did Uncle Willy do when you saw him showing Uncle Dock the coin?" Crystal asked quickly as Jake looked like he was going to give Cody a third kick.

"Told me I was imaginin' things. Willy brought out some pea-sized gold nugget. Said he found it, an' tried to convince me that's all I'd seen. Tried to involve me in some cockamamie mining venture he an' Dock had cooked up, but never got off the ground after Cody got into trouble an' left."

Jake cackled, evidently still delighted the uncles had failed without Cody's help. "I faked my disappearance so's I could follow 'em back up to the Dutchman," he said. "But they never went, so I figured I'd just get rid of 'em an' search for the doubloons. I knew they had to be hidden somewhere around Cactus Station, an' I figured I had plenty of time to look."

"So you waited until they went into the mine and then detonated it." Cody shook his head. "They were two harmless old men."

"Which you two are not." Jake put the lantern on a rock closer to Cody and Crystal. "I figure Willy n' Dock left you both the town so's you'd find the doubloons."

"But they never told us anything about Spanish gold being hidden there," Crystal protested. "I don't know how they expected us to find it."

"I bet they were planning to tell one or both of us," Cody said. He struggled into a sitting position and looked at Jake. "But then you blew them up before they could do that."

"The gold belongs to *me*."

Jake kept moving the rifle around, and Crystal worried that he was beginning to point it more in Cody's direction than anywhere else.

"Why the hell didn't you just give up, damn it?" Jake asked. He sounded frustrated more than angry. "Things were goin' so badly, you should've. Hell, everyone else had left town. *She* wasn't even talkin' to you..." he jerked his head toward Crystal.

"I had to have the doubloons," Cody said. "They're all I've got to offer Crystal."

She looked him straight in his one open eye. "You're all I want. I don't need gold."

"Very touchin'." Jake spat on the floor to show his appreciation. "Too little, too late. I'm not takin' any chances you'll escape my dynamite. Cody's too sly for my likin', an' he might figure out a way to get out of here."

He stopped waving the rifle around and pointed it straight at them. Crystal closed her eyes. She and Cody were going to be together, all right, but in the hereafter, not the present.

Snarling made her open her eyes back up in a hurry. Jake was on the ground with the dog on top. The gun discharged and Jackson yelped.

Cody struggled to break out of his bonds. Crystal didn't know what to do. The only weapons that presented themselves were an ancient pickaxe leaning against a wall and a shovel on the floor behind Jake, who was already scrambling to his feet. Inexplicably, instead of shooting them he grabbed the flashlight and ran down one of the tunnels.

Crystal managed to loosen the knots in the rope enough for Cody to slide his hands through. He untied his ankles.

"How did you get here?" he asked. He kissed her quickly before running over to check on the dog.

"Jackson brought me. I don't know if Jake was at the bottom of it, or Jackson did it on his own."

"It's a toss up," Cody said. "I never told you, but Jackson used to belong to Jake." He ran his hands over the dog's fur and came up with bloody palms. Jackson whined.

"Where do you think Jake's gone?" she asked.

"To blow up the mine."

"Cody, I can't believe you're just standing there." She tore at his arm. "Let's get out of here."

"Not up the slope you came down. It's too steep, and we'd be climbing forever. Besides, I'm not leavin' the dog here. He just picked sides and saved both of us." He looked at the tunnels. "We can't go where Jake went, so I guess that leaves the one on the right. I have no idea where it goes, but we're gonna find out." He picked Jackson up in his arms. "Damn, he's heavy."

"You can't ask me to go down that tunnel," she said, dread filling her.

He was used to fumbling around in total darkness. Miners didn't even use candles when they ate lunch, they were so set on conservation. She was no miner. "I'll die in there," she told him. "It's hot and airless. I'll pass out."

"Listen to me," he said. "There's no choice. Either we stay here and die when Jake blows this place up, or we take a chance we can get out."

He was asking too much. If she was going to die anyway, she'd rather do it right where she was in the large open space lit by lanterns.

"I love you," Cody said. "Come with me. Take a chance."

She looked at his face, deeply lined with worry. "Ooh, you had to pull an ace out of your back pocket, didn't you?"

"Hold onto my belt," he said.

"I...I..."

"Don't think. Just do it." He started walking toward the tunnel. "Come on, let's go."

He wasn't going to hang around and wait. She looked at the flickering lights one more time and held on tightly to his belt. The knowledge that he loved her did more to keep the panic at bay than anything else could have done. As the last vestige of light disappeared, she closed her eyes and depended on Cody to guide her.

"You'll be fine," he reassured her.

"Tell me again that you love me," she managed between gasps.

"I love you. I've always loved you. But since I'm not good enough for you, I've kept it to myself."

Crystal wanted to protest, but she didn't have the strength. "I'm not going...to...make..." She tried to take in air and found none. "I can't...breathe." She started hyperventilating.

"Calm down." His voice was so soothing. "You know it's panic taking your breath. There's plenty of air down here. In fact, there's so much, I think this shaft must go up to the surface."

"Really?"

She let go of him to unfasten two more buttons on her shirt. Maybe if she did, her lungs would be able to expand again. Her clothes were too tight. She reached out for him and felt only emptiness.

"Cody?" Arms outstretched, fingers clawing at darkness that felt as thick and impenetrable as a blanket, Crystal whirled in circles.

"It's okay. I'm here." His arm curved around her shoulders. "We're under an air shaft." He kissed the tears from her face. "Look up, honey. You can see daylight."

She raised her head and saw a yellow light high above them. "How are we going to get up there?"

"A ladder." He guided one of her hands to the wall and pressed her fingers over an iron rail. "Go on."

"What about you? How are you going to get Jackson up there?"

"I'll manage. Get goin'. Jake always sets his charges on a timer, and he usually gives himself ten minutes to get out of the area. Seein' as he's older now, he may even make it fifteen, but I'm not countin' on that."

Crystal scrambled up the rungs, her sweaty palms sliding on the cold iron surface. The higher she climbed, the brighter and wider the light became, until she felt dirt with her groping fingers and heaved herself into some short of shack. Holes between the boards let in sunlight, producing the yellow glow she had seen from the bottom of the shaft.

"Give me a hand with Jackson, would you?" Cody said from behind her.

He had placed the dog around his neck, like a scarf. She helped pull them both out, and Cody lay on his back, his chest heaving.

"Get up." She tugged at him. "If you take the time to rest, we may get blown sky high."

A large, furry head came between them and Jackson licked Cody's face.

"Hey. Now you're awake after I carried you all this way?" Cody laughed. "I thought you were dyin'."

Jackson shook himself and limped out through the open door, favoring one leg.

Crystal watched him as they ran hand in hand toward town. "I guess he was in shock."

"Or playin' possum. He's much happier when I'm payin' attention to him instead of you."

"He and I are going to have a long heart to heart about that when all this is over." Crystal held tight to Cody's hand. "I'll never let go of you again, and that dog is going to have to take a back seat in your affections."

"I hope so." Cody pulled her behind an outcropping. "I think we're far enough away to be safe," he said. He took her face in his hands. "Without those doubloons, I don't have anything else to offer you but myself. I've got rough manners an' ways that will offend all your friends, an' maybe you, too in the end. I can't make you wealthy an' I don't know how to do anythin' except get grubstakes or dig mine shafts. Why do you want me?"

Crystal couldn't believe he still doubted his worth. "You just saved my life--again," she told him. "You've done it three times in as many weeks."

"Who's countin?"

"Me," she assured him. "You always look after me, even when you're mad at me." She smiled when he raised his eyebrows. "You're easy going and even easier on the eye."

"I'm gonna get a swollen head," he protested.

"You said you don't know why I want you, so I'm telling you," she said. "Cody, you can even be charming when you want to be."

"That's how I get people to do what I want them to." He lowered her to the ground.

"Now, now," she said. "You're trying to sidetrack me, and that's not playing fair. We're talking about what makes you so special to me."

He tried to kiss her, but she turned her head.

"Let's see. Oh, yes--you know more about dynamite than anyone I've ever met." She cupped his chin in her hands. "You could make a career out of that talent, and I can steer you to the right people, if that's what you want." She kissed him sweetly. "And finally..." She placed her cheek against his and whispered in his ear. "You made a woman out of me."

A dull rumble interrupted further conversation. The ground beneath their feet trembled, then shook. The shack and a considerable portion of the cemetery disappeared inside a gaping hole.

"In my opinion, he overdid the dynamite," Cody said. "An' those charges were set for closer to twenty minutes. He's really slowed down."

"Now I can see how he managed to come and go so easily the night we left the doubloons." She gazed in awe at the chasm that had once been the last resting place of Cactus Station's population.

"I bet he used tunnels under the town, too," Cody said. He took her hand again. "Come on, let's go see what's left."

As soon as they arrived at the edge of town, they saw all the rubble. A porch was the only reminder of the convenience store. The sign for the Branch Water Bar lay in the middle of the street, announcing the opening hours of a place that no longer existed.

"Look at the hotel," he said.

Her gaze followed his. The Gold Rush had all but collapsed. Part of the outer walls still stood while the rear, already damaged by fire, had toppled onto Cody's vehicle.

"I guess you'll have to total your Blazer," she said.

He picked his way around the debris to look. Crystal followed. He quickly drew his head out of the cab and led her away. "I don't think you want to see this," he said.

"Don't be so bossy. I hate it when you do that." She tried to shake herself loose.

"Jake's in there, crushed," he said.

"Crushed?" She stopped struggling.

"Yeah. It's pretty bad."

"I guess that's the end of it, then."

"No." Cody drew her close. "It's only the beginning for us. The doubloons are on the front seat, too."

~

Reed Dalton's squad car crawled slowly around all the debris and stopped in front of the hotel. Hoyle Bixby sat in the front passenger's seat.

Reed opened his door. He pointed his finger at Hoyle, who was about to get out on the other side. "You stay right where you are, Hoyle, an' don't you touch *anything.*"

Hoyle nodded vigorously. "No, sir, Sheriff," he said.

"Harold and Jolie Webster called me." Reed pushed his hat back on his head and whistled as he looked around at the remains of Cactus Station. "Harold said they'd been trying to reach you since this morning, an' they were real worried about you. So I called myself, an' I knew something was really wrong when Hoyle answered the phone. There was no way either of you would let him do that unless you weren't around to stop him." Reed hooked his thumbs through the belt loops of his pants. "What the hell happened here?"

"A little remodeling," Cody said with a wide grin. "Ouch." He touched his swollen eye and cheek. "That hurt."

"Serves you right," Crystal said, but she found herself smiling, too.

Suddenly the day seemed brighter, and the destruction of Cactus Station didn't matter any more. Cody loved her. He'd finally admitted it and despite his reservations, she could dream of a future that included the man she had wanted to be with for so many years.

She'd even put up with the dog, she thought as she held Cody close. Jackson was a small price to pay when she'd been given so much happiness.

Sheriff Dalton interrupted her euphoria by clearing his throat loudly.

"Crystal, I did the checking you asked me to," he said. He had the grace to look embarrassed. "You were right--Cody was workin' in Utah at the time of the murders. I've got the faxed pay stubs to prove it, along with his time sheets." Reed scratched his head. "I don't know how you do it, Cody," he said, "but you always manage to come out ahead."

"Not always, Sheriff," Cody said. "But this time, I caught a lucky break. A real lucky break." He looked at Crystal and smiled.

"Jake murdered the uncles," Crystal told Reed. "He confessed to us before he tried to blow up the mine shaft he had taken us to."

Cody jerked his head in the direction of the hotel. "He's over there, Reed. Dead inside my truck. He blew himself up as well as the town. Why don't you go check it out?"

Jackson brought a doubloon and dropped it beside Cody's boot.

"Not now," Cody said as he took Crystal in his arms. "I'm about to ask the woman of my dreams to marry me."

Reed looked at the coin glinting in the bright sunlight. "Come on, Jackson," he said. "They want to be alone an' you can show me where the rest of these things are." He ambled off with the dog.

"You're way more important than gold," Cody said.

"I think you were about to ask me to marry you," Crystal reminded him.

"I was," he said. "I am."

"Good," she said. "Because the answer's 'yes,' and as quickly as possible. We've got a lot of lost time to make up for, you know."

"I'm sure we'll manage," he said.

And then he kissed her. And Crystal forgot all about lost time, gold doubloons and dogs.

~The End~

ABOUT THE AUTHOR

Heather Ames knew she was a writer from the time she won first prize in a high school novel contest. An unconventional upbringing gave her opportunities to travel extensively, leading to nomadic ways and an insatiable desire to see the world. She has made her home in 5 countries and 7 states, learning a couple of languages along the way. She is currently pitching her tents in Salem, Oregon, and after a long career in healthcare, has achieved her dream of writing full-time.

Heather is a current board member of Sisters in Crime's Harriet Vane Chapter in Portland as well as an active member of Northwest Independent Writers Association (NIWA.)

Visit her website at
www.heatherames.com

ALSO BY HEATHER AMES

Mystery/Suspense series

Indelible (Book 1)

A Swift Brand of Justice (Indelible — Book 2)

Suspense

Night Shadows

Contemporary Romance

The Sweetest Song

Upcoming Books

Swift Retribution

(Indelible mystery/suspense series — Book 3) Fall 2019

Ghost Shop series

(mystery/suspense with a paranormal twist — Book 1) 2020

www.ingramcontent.com/pod-product-compliance
Lightning Source LLC
Chambersburg PA
CBHW071331250626
47159CB00004B/1559